"We don't have to jump into bed together right away." Mirth shimmered in the golden flecks of Bodie's eyes.

"Are you insane?"

"Oh, well if you're all for it, so am I. How soon can we start?"

Ronni's nerves lit up, unleashing a flood of hormones. Tingling rose from her core. Where was the full moon when she needed something to blame on her total lack of self-control?

"I don't need any more complications in my life." Ronni shook her head to clear the riotous uproar going on internally.

"Boy likes girl, girl likes boy. Boy and girl have wild, crazy, sweaty sex." His dark eyebrows wiggled. "Can't get any less complicated than that."

Oh yes. Yes, it could.

Southern born and bred, **Kristal Hollis** holds a psychology degree and has spent her adulthood helping people and animals. When a family medical situation resulted in a work sabbatical, she began penning deliciously dark paranormal romances as an escape from the real-life drama. But when the crisis passed, her passion for writing love stories continued. A 2015 Golden Heart® Award finalist, Kristal lives with her husband and two rescued dogs at the edge of the enchanted forest that inspires her stories.

Books by Kristal Hollis

Harlequin Nocturne

Awakened by the Wolf
Rescued by the Wolf
Charmed by the Wolf
Captivated by the She-Wolf

CAPTIVATED BY THE SHE-WOLF

———

KRISTAL HOLLIS

HARLEQUIN® NOCTURNE™

Recycling programs
for this product may
not exist in your area.

ISBN-13: 978-1-335-62949-4

Captivated by the She-Wolf

Copyright © 2018 by Kristal Hollis

Printed in U.S.A.

Dear Reader,

Years ago, I was introduced to the legend of the Native American Tlanuwa, a giant mythological birdlike creature once believed to have terrorized the area in northeast Georgia where the fictional town of Maico and the Walker's Run territory are set. I've long since wanted to utilize this vibrant lore but every idea fell flat until I learned of the symbiotic relationship between real wolves and ravens. Suddenly, I had an organic way to incorporate the legend into this project, by reimagining the Tlanuwa as raven-shifters.

Now I'm excited to present to you the fourth story in the Wahyas of Walker's Run series, the tale of a raven falling in love with a wolf.

I hope you enjoy Bodie and Ronni's adventure.

Kristal

I love hearing from readers. To connect with me, visit www.kristalhollis.com.

To the Cradle of Forestry employees and volunteers at the Brasstown Bald Visitor Information Center, thank you for your dedicated conservation efforts and diligence in maintaining one of my favorite places to visit.

Chapter 1

Watching two wolves copulate wasn't how Bodaway Gryffon wanted to spend his evening.

In his raven form, he'd flown into the Walker's Run Cooperative's wolf sanctuary to scout possible locations for his daughter, Willow. Her Transformation Ceremony would take place on her sixteenth birthday, the age their kind, the Tlanuhwa—an ancient Native American clan of raven shifters—developed the ability to shift into their bird forms.

Bodie had first learned of the Walker's Run Cooperative and their commitment to conservation and the preservation of wildlife a few years ago while working with other state, federal and local agencies to contain a massive fire within the Chattahoochee National Forest.

Recently moved to the area, Bodie now had the opportunity to explore the Co-op's protected lands with the hope of finding a safe and permanent home for Willow, his mother and himself.

Ignoring the activity below his perch, Bodie lifted his gaze to the full moon, a large, bright, unblinking eye that watched over the earth—or at least the wolf sanctuary. He wondered if its bluish glow served as an aphrodisiac for the wolves, considering the number he'd seen mating tonight.

Peripheral movement in the distance drew his attention and he launched from his perch to investigate. Weaving through trees with branches still weighted with lush, green leaves, he honed in on the she-wolf leisurely padding ahead. Thick reddish-gold fur covered her sleek, toned body. Nose twitching, she tilted her head and watched Bodie alight in a nearby tree. Curiosity shimmered in her cobalt blue eyes and as she examined him inch by inch, an indelible warmth spread across Bodie's skin beneath his dark feathers.

Inspection complete, she continued on her trek and he felt an unusual tinge of sadness at her departure. Before the she-wolf disappeared completely from view, she looked over her shoulder directly at him.

Bodie wasn't presumptuous enough to simply assume that he was her visual target. His vision was as sharp as any raptor and he could see her blue gaze fixed on him as clearly as if they were standing nose to beak.

She smiled.

Whoa!

Could wolves actually smile?

Damn curious, Bodie took off from his perch and landed in a tree near where the she-wolf waited. No sooner had he settled than she restarted her journey.

Following along, he flew from limb to limb. She didn't look back at him again, but if he waited too long to catch up, her pace slowed.

That she wanted Bodie's company gave him a rush. Although he couldn't physically smile with his beak, mentally he couldn't seem to stop himself. If all of the Co-op wolves were this friendly, then the sanctuary would be ideal for Willow's ceremony and a great place to teach her how to fly.

The she-wolf made her way to a wide, peaceful stream. Gently flowing water sparkled with the moonlight. She eased into the water, as graceful as a nymph, and Bodie landed on an outcropping of rocks at the water's edge. Leisurely, she swam without once casting her gaze in his direction. He shook off the unexpected annoyance, ruffling his feathers.

A few minutes later, she leaped from the stream and shook. Hopping backward to avoid the spray, Bodie slipped on a slick spot and one of his three-toed feet wedged inside a small crack in the giant rock. A shock of pain shot up his leg and he squawked.

Wiggling his toes didn't cause further pain, so nothing was broken. Gently, he tried to pull his foot free. But again, something sharp in the slim crevice kept him pinned. Even clenching, then unclenching his toes as he lifted his foot didn't work.

He tilted his head and peered inside the crack at the jagged piece of debris. With a spaghetti-thin stick or perhaps a pine needle, he might be able to dislodge the obstacle. Too bad nothing was in reach of his beak.

An ominous prickle crawled up his spine and he became aware of the sound of nails clicking against the rock. Slowly, he turned his head and saw the she-wolf peering down at him.

Oh, boy!

Trying to remain calm, still and avoid sudden movement, Bodie tried again to lift his foot free of the crack. He got the same result—a stabbing pain when he bumped against the sharp debris.

Nudging him, the she-wolf snorted softly, blowing air through his feathers. His heart stopped and panic exploded in his mind. He didn't think about death often, but on the occasion he did, getting eaten by a wolf was not one of the scenarios his mind conjured.

Attempting to shoo her away, he squawked and flapped his wings. Her nose wrinkled in a grim expression, then she planted her rump on the rock.

The silvery light that flashed along the tips of her fur wouldn't have bothered Bodie in his human form. However, to his bird sight, the brightness was blinding. When he finally lowered his wings from his face and the black spots faded from his vision, he saw a beautiful, naked woman crouched where the she-wolf had been.

Shock threw his brain into flight mode and the only clear thought he had was to escape. Wings flapping, he intended to soar upward. Pain anchored his trapped leg and he fell flat on his beak.

"Easy, little one."

Little one?

Indignation nearly overrode his sensibility. Too bad it would be really awful for him to shift right now.

"Ouch!" The woman drew back her hand. A perfectly round drop of blood formed in the spot where Bodie had pecked her.

"I'm only trying to help." She pressed the small wound against her mouth.

Yeah? Well, Bodie didn't know that when she'd reached toward him and he had defended himself with the only weapon he had, his beak. He felt bad about breaking the skin, though. But his reflexes were hyped on adrenaline. Having never encountered a shifter species outside of his own, his linear view of reality had suddenly turned kaleidoscopic. As a matter of survival, Tlanuhwas like himself were extremely secretive about their ability to transform into ravens.

"I know what it's like to feel trapped and afraid," the woman cooed.

Now sympathy overran the adrenaline, awakening Bodie's protective nature and flooding him with an undeniable need to safeguard the she-wolf. Instinctively, his chest puffed and his feathers fluffed.

"Don't worry, I won't hurt you in my human or wolf form. Wahyas are forbidden from harming other creatures, especially inside the sanctuary."

So that's what they called themselves. Bodie repeated the word in his mind. *Wa-hi-ya.*

Filled with suspicion, her eyes inspected every inch of him. "You look different from the ravens in these parts."

That's because I am.

Double the size of ordinary ravens, Tlanuhwa had inky

black feathers that shimmered with a silver iridescence in moonlight and their eyes were golden rather than black.

"If you're scavenging for leftovers, you won't find them here." She eased forward. "No hunting of any kind is allowed inside the sanctuary. Our sentinels will hunt down anyone who tries."

No hunting allowed.

Bodie wanted to kiss her. Would have in fact, except for…well, him being a bird with his foot stuck in a crack.

He looked at her. Really looked to see the woman, not the she-wolf.

Her long, strawberry blonde hair was damp, rumpled and sexy. Her captivating eyes had remained the same beautiful blue as her wolf's had been. Tiny crinkles around her mouth and the faint lines in her forehead said she experienced the ups and downs of life head-on. He'd expect no less from a she-wolf.

High cheekbones flanked her straight nose, neither too long nor too short, and the slightly upturned tip was the perfect place for a teasing kiss. The faintest freckles dotted her creamy skin and the delicate expanse of her slender throat inspired visions of delicious nips and licks.

Any man would be honored to be held by such soft, round shoulders and sleek, strong arms. Her breasts were full and perfectly shaped and the pale, pink nipples made his mouth water even though his throat went dry.

"Hey!" She snapped her fingers in front of his face. "Unbelievable!"

Sorry.

His gaze naturally found her chest again.

Oh, so not sorry.

"Show some respect or I'll leave your feathered ass here. None of the animals will hurt you, but the ants are bitches."

The threat snapped Bodie's mind back to where it needed to be.

"So you do understand me."

He answered with a deep-throated croak.

"If I'm going to get you unstuck, I need to see what your foot is caught on." Slowly, she leaned down.

He froze, unable to breathe. His form might be that of a raven, but he was still male. Hot-blooded and drowning in testosterone.

"How in the world did you manage to get stuck like that?" she said, staring down into the crack.

Funny story. Maybe I'll tell you one day.

"I'm gonna need something to dislodge that pebble." Frowning, she glanced around.

Hey, beautiful, what's your name?

Crouched on her hands and knees, she leaned over the boulder and reached into the water.

Come here often? I'd really like for you to show me around. Show me a good time.

Unable to resist, he cautiously stretched out his wing so that the tips of his feathers grazed her backside.

"Hey!" Clutching a thin reed, she sat up and looked around.

Bodie quickly pointed his beak in the air looking everywhere except at her gloriously naked body.

"Weird," she mumbled, moving back into position to peer into the crack.

He couldn't see what she was doing but he felt the debris fall away from his foot. In his excitement to be free, Bodie accidentally slapped the woman's face with his wing.

"Gee, thanks."

Sorry! This time he meant it.

On his good leg, he hopped in circles, trying to inspect his other foot. Thankfully, it wasn't bloody or mangled.

"You should be all right now."

He eased his foot down until it was flat against the boulder. After a few tentative steps, he put his full weight on it. It didn't buckle and he felt no pain.

Croaking gratefully, he bowed to his lovely rescuer.

His reward was a soft smile. This time, when she reached toward him, Bodie didn't strike back.

She gently stroked his chest. His insides got all warm and fuzzy, and he felt a little drunk. He blamed the sensation on his relief at being freed.

"Aren't you cute."

Cute? Seriously?

Cute was for teenagers. When she saw him in his human form, that would not be the first word that popped into her mind.

A howl rose in the distance.

"Gotta go, little one," she told Bodie before shifting into her wolf and leaping from the boulder.

Little one.

Oh, he couldn't wait to show her how little he wasn't.

Chapter 2

The hypnotic whir of the sewing machine was as near to heaven as Veronika Lyles could get, except for the moment of ecstasy when being loved by her mate.

Since Zeke had died, owning her own business was near enough.

Inside The Stitchery, the aromatic scent of dye from the bolts of fabric lining the shelves had taken a while to get used to, but now Ronni barely noticed them. She loved the feel of fabric between her fingers, taking yards of shapeless cloth and fashioning them into something useful and beautiful.

The Walker's Run Cooperative, the public human face of her new wolfan pack, had spared no expense on the renovations of the abandoned store next to her cousin's automotive repair shop. Not only had they given Ronni a place within their pack but also a purpose.

In Pine Ridge, her poverty-stricken and turmoil-plagued former pack in Kentucky, she'd mended threadbare clothes, patched thrift store finds and reshaped garage sale discoveries into whatever her family had needed. Now she and her teenage son, Alex, lacked for nothing, including the freedom to live a life of their own choosing and the safety in which to do it.

Gratitude swelled in her heart. The Co-op really took care of its own. Even those adopted into the pack.

Having lost and gained so much over the last nineteen months, she was finally starting to feel settled and relaxed. Time did eventually heal even the deepest wounds. She had expected last week's full moon to be a difficult night, since it fell on the anniversary of her claiming—the night Zeke had bitten her during a sexual encounter and marked her as his life-mate.

His death had been the catalyst in expediting Ronni and their son Alex's relocation to Walker's Run, saving them from the deadly uprising within her birth pack. The tug-of-war between the grief of losing her beloved mate and the downright thankfulness for a new and better life was a battle she fought daily.

Since the encounter with the unusual raven a few nights ago, Ronni had found the struggle a little easier to bear. Every night since, he perched in a tree outside her house and watched over her as she sat on the back porch swing. Ravens were infamous thieves, so maybe he was stealing her troubles away, one night at a time.

Whatever his reason for visiting, she now looked forward to his company. Preferred it, actually, to the males who figured her mourning period was over and that she was back on the market. Most of them would make fine mates for some other she-wolf. Having been loved and loved hard, she wouldn't be content with anything less and she simply hadn't connected that strongly to any potential suitor. Except the raven.

She laughed at the absurdity.

The delicate chime of bells jingled from the front of the store.

"That you, Elliott?" Ronni rolled her chair away from the sewing table and stood, arching her back and stretching her arms above her head. The bunched muscles relaxed.

"Yep." Without fail, postal employee and fellow packmate Elliott Dubois delivered Ronni's mail at ten fifty-five every morning.

She walked into the front where slanted teak shelves were loaded with bolts of every imaginable color of fabric.

More for show than actual use, the rainbow effect reminded her that this store, this pack, this *life* was her pot of gold.

"You have to sign for this one." In his late fifties, Elliott had dark springy hair clipped close to his head, smooth brown skin, sepia-colored eyes teeming with intelligence and a tightly trimmed beard framing a generous mouth that usually dazzled her with a flash of straight white teeth. Today, Elliott clenched his jaw hard enough to flatten his lips until they whitened around the edges.

"Well, it can't be an eviction letter." The Co-op owned her building and she paid a portion of her profits to the Co-op, as all members did.

Ronni stepped behind the sales counter and picked up a pen from the cup beside the register.

"It's from the Woelfesenat." He handed her an overnight, certified letter.

Ronni's heart stopped. As did time itself.

The air inside The Stitchery stilled. Neither she nor Elliott breathed. The ticking of the pendulum clock on the wall behind her ceased to tock in her ears.

Although all Wahyan packs were independently governed by their respective Alphas, the Woelfesenat was the international wolf council that ensured their species continued to live peaceably among the unsuspecting human populace. They held the ultimate ruling power over all wolf shifters, world-wide. A communique from them was either really good news or it wasn't. There was no middle ground with them.

Since Ronni preferred to stay off their radar, she doubted they were awarding her a commendation.

Nervously, she signed for the document.

"Maybe it's not too serious." Elliott offered her a hopeful smile.

"Probably paperwork involving my mate's death," she said, even though Zeke had died over a year ago. "It all happened so fast, Alex and I just packed up and left."

"I'm sure that's all it is." Relief eased Elliott's worry. "I'll see you tomorrow."

Ronni kept her smile in place until Elliott walked out of The Stitchery and across the street. Hands shaking, she tore into the letter.

It wasn't about her deceased husband, Ezekiel. It was about his brutal older brother, Jebediah.

Ronni's heart dropped into her stomach with such velocity it could have passed right through her pelvis to make a crater on the concrete floor.

Jeb wasn't dead like everyone had believed. And despite the many prayers and supplications Ronni had made to never lay eyes on that man again, the Woelfesenat was officially informing her that Jeb had petitioned for the assertion of his blood-kin rights and would be contacting her shortly regarding visitation with her son, Alexander.

The letter slipped from her fingers. Her knees gave out. She sank to the floor. Her heart climbed back into her chest and beat in a furious attempt to make up for lost time. A sudden deluge of adrenaline made her head spin. Her breaths grew short from the tightening of her chest and the closing of her throat. Even her nose seemed unable to draw in air.

As her mate's brother, Jeb had a stronger blood-kin relation to Alex than Rafe Wyatt, Ronni's distant cousin, who had given them refuge after Zeke's death, providing a home and helping to establish them in the Walker's Run pack.

Zeke had risked his life to protect her from Jeb, who had begun obsessively stalking her with a mind to forcibly claim her if she resisted. And later, in hopes of giving his family a better life, Zeke had been coordinating with Rafe on their transference to Walker's Run when he was killed by rebel packmates.

If allowed to go unchecked, Jeb would undo everything Zeke had sacrificed to give them.

Under no circumstance would Ronni allow that to happen. Taking a calming breath, she forced down her panic.

The clock on the wall behind her chimed and she jumped.

Irritated with herself, Ronni stood and shook off her momentary weakness and flattened her hands on the counter. She couldn't stop Jeb from coming to get them, but she would make damn certain he left Walker's Run empty-handed.

"Who are you again?" Mary Jane McAllister, an elderly woman with short, gray curly hair and wearing overalls, squinted at Bodie from behind her screen door.

"Sergeant Gryffon." The wooden porch squeaked as he shifted his weight. He'd been interviewing tight-lipped Co-op residents all morning about the gunshots he'd heard inside the wolf sanctuary last night. "I'm with Georgia DNR."

"What's that?"

"Department of Natural Resources," he answered, for the third time. Noting the hearing aids in her ears, he swallowed his impatience.

Again, she inspected him head to toe. "Are you a game warden or something?"

"Yes, ma'am." Though as a DNR conservation ranger in the law enforcement division, Bodie had the same investigative and arrest powers entrusted to all local, state or federal law enforcement officers.

"Well, whatcha doin' here?" She crossed her arms over her full chest.

That was a loaded question.

In recent years, there had been a number of fatal wild boar attacks in and around Maico. DNR's growing concern with the feral hog situation was, in part, responsible for Bodie's reassignment here. And since his arrival, he had combed the entire area, on foot or in the air. And there wasn't a single boar to be found, wild or otherwise.

There were, however, wolf shifters who in all likelihood did not take kindly to trespassers or interlopers.

"A witness reported shots were fired inside the Walker's Run wolf sanctuary last night." Bodie didn't elaborate that he'd been the one to hear the shotgun blasts while perched in a tree at the she-wolf's house.

After following her home from the sanctuary a few nights ago, he couldn't seem to stay away, returning nightly to watch over her as she sat on the back porch swing. During the day, wherever his job led, he searched the faces of every woman, hoping to find her and introduce himself.

This morning as he began to interview residents living near the wolf sanctuary, Bodie had thought he would finally meet her. But when he knocked on her door, no one answered. Somehow, he had to find a way to meet this woman while in his human form. Maybe then, visions of her would stop invading his dreams.

"Did you hear gunshots last night, Ms. McAllister?"

"What if I did? It's hunting season."

"Yes, ma'am, but it's illegal to hunt inside a protected wildlife refuge."

"You ain't got nothing to worry about," she said. "The Co-op will take care of any poachers caught on their land."

The thought had crossed Bodie's mind more than once. In the sanctuary, the she-wolf-turned-beautiful-woman had said sentinels would hunt down anyone who harmed an animal on Co-op lands.

"I'm trying to do my job, ma'am." *Before someone gets hurt.*

"Well, go do it somewhere else." Ms. McAllister stepped back and gripped the hardwood door. "I ain't got nothing to say."

The door closed hard enough to rattle the metal screen. Definitely not the first one slammed in his face this morning, but since this was the last house bordering the Co-op's wolf sanctuary, it would be the final interview for today.

He descended the porch steps, walked to his state-supplied, double cab truck and climbed inside. Shaking off the autumn chill, he studied the McAllister homestead. It was different from the other homes bordering the Co-op's wolf sanctuary in that she had a dozen or so chickens running around her yard and an empty pig sty. There had been no indication of pets or farm animals at the other residences.

The house appeared more weathered than the others he had seen, but still in good repair. In the front window, one slat in the blinds parted. His intent when questioning the residents wasn't to antagonize them, but to offer help.

Help that no one seemed to want or appreciate. If indeed they were wolf shifters, as he suspected, perhaps the Co-op residents believed they were safe living among their own kind. Estranged from his clan and under constant scrutiny, Bodie could only imagine how comforting that feeling must be.

He turned the key in the ignition and waved to the woman in the window. The blind snapped closed.

In the rearview mirror, he saw a white pickup truck pull in behind him. An older man got out, his movements stealthy and predatory.

Wahya! The term the she-wolf had used when referring to her species pierced his mind. Whereas her spirit had been kind and gentle, the aura emanating from the man stalking toward Bodie's vehicle caused his feathers to ruffle.

Bodie rolled down his window. "Good morning, sir. I'm Sergeant Gryffon with DNR."

"I know who you are." The man's dark eyes narrowed. "Appreciate your interest in the shots fired last night, but it's a Co-op matter. Best you stay out of it."

"If it involves poaching or any other illegal activity, I'm inclined to disagree."

"It doesn't."

"Then you know who discharged the firearms?"

The man sucked his teeth and his gaze flickered right. "A couple of the Co-op's teenagers were horsing around. Won't happen again."

It was an outright lie. In his raven form, Bodie had seen the shotgun casings on the ground and the cut fence. He'd also followed several wolves tracking the perpetrators' trail, which stopped abruptly at the tire tracks that disappeared at the asphalt road. Since he couldn't very well admit to it, he was at a dead end, too.

Bodie picked up the notepad and pen on the seat next to him. "Do you mind telling me your name, sir?"

The man's wizened face darkened. "Don't see why I should."

"For the record," Bodie said. "If I'm going to close out the incident report, I need to know who provided the information."

"Henry Coots." The man exhaled heavily. "Most people call me Cooter."

Bodie jotted down the name. "Who are the juveniles involved?"

"I don't think their names are necessary. They got a good scolding from the sentinels. It won't happen again."

"The sentinels?" The she-wolf had mentioned them, too.

"The Co-op's security force." Cooter nodded. "Put down in your book that they handled the situation. There's nothing more to it."

Oh, there was a hell of a lot more to it. "Thank you for your time, Cooter."

"Next time, before you stick your nose into the Co-op's matters, you should talk to Tristan Durrance. He's been in charge of security since I retired."

"Yes, sir." Bodie had left a message for Tristan but hadn't received a call back yet. Having first met while working the fires in the Chattahoochee National Forest a few years ago, they had reconnected when Bodie moved to Maico.

Cooter returned to his truck and drove around Bodie's vehicle toward the house. Bodie checked the rearview mirror.

At least no more Co-opers were driving up to tell him not to stick his beak where it didn't belong.

Thankfully Willow was having a better time integrating with the locals than her father. She loved her new classmates. Had to be a first. Quiet and heartbreakingly shy, Willow had hated every school she'd attended. Bodie suspected bullying though she never admitted it.

But on her first day at Maico High, she had come home all smiles and talking more than she had the entire summer before they'd moved. Coming out of her shell, she had made friends and was growing more confident in herself every day. Perhaps it had something to do with the nearing of her first transformation, but he hoped that it was because she was happy.

The gnawing in his belly turned into an obnoxious rumble. He'd missed lunch and now his stomach was trying to devour itself. He lifted the phone from its holder on the dashboard and called the local diner.

"Mabel's," a woman answered.

"I need to place an order."

"Bodie?" She drew out his name with her Southern drawl. "Is that you?"

"Yeah."

"Well, hey, cutie pie. I wondered if you were comin' by today to see me."

Bodie had no idea which server was talking to him.

Being a new face in a small town always made one stand out. Being a new single face was like wearing a neon sign. But after Willow and Bodie's mother had joined him in Maico, the neon sign went nova.

"I'm running late and need to pick up something to go."

"Want the usual?"

"That'll be fine." Bodie glanced at the clock. "I might not get there until after the diner closes."

"I'll keep it warming in the window. You drive safe, now. See you soon."

Bodie backed out of the driveway onto the road. Heading into town, he passed the KOA campground and the weight on his shoulders increased. Living in the camper had been a temporary plan when he'd arrived in Maico, alone. He'd expected to have time to find a place before bringing up his daughter and mother.

However, plans changed after two Tlanuhwas had unexpectedly approached Bodie, hoping to recruit him into a small faction wanting him to pick up the mantle of modernization among their kind that had gotten his forward-thinking father killed. Not knowing if they were sincere or informants for the Tribunal—the Tlanuhwas' governing council—Bodie had adamantly declined.

Still, if something was going on among his clansmen, he wanted his family close. Of course, his mother had squawked about the move. But she didn't know about the incident and he wasn't inclined to worry her over something that might not come to fruition.

Clipped to the dashboard, his phone chirped. He tapped the speaker button. "Gryffon."

"Hey." Tristan sounded like his usual friendly self. "Just got your message. Nel turned my phone off so I could get some sleep."

"Nel is in town?"

"Yeah." Tristan's voice faded into a contented sigh. "This time, she's staying."

"That's great," Bodie said, now making sense of how devastated his staunch bachelor friend had been by the break-up with his summer fling. Wolves mated for life; apparently wolf-shifters did, too, when they fell in love.

Not that Bodie was looking for love, but maybe Tristan could help him connect with the she-wolf. Never far from his mind, she captivated him in a way no woman had. He needed to meet her in person, gauge her reaction to his human form. Find out if the strong attraction he felt was mutual.

"About the gunshots last night," Bodie began before his thoughts continued to lead him elsewhere.

"Yeah, that's why I'm calling." Tristan paused. "Can you meet me at the Walker's Run Resort? We need to discuss a few things."

Oh, yes, we do.

Chapter 3

The gray gloom in the early afternoon sky matched Ronni's mood and she barely felt the nip in the light autumn breeze. Strolling past Wyatt's Automotive Service, she gave a finger wave to Rafe inside the garage and then crossed the side street to Mabel's Diner.

After an explosion at Rafe's business last year had caused damage to the diner, the aging owner, Mabel Whitcomb, had considered retiring instead of reopening. She—like most humans—was unaware of the existence of wolf shifters and was not a member of the Walker's Run Cooperative. But, because she was a pillar in the community and a friend to many Co-op members, Gavin Walker—the pack's Alpha—had directed funds from the Co-op's reserves to finance the diner's remodeling project.

On the outside, the town landmark still looked the same with its bright yellow walls and white trim. The interior, however, had been given a significant overhaul. Gone was the faded eighties decor, the stained and threadbare commercial carpet, the ripped vinyl booths, the wobbly aluminum tables and a lunch counter with a large, face-like coffee stain the servers had named Fred.

Now the palette matched the cozy feel that Mabel's always generated. The walls were creamy yellow with white accents, though some rich wood paneling kept customers from feeling like they'd been swallowed by a lemon meringue pie. Instead of carpet, the floor was now wood laminate. The worn and rickety booths, tables and chairs were replaced with solid, sturdy wooden ones. Red-and-white-checkered cloths decorated the tables, and lacy curtains hung over the windows.

The menu was as Southern as ever. Just walking into the diner, one could hear the patrons' arteries hardening. In an effort to not kill off all the customers with cholesterol-induced heart attacks, a few lighter and healthier menu options had been introduced.

Mabel herself remained the most prominent fixture. Sporting her iconic red beehive hairdo and sky blue eyeshadow, she perched on her stool behind the cash register, ringing up the last customer in the restaurant.

"Put your order in about five minutes ago, hon," Mabel said. "Should be out any time."

"Thanks." Ronni smiled as if she hadn't received a letter announcing her entire world could come crashing down at any time.

She continued on into the women's restroom that wasn't much bigger than a closet. After washing her hands, she splashed cold water on her face. The harried look her eyes had held after Zeke died was back. Fear, mostly, of what an uncertain future held.

She stared at her reflection until the fear cowered beneath her determination. No man, no wolf, would take her son.

This was the twenty-first century. Wolfans had evolved alongside humans. It was about time their laws did, too.

Ronni returned to the dining area, empty except for one other person. A man. Sitting on her stool. Eating her lunch.

A growl rumbled in her throat. Stealing a wolfan's food could be a deadly mistake.

"Hey!" She marched over to *her* seat. "What do you think you're doing?"

The Native American man wearing the green slacks and gray button-down of a Georgia state ranger uniform didn't startle. He merely finished chewing and slowly turned in her direction.

Straight black hair fell to his shoulders and the shadow of

a beard shaded his jaw and mouth. Leisurely, his gaze rose from her midsection to her face. Recognition flared in those whiskey-colored depths, though she'd never met the man.

She had, however, heard talk about Bodie Gryffon, the town's newest bachelor. Tall, handsome, mysterious.

In a place as small as Maico, the rumor mill never ceased, especially when a single man was involved. There had been speculation as to why he'd declined interest from all the ladies who'd put themselves in his path.

Ronni could tell by the way his eyes dilated and his nostrils flared when assessing her that at least one of the rumors was dead wrong.

He was nice-looking, with high cheekbones balancing a well-proportioned nose that turned down slightly at the tip. And his naturally bronzed skin was simply flawless. Still, Ronni wouldn't agree that he was as handsome as the gossip mill reported until she saw his chest. Broad and taut with muscles sculpted by hard work, yet warm and comforting when she needed to be held—that's what made a man desirable in her eyes.

It was difficult to really ascertain much about Bodie's chest from the way he filled out his shirt because he wore a bulletproof vest beneath it.

"I'm eating lunch." His broad and toothy smile held no apology for pilfering her food, but it did speed up her heart. "Care to join me?"

"I might've considered it, if you weren't already eating *my* lunch." Wahyas took food very seriously.

Her inner wolf didn't care and urged her to take a seat.

"This is mine. I called in a to-go order."

Ronni flattened her hand on the counter and leaned close. "Does that look like takeout?" she said, catching a whiff of his clean, masculine scent. Hormones that had been dormant for quite some time took notice. Awareness spread through her body while bewilderment distracted her brain.

Bodie wasn't wolfan. Wahyas had a special sense that

helped them recognize their own kind. But something about him was setting off her intuition.

He stared down at the platter of food and drink. "You ordered a fried fish sandwich minus the tartar sauce, pickled okra, cheesy tater tots and an orange soda, too?"

Ronni nodded.

The double doors to the kitchen swung open and Mabel sauntered out carrying a takeout bag. "Here ya go, hon." Her gaze slid from Bodie to Ronni.

Eyes wide and apologetic, Bodie hopped off the stool. "My mistake."

"We can swap." Smiling, because he was a gentleman after all, Ronni took the seat next to him.

"Actually, I have a meeting and was going to eat on the way." He tugged his wallet from his back pocket. "I ate a couple of your tater tots, so I'll give you mine and pay for your lunch."

"Don't worry about it. I won't miss a few tots."

He handed Mabel his money and shoved his wallet back into his pocket. "By the way, I'm Bodie Gryffon."

"I know. Small town." She shrugged. "I'm Ronni Lyles. I own The Stitchery down the street."

"Lyles?" Bodie studied her. "Do you have a son named Alex?"

Ronni's hackles rose along her spine. "I do, why?"

"My daughter, Willow, is very shy. Alex and his friends have been very kind to her at school."

Ronni relaxed. "I would be disappointed to hear otherwise."

"The Stitchery? Is that a dress shop?"

"Fabric store and sewing supplies, mostly. But I also do custom orders and alterations."

"Willow needs some things for a school sewing project." He fished his cell phone from his pocket. "Do you have any of this?"

Ronni read the list: two or more cute pieces of fabric,

matching felt, piping, color-matched thread, straight pins, a sturdy needle, fabric glue.

"I do. What is she making?"

"Beats me." He started to put the phone away and hesitated. "What's your number?" The golden flecks in his curious eyes glittered.

"Why do you want my number?"

"To text you the list." On any other man, the smugness in his smile would have immediately turned her off. Somehow on him, it worked. Maybe it was the tease in his eyes which she found more playful than arrogant.

She took the phone from him, ignoring the static charge that nipped them both, and put in her name and number before returning the device to him.

"Great. I'll ask my mom to bring Willow by your store tomorrow." Bodie glanced at his watch. "I have to go."

He picked up the takeout bag and his drink. Going out the door, he flashed a sexy grin. "See ya later."

"You might be the first woman in town he's asked for a phone number." Mabel sidled over to Ronni.

"It's for business." Her phone pinged with a text.

Hey, beautiful. You're a lifesaver and made my day. :)

His daughter's list followed.

"I don't think he got your number just for business." Mabel chuckled. "He can't take his eyes off you."

Ronni turned to look out the window and met Bodie's gaze. She couldn't explain it, but something about him seemed very familiar.

The morning might've been a bust, but starting the afternoon meeting his she-wolf in person had overshadowed the disappointment.

Ronni Lyles.

Now Bodie had a name to go with the beautiful face that

haunted his dreams. And an excuse to see her again. Once Willow picked up her supplies, he planned to stop by Ronni's store and take her to lunch to thank her. He couldn't wait to see what developed from there.

Walking inside the rustic-themed lobby of the Walker's Run Resort, he noticed a huge wolf totem with a large black bird at the top in one of the far corners. The irony wasn't lost on him, but maybe it was on the wolfans.

Legends often associated wolves and ravens. He wondered if and when the two shifter species had been allies and what had come between them.

A tall, blond man appeared in a hallway near the registration counter. Bodie met him halfway across the lobby.

Smiling, Tristan extended his hand. "Glad you could make it."

Bodie accepted the cordial handshake, feeling a little awkward suspecting his friend's wolfan secret yet remaining quiet about his own shifting abilities. But, until he knew more about the Wahyas, caution was paramount.

"I've been meaning to catch up with you." Tristan led Bodie down a carpeted hallway decorated with rich tapestries. "Between getting our security force up and running and Nel coming home, I've been short on time."

Having long hours and an erratic schedule with his own job, Bodie completely understood.

"Speaking of which, I'm not able to stay for the meeting. I need to pick up Nel for a doctor's appointment."

"Then why am I here?"

"I want to introduce you to Gavin Walker, the man in charge of the Co-op. He wants to discuss what happened in the wolf sanctuary last night."

Bodie hoped it wasn't more of the same stone-walling he'd received from Cooter.

They stopped in front of a large wooden door. Before Tristan's knuckles rapped against the wood, a strong, masculine voice called out, "Come."

Bodie's palms began to sweat. Wolfans must have damn sensitive noses if the one inside the room had smelled them coming.

Tristan pushed open the door and ushered Bodie into the office. "Gavin, this is Sergeant Bodie Gryffon from DNR."

"Welcome to Walker's Run." The older man sitting behind the mammoth mahogany desk slowly rose. Intelligence and wariness shone in his icy blue eyes. His hair and close-cropped beard might be snow-white but he exuded health and vitality and more than a little cunning. He waved at the two captain's chairs in front of the desk. "Please have a seat."

Bodie took the one on the right, closest to the open window. He might not be able to outrun a wolf to the door, but he could fly out the window if necessary.

"Sorry to make introductions and run," Tristan said to Bodie. "But I promise we'll catch up later."

"Today is the ultrasound, isn't it?" Gavin asked.

"Yep." Tristan grinned. "Boy or girl, doesn't matter. We just want the baby to be healthy."

"So do Abby and I." Gavin gave a slight nod. "Do let us know."

"Will do." Tristan ducked out of the office.

Bodie had yet to meet Tristan's girlfriend, but he wished her all the best. Pregnancy, even in modern times, was risky. So was the post-delivery, which was when Bodie had lost his wife.

"Are you all right, Sergeant Gryffon?"

"Yes, sir," he said, a bit more solemnly than intended. He hadn't thought of Layla in a long time. They married out of duty, not love. Because the Tlanuhwa numbers were alarmingly low, marriages were arranged by their Tribunal to ensure the best matches for healthy offspring. Despite the emotional distance between them,

Layla had given him a daughter. For that, he would always be grateful.

"I had a number of calls this morning about you," Gavin said.

"It wasn't my intent to alarm anyone. I was simply following up on a report regarding a possible poaching incident in or near the Co-op's wolf sanctuary," Bodie answered.

"The Co-op has dealt with poachers in the past."

"So I've heard." Bodie didn't want that happening again, especially on his watch. "However, I've been assigned to this area and it's my job to deal with these situations."

"We appreciate your commitment, but whatever happens on Co-op property is not your concern."

"Actually, it is. I have the same power and privileges as any law enforcement officer. And, in situations regarding game and wildlife, I actually have more authority. Which means your wolf pack is completely within my realm of responsibility." And it was a responsibility Bodie took seriously.

A subtle tension crept into Gavin's body. Bodie knew to tread carefully. He did not want to get on the bad side of the man who had the power to help him on a personal level.

"The problem I face is that I work alone and I can't be everywhere," Bodie said. "I've noticed the Co-op's security teams patrol well beyond the wolf sanctuary."

"They do." Gavin leaned back in his chair. "The Co-op owns a lot of property, which is why we maintain a separate town charter. Our lands, including our wolf sanctuary, lie outside the jurisdiction of the Maico sheriff's department and emergency services, so we created our own."

"The Co-op is its own public municipality?"

"Municipality, yes. Public, no. We maintain an exclusive membership."

"What are the requirements?"

"Most of our members were born into a Co-op family," Gavin said.

Well, Bodie wouldn't be joining their ranks that way.

"Others married members or were inducted because of determinable loyalty to the Co-op and our mission."

Things were looking up again. "And your mission is?"

"To safeguard and provide for our families and community, and to protect our way of life."

"An admirable mission close to my heart."

"Then perhaps you are a kindred spirit." Gavin smiled. "I hear your family came with you to Maico."

A reactionary sliver of alarm pulsed beneath Bodie's skin. He didn't detect any hint of malice or threat coming from Gavin but Bodie was overly cautious where his family was concerned. "Yes, my daughter and my mother."

"Your wife?"

"She died following childbirth."

"Now I understand why you paled when Tristan mentioned Nel's pregnancy." Something in Gavin's demeanor softened. "My condolences."

"It's been almost sixteen years, but thank you." Bodie hadn't realized he'd reacted at all. He needed to school his expressions more carefully. "I would do anything to protect my daughter and I'm sure you would do the same for your family." *Or pack.*

Gavin nodded. "I'll speak with Tristan about coordinating efforts regarding last night's poaching incident."

"So there *was* an incident. I was informed the shots were an innocent kids' game." Not that Bodie had believed it.

"Cooter told me what he said to you. He doesn't like outsiders nosing into Co-op business." Gavin gave a look that silenced Bodie's interjection. "However, I believe it can be mutually beneficial if we work together to curtail this threat."

"I appreciate your cooperation." A weight didn't necessarily lift from Bodie's shoulders but he did feel a small sense of relief. "Were any of your wolves harmed?"

"Thankfully, no. But the hunters did kill a young deer inside the sanctuary," Gavin said.

A chill passed through Bodie; he knew the Co-op's sentinels wouldn't stop until the perpetrators were found and he hoped to avoid another situation that might be blamed on the nonexistent wild boar.

"Reed Sumner, one of our security officers, said three men escaped through a cut portion of the sanctuary's fencing. The breech is being repaired and we've doubled our patrols."

"Did Sumner get a good look at the men? Or their vehicle?"

Gavin shook his head slowly and Bodie got the feeling that if the men's identities had been known, they would not be having this conversation. "We do suspect that the vehicle was a truck, based on the tire tracks."

"At least I know to look for a trio in a truck." Bodie stood. "Thank you for your time."

"Tristan has your number?"

"Yes, sir."

"Excellent." Gavin stood. "I'll walk you out."

"Just out of curiosity," Bodie began as they headed down the corridor.

Gavin chuckled. "I thought you might have a question or two."

"How did the select few you mentioned earn membership in the Co-op?"

"Quite frankly, they put themselves in jeopardy to defend and protect one of our own."

"So basically, they honored your mission by nearly dying for it."

"Exactly." Gavin patted Bodie's shoulder.

"Thanks for the tip." But it was one too risky to consider. If Bodie decided to pursue membership in the Co-op, a safer and more pleasant way would be to court Ronni and take her as his mate.

He'd married out of duty before and would do so again if necessary. Maybe this time, it would be different. Bodie already knew he was sexually attracted to Ronni. The warmth of her kind touch still lingered in his mind. Too easily, he could recall every luscious curve and line of her naked human form. Fully dressed in jeans and a flowy blouse, she was still beautiful.

For a moment at the diner, when she had leaned close to him, he'd had to force his gaze away from her before he reached to touch the reddish-blonde tendrils that had worked loose from her relaxed braid. And those cobalt blue eyes… He'd seen more than a flicker of interest in their depths.

Even if they didn't fall in love, she could be a good match. And as long as his family was safe, having Ronni warm his bed wouldn't be too much of an inconvenience. He almost smiled.

Chapter 4

"It's past quittin' time." Ronni tried to turn her grin into a frown as Rafe and Alex ducked their heads from beneath the car hood and stared wide-eyed at her with identical "oops" expressions.

"Rafe was showing me the guts of Brice's Maserati." Excitement flushed Alex's handsome face. Every day, he looked more and more like his father.

Except his eyes. Those cobalt blues were a gift from Ronni's maternal line. A gift that Rafe had also inherited.

Over the last year, Rafe had become like a brother to Ronni. And, at the very least, a favorite uncle to Alex. Rafe's quiet strength and patience had helped steer Alex through the maelstrom of emotion the last year and a half had wrought. Alex was in a good place now.

So was she, until this morning.

When coming to Walker's Run, they had nothing to lose and everything to gain. After receiving today's letter from the Woelfesenat, the exact opposite was true.

"I meant to call," Rafe said, cleaning his hands with the shop towel he drew from the back pocket of his gray coveralls. "I'm dropping off Brice's car and I told Alex he could come along, if it's okay with you."

Blood pressure inching up, Ronni eyed the expensive sports car. "By come along, you mean as a passenger, right? Not the driver?"

"Mom!" Alex's brow scrunched in tandem with a ferocious frown. "I do know how to drive."

"My four cylinder." Ronni swallowed the screech in her

voice. The upcoming drama with Jeb paled in comparison to the thought of her son speeding along a narrow, crooked road, missing a sharp curve and sailing off the side of the mountain. "Not something with a rocket engine."

"It doesn't have quite that much horsepower." Rafe snorted. "And I'm not crazy. I didn't agree to let him drive."

"Brice said I could and he's the Alpha-in-waiting."

"Brice isn't your mother. I am." She raised one eyebrow, her signal to Alex that the discussion was over.

Alex humphed resoundingly, indicating his compliance under protest.

"I'll see you after school tomorrow," Alex said to Rafe, then glanced longingly at the flashy car.

"We're not leaving yet. It's time for a family meeting with Rafe."

"Let's go inside." Rafe punched the buttons on the wall. Motor humming, the bay doors descended slowly to close up the service area. He held open the interior door leading into the empty customer service lounge. Ronni and Alex followed him through the short hallway to the employee break room.

The layout of Wyatt's Automotive Service was similar to Rafe's first repair shop, which had burnt down in an industrial fire caused by the same deranged wolfan who had torched the home Rafe had given Ronni and Alex upon their arrival in Walker's Run. Only Rafe's new building didn't have an apartment like the old one did. Of course, now happily mated and a new dad, Rafe no longer cared to sleep where he worked.

She and Alex sat at one of the round tables in the kitchenette. Rafe pulled three bottles of water out of the refrigerator. Alex accepted the one offered to him, but Ronni waved hers away. Anything in her stomach might come right back up.

Rafe sat in the chair directly across from Ronni, concern weighting his gaze. "Whatever is eatin' at you, just spit it out before it chokes you."

"Remember how we thought you were our only blood-kin?"

Nodding, Rafe swallowed a gulp of water.

"Well, Zeke had an older brother."

"Uncle Jeb," Alex announced. "Dad said he left the Pine Ridge pack and was killed in a bar fight before I was born."

"That's what we thought, hon. But I got a letter from the Woelfesenat." She handed it to Rafe. "Jeb isn't dead."

Alex blinked and gave a slight shrug. "What do they want us to do? Let him live here? Like Rafe did for us when Dad died?"

"Jeb doesn't need a place to live. He's the Pine Ridge Alpha now."

No emotion registered on Alex's face. The loss of his father, relocation to a new pack, a devastating home fire and nearly losing Rafe, whom Alex idolized, in a deadly wolf fight… How much more could a teenage wolfling handle?

On the flip side, plenty of emotion flickered in Rafe's laser-intense eyes. She didn't need to explain the gravity of the situation to him.

"Well, he can't be any worse than the last Alpha," Alex said.

Oh, he certainly could. Jeb had been a terror in his own right. He liked to hurt people, something he learned from his abusive father. Jeb hated his sire and eventually put him down, but the fallen apple hadn't rolled away from the tree in his case. Those violent seeds took root and Ronni doubted the years had wormed out those traits.

"The Woelfesenat said Jeb wants to get to know us." Ronni's brain silently screamed furious defiance and she had to force herself not to shake.

"When?" There was a cold edge in Rafe's voice. Likely, he was sensing her outrage and his protective instinct had kicked in.

"Soon, I imagine." The thought of running had crossed her mind more than once, but she had no doubt that Jeb would track them down. Better to face him in Walker's Run where she had the protection of her pack. "I asked Brice to schedule a video conference with the councilman he knows." The Alpha's son was highly respected within the Woelfesenat and he had promised to do all he could to keep the situation from escalating. "I'll know more after speaking with them."

"If you want me to be there..." There was a pregnant pause.

"Of course I do." Ronni's heart squeezed. As the oldest male blood-kin in her family, he could make significant decisions concerning her and Alex, until she took another mate or Alex turned eighteen. However, Rafe allowed Ronni the freedom to make choices and act in her and Alex's best interest without interference. "I'd appreciate the support."

"Where do you think he's been all this time?" Alex toyed with his empty water bottle.

Not dead and buried as she had believed. "I don't want to imagine where he's been or what he's done. Jeb isn't like your father, Alex. Your father was a good man. The only decent thing Jeb ever did was leave Pine Ridge."

"Why did he go back?" Rafe leaned in his chair, arms crossed high on his chest, his default posture when mentally digging in his heels on an issue.

It warmed Ronni's heart to know he really cared about them.

"I guess he finally heard about Zeke's passing. Alex is now his only blood-kin." And Ronni was the she-wolf Jeb had been dead-set on claiming, until Zeke beat him to it.

Finally understanding the significance of Jeb's return caused the bright blue of Alex's eyes to turn icy. "I'm not leaving Walker's Run. If Uncle Jeb wants to see me, he can come here."

Ronni would inform the Woelfesenat of the same. Both she and Alex had finally settled into a comfortable routine within the Walker's Run pack. It wasn't fair to uproot them because a stranger with a closer genetic relation to Alex had suddenly risen from the dead.

Regardless of wolfan law, she was Alex's mother. It was her right to decide what was best for her son and that definitely wasn't Jeb Lyles.

"What's going on?" Stepping into the camper serving as their temporary residence, Bodie nearly choked on the tension between Willow and his mother, Mary.

"Enisi!" Willow ground out the Tlanuhwa word for grandmother. "She never lets me do anything fun!" Willow sat at the small dining table, her arms folded across her chest, an uncharacteristic, cross look on her angelic face.

Equally visibly vexed, Mary took a plate of food from the refrigerator and shoved it into the microwave.

Really, Bodie could warm up his own supper without his mother's assistance, but the last time he tried, she'd gotten upset. A full-time homemaker when Bodie was growing up, Mary continued to fulfill the role after his daughter was born. Now that Willow was on the cusp of early adulthood, Bodie guessed his mother was feeling like she was no longer needed.

"I'm almost sixteen." Willow's jaw jutted, reminding Bodie of himself.

Even without hearing both sides of the story, he was sympathetic to Willow. At her age, he'd been eager to stretch his wings, too.

"What is it that you want to do?" he asked her.

Still frowning, she watched him with guarded eyes. "There's a football game Friday night and Lucas asked me to go."

Bodie's first instinct was to agree with his mother. His little girl, out with boys? He shuddered, remembering very well what teenagers were like.

But his mother had tried to keep him under an iron thumb

and he had rebelled, sneaking out at night, keeping secrets. Bodie didn't want Willow to engage in similar behavior.

"Just you and Lucas?" Bodie sat across from Willow.

"Alex and Ella are going, too. Alex said his mom will take us."

Now Bodie's interest was definitely piqued. "Is she staying or dropping off?"

"I guess she's staying." Willow bit her lip, her eyes growing wide. "Please, Dad. I've never had friends before and I want to do stuff with them."

"How about I take you to the game and meet your friends? Afterward, I'll consider taking everyone out for pizza."

Sunshine burst on Willow's face. She squealed and slid out of her seat to hug him.

He squeezed her, wanting to hold on to his little girl. But she wasn't little anymore. Soon she'd experience her first shift and in a few years, she'd likely take a mate.

His heart sank. The Tribunal would select a match for her, as it had done for him. Bordering on extinction, the Tlanuhwa had one priority: increasing the flock.

Bodie had resented being forced into an arranged match. He'd wanted to choose his own path, his own mate. In the end, he'd been forced to submit. Still, he never regretted his decision. How could he when he'd been gifted with Willow?

As Tlanuhwa, he understood the dire need for the propagation laws. But as a father, he had a difficult time supporting an archaic mandate that might not be in the best interest of his child.

Willow gave her grandmother a triumphant look. "I'm going to call Lucas." She grabbed her phone and plopped on the pullout couch in the small living area which also served as Bodie's bedroom.

Shaking her head, Mary retrieved the plate from the microwave and placed it in front of Bodie. He nodded his thanks without meeting her gaze.

"You're too soft with her," his mother said. "It gives her false hope."

"How?" Bodie swirled his fork through his food.

"She cannot escape the law." Mary hovered over him. "Unless you want her thrown to wolves, defenseless and shunned."

Mentally, Bodie snorted. The wolves he'd encountered at the Walker's Run sanctuary might not be as ruthless as the threat his mother intended.

"I want Willow to be happy." Bodie watched his daughter. All smiles and giggles as she lounged on the couch and video chatted with Lucas.

"How happy will she be when our race becomes extinct?"

"The Tlanuhwa's survival isn't dependent on one girl."

"What if more fathers think like you?"

Considering the recent conversation that he had with a couple of clansmen, Bodie suspected some already did.

"The Tribunal will be unable to pair the best matches. What then?"

"Maybe we'll evolve into something more than a tired, frightened people." Bodie shoveled a forkful of food into his mouth and swallowed without tasting it.

Mary tossed her hands in the air. "If your father were here!"

"We wouldn't be having this conversation." Because Bodie would've made an entirely different choice. But when his father died, Bodie did what he had to do for his mother's sake.

"It's cruel to give her so much freedom. It will only break her heart in the long run." Huffing, his mother moved into the kitchenette to wash the few dishes in the sink.

Bodie's heart pinged. His own heart had been broken after falling in love with his college girlfriend. His mind's eye had even created a reality in which they could've lived happily-ever-after, if he had been human.

But he wasn't, and the Tlanuhwa were the monsters in fairy tales, not the princes and princesses. How many times had his mother told him that there were no true happy endings for their kind? Survival was all that mattered.

He yearned for something different for his daughter.

Maybe that was how the end began. One father breaking with tradition, hoping to give his daughter what he and her mother had been denied.

"Times have changed," he said quietly. "The Tlanuhwa should, too."

"Remember," his mother warned. "That kind of thinking is what got your father killed."

It wasn't something Bodie would likely forget.

If he met his father's fate, his mother and daughter would be all alone and without support. He hoped forging an alliance with the Co-op would ensure that his family would be looked after if anything should happen to him.

"Dad?"

"What, chickadee?" Turning toward Willow, he cleared all worries from his expression.

"Did you get the stuff I need from the craft store in Gainesville?"

"No, but I met Alex's mom. She owns The Stitchery in Maico and she has everything you need. *Enisi* can take you after school tomorrow." He glanced at his mother. "It's off Sorghum Avenue."

Bodie wished he could take Willow himself but by the time he got off, Ronni's store would be closed. He would have to wait until Friday night to get up close and personal with her again. Until then, watching over her from his perch in her backyard would have to suffice.

Chapter 5

"Boy or girl?" Ronni asked the pregnant woman walking into the store.

"I didn't want to know." Nel Buchanan's unexpected visit was a bit of sunshine in Ronni's gloom.

"I bet Gavin had a conniption, or did Doc tell him?"

"Nope. I pulled the HIPAA card. Doc can't release any of my information without my explicit permission."

"That's an advantage of being human," Ronni laughed. "A wolfan can't keep a secret from the Alpha." Something she'd learned when Gavin called about the situation with Jeb minutes after she had received the news and assured her that she had the pack's support.

Ronni knew she would, but having the Walker's Run Alpha tell her that personally had meant a lot.

"Which is why Tristan doesn't know either." Nel's skin had a radiant glow, not just from the pregnancy; she was truly happy.

Ronni's heart pinched. Tristan was lucky to have recently reclaimed his mate after she left him. Having lost her own mate, Ronni had sympathized with his pain. However, Tristan's mate had returned to him and Ronni's never could.

Still, that didn't diminish her happiness that her friends had reunited. And everyone in the pack loved it when a new wolfling was on the way.

"He's okay with not knowing?"

"Said he didn't care. He only wants the baby to be healthy." Rubbing her stomach, Nel walked up to the counter where Ronni stood. "No matter what, he's going to spoil this little one rotten."

"As well he should," Ronni said. "How are the house plans coming?"

"That's why I'm here." Nel withdrew a folder from her flashy designer bag. Likely a gift from Tristan's socialite mother. Nel's personal style was more subdued.

"Meeting Suzannah today?"

"We had lunch." Nel grinned. "She was not happy when I told her no one would find out the baby's sex until delivery. I may not get any more highfalutin gifts." *Thank goodness*, Nel mouthed.

"What are these?" Ronni picked up one of the papers Nel had laid on the counter.

"Rough sketches of the interior of the new house. We finally agreed on a floor plan. Tristan is meeting with his dad today to work out the construction plan. If all goes well, we'll be able to move in by the end of January."

"That's wonderful."

"It will be. I'm grateful Gavin is letting us live in one of the resort's rental cabins, but I'm counting the days until we have our own place."

"I know the feeling." Ronni and Alex had temporarily lived in a resort cabin after the fire that destroyed their home.

Nel handed Ronni sketches of each room's decor. The patterns and color choices were spot-on, but Ronni would expect no less from an artist whose future mother-in-law was an interior designer.

"I know your schedule is pretty full, but I'm hoping you can squeeze in an order for custom curtains, bedding and some accessories."

"Of course," Ronni said. "I'll order the fabrics and call you when it comes in. Before I start cutting, I want to make sure it really is what you want."

"Great! Here are all of the window measurements. Tristan promised he wouldn't make any more changes."

Ronni tucked all the papers into a manila folder.

"Grace, Cassie and I are having a spa day at the resort on Sunday. Would you *please* join us?"

Ronni nearly defaulted to her usual "thanks, but no thanks" response. Grace, Rafe's mate, often tried to include Ronni in her girls-only outings. She had always declined because Grace and her friends were human, they were younger than her and Ronni wasn't quite sure how she would fit into their group.

"Everything you do is either for Alex or the store. Once in a while, it's okay to do something just for you. Besides." Nel made an exaggerated pouty face. "It's unlucky to make a pregnant woman sad."

Ronni didn't need any more bad luck. "What time?"

Surprise lit Nel's face. "Ten o'clock. We do a leisurely brunch in the resort's restaurant, then a full massage, followed by a manicure and pedicure which is a-mazing."

"Sounds nice." Ronni's voice fell unintentionally flat.

"Don't tell me you're coming and then skip out," Nel said. "It'll hurt my feelings."

"I'll be there."

"Good." Nel slipped the straps to her bag onto her shoulder. "We'll see you Sunday at ten."

After Nel left, Ronni pulled the laptop from beneath the counter. As her nails clicked the keyboard, Ronni silently admitted it was time for a good manicure and decided she was actually looking forward to spa day.

By the time the chimes above the door jingled, Ronni realized she'd spent nearly two hours searching online fabric wholesalers for Nel's project.

"Welcome to The Stitchery," she greeted the newcomers, an older Native American woman and a teenager.

"You're Alex's mom, right?"

"Yes. You must be Willow." The girl's long, black straight

hair fell midway down her back and her flawless skin was a shade lighter than her father's.

The teenager's eyes, a light brown with golden flecks just like her father's, widened. "I am."

"I met your dad yesterday. He said you would come by today." Ronni walked from behind the counter toward the older woman. "I'm Ronni." She extended her hand as human custom dictated. "You must be Bodie's mother."

"Mary." The woman accepted the greeting but there was no warmth in it. She had the same sharp angles in her face as Bodie, but her eyes were an espresso color and the black hair pulled back in a severe bun was laced with threads of silver.

"I have the list of supplies you need," Ronni said to Willow. "What are you making?"

"A study pillow." Willow took her phone from her book bag. "Like this, but cuter."

The photo was a basic blue rectangle throw pillow with a small red pocket in the top left corner to hold pens and pencils and a gray pocket on the right side large enough to tuck a small book and homework papers inside it.

"Pick out the fabrics you like." Ronni pointed to the upright bolts of material loaded on standing shelves and stacked on wall racks. "I suggest a neutral main color, such as something in a gray or taupe pattern. Brighter colors will fade with use."

"Gray and taupe aren't cute," Willow said.

"No, but they are a good balance if you're using fun, colorful fabric for the pockets."

"Okay." Willow strolled through the aisles, running her fingers over the bolts of material.

"Please, have a seat, Mary." Ronni motioned to the table and chairs in the corner. "Would you like some coffee or tea?"

"Black coffee."

Ronni went into the small kitchenette in the back, filled

a medium-size disposal cup with hot coffee and gave it to Mary.

"You shouldn't have given Willow so many choices." Mary waved her hand. "She'll take forever."

"I don't mind," Ronni replied mildly, joining her at the table. "If Willow takes her time, she'll be happier with her selections."

"It's just a school project. As long as she gets a good grade, what difference does the material choices make?"

"Kids should be happy as much as possible. When they become adults, those moments may become few and far between."

"You sound like my son," Mary said. "Willow is his whole world."

"My son, Alex, is mine."

"Oh, yes. Alex." The flat corners of Mary's mouth dipped. "Willow talks a lot about him and a boy named Lucas. She wanted to go to the football game with them Friday night but Bodie decided to take her himself."

Ronni's heart flip-flopped. "Bodie is going to the game?"

"Apparently." Mary's frown deepened.

With the situation with Jeb looming, this was not the time for Ronni to feel all giddy and such. Still, her hormones switched on and she had a difficult time containing her smile.

As long as Friday morning's video conference with the Woelfesenat went well, then Ronni would be more than ready to explore the spark between her and Bodie.

"This space is a temporary location." Tristan chowed down on the burger delivered by room service to his office, a small conference room on the second floor of the resort. "We have plans to build an actual emergency services building to house the Co-op's LEO, EMTs and fire rescuers."

"Your Co-op really is becoming its own city." Bodie

swiped a paper napkin across his mouth, greasy from his burger.

So far, he'd learned the Co-op was an entirely member-supported entity. They prided themselves not only on their thriving wolf population but also on taking care of their own. From education to healthcare to homes and business start-ups, the Co-op made sure no member was left struggling.

To Bodie, whose own people were few and scattered, the Walker's Run Cooperative's close-knit, family-style operation sounded like paradise.

"Yes and no," Tristan said. "We still rely on water and power from Maico's public utility services. And all Co-op businesses are in and around Maico."

"Is The Stitchery one of those businesses?"

Nodding, Tristan swallowed another bite of his food, confirming what Bodie had suspected. "Why do you ask?"

"I met Ronni at Mabel's the other day. I figured if she was a Co-op member, you would know her."

"I know pretty much everyone in these parts. Co-op or not."

Bodie wasn't surprised. When he'd worked with Tristan during the fires, the man never seemed to meet a stranger.

"Word of advice," Tristan said. "Since she's been here, Ronni has shot down all suitors. Don't take it personally if she gives you the cold shoulder."

"Does she usually give out her number?"

Tristan looked up from his food. His chewing ground to a stop. "Not her personal one."

"Oh." Bodie hid his smile behind his burger, taking a giant bite.

"Ronni has been through a lot." Tristan's expression turned serious.

"Is that a warning to tread lightly?"

"What do you think?"

"I think Ronni is someone I'd like to get to know better." Pretty in a natural way, she was comfortable in her own skin. Kind, gentle, but definitely not a pushover, considering that she had confronted him over unintentionally stealing her food. What impressed him was that once they'd figured out the mistake, Ronni didn't stay mad at him. Even perturbed, she was still rather pleasant. Plus, she was beautiful naked. "In the time I've spent with her, I've felt a connection that I'd like to explore."

Tristan merely looked at him. His dark brown eyes bored through Bodie but not in a menacing way.

Bodie resumed eating. "If you want me to back off, I will. I won't like it, but I don't think you would ask without a damn good reason." One being that wolves didn't get involved with non-wolves. If that was the situation, better to know now than after he'd invested time and energy into pursuing a she-wolf.

"If Ronni wants you to back off, she'll tell you herself. If she does, respect her decision."

"I will." But Bodie intended to do everything possible to ensure that she didn't want him to back off.

Chapter 6

Cold throbbed deep inside the marrow of Ronni's bones but it wasn't from the chill in the night air. The video conference with the two Woelfesenat councilmen presiding over the Southeastern Wahya packs had not gone entirely in her favor.

Because Jeb had no children of his own, and Alex was his only blood relative, the council had decided not to deny visitation rights.

After the meeting, Rafe assured her that he would be present for all visitations, if she wanted him to be. And Brice explained that Jeb could only meet with Alex within the Walker's Run territory and visits had to be arranged through Gavin.

Ronni let out her breath, a puff of steamy fog forming as it left her lips.

Twenty years ago, Jeb had been a cruel, frightening man. He didn't care for anyone or anything, except Zeke.

Jeb could have changed in the years he'd been gone, the years she'd thought him dead and buried, fattening the insects feasting on his rotten carcass.

Maybe now all Jeb wanted was assurance that his baby brother's family was taken care of and safe.

Jeb was now the legitimate Alpha of the Pine Ridge pack. If he violated any law, including the Woelfesenat's current ruling, not only would he face hostilities from all the Alphas who had a treaty with his pack, he'd also face the Woelfesenat's wrath.

Jeb was a lot of things. Stupid wasn't one of them.

"Willow!" Seated two rows below where Ronni sat, Lucas Grayson, Alex's best friend, jumped up and waved.

A girl at the bottom of the bleachers looked up, her uncertain eyes widening a moment before a relieved smile lightened her anxious expression. She waved and carefully climbed the steps, her father trailing behind her.

There was no uncertainty in the look he gave Ronni. Sexy, confident, predatory.

Her skin prickled and she gritted her teeth, willing him to sit anywhere except next to her. She had enough to deal with without adding her hormones into the mix.

Alex and Ella, his girlfriend of the month, scooted over to allow Willow room to sit next to Lucas. Usually the quiet, awkward one among Alex's expanding group of friends, Lucas beamed and chattered excitedly with Willow.

Young love. The wolflings in Walker's Run had no idea how fortunate they were.

Bodie inched past the people sitting on the same row as Ronni. Her heart raced, even though she willed it to beat at its normal pace.

"Hi." Though a smile hung on his face, the crinkles around his eyes seemed to be more from fatigue than excitement. "I was hoping to find a friendly face in the crowd."

"Considering the number of women's heads turning in your direction as you climbed the bleachers, I'd say there are at least a dozen to choose from." In her current mood, Ronni was fairly sure even a blind man would sense that she wasn't in a friendly state.

"Didn't notice them," Bodie said easily. "I was focused on you."

"You might want to adjust your sights. I've had a bad day and won't be good company tonight." Ronni watched the players rushing onto the field.

"My sights are fine. Your company will be, too." Bodie sat closer to her than necessary since there was plenty of space on their row. "By the way, you look lovely."

"Thanks." She wasn't wearing anything fancy, just a pair of dark blue jeans and a buttercream sweater that complemented her peachy complexion and the red tones in her hair. "You should've brought a jacket."

With sleeves rolled to his elbows, the blue button-down shirt he wore wouldn't keep the chill out for long. Fall would likely come early, with temperatures beginning to dip into the low sixties at night.

Bodie's gaze fell on the blanket covering her lap. "Maybe we can make a deal. You share, I share." He dangled a large thermos and winked.

She was sure he meant it only as a tease, still her nerves tingled and her body warmed. "What's in it?"

"Coffee, strong and black." He set the thermos between their feet.

"Lucky for you it isn't hot chocolate." Ronni returned her gaze to the activity on the football field.

"Yeah?" Inching closer, he bumped her shoulder.

"I'm allergic to chocolate." She refused to look at him or encourage his flirtatious behavior. "You would've lost your only bargaining chip." She saw his arrogant male grin without even looking at him.

"Oh, I doubt that."

Ronni did, too. Especially since his shirt molded around his shoulders, back and torso, teasing her with glimpses of his solid, sculpted, muscular chest.

Bodie gazed up at the clear, dark sky. "Beautiful night to be outside."

Ronni agreed. Ordinarily on nights like this, she would run the woods behind her house, only entering the sanctuary on full moon nights to avoid prowling, unmated males. Since learning of Jeb's reemergence, Ronni had stayed on her back porch swing. Every shadow that flickered beyond the porch light elicited an involuntary shiver and she hated that the mere thought of Jeb Lyles induced such unease.

Something brushed her thigh and Ronni jumped.

"Everything okay?" Bodie's deep, soothing voice drew her attention. Warmth spread beneath his palm, flattened against her leg.

"Yes," she said, swallowing the tightness in her throat.

Doubt lingered in his gaze, but he offered a reassuring smile. He opened the thermos and poured a steaming cup of coffee, then handed it to her. "This should help you shake that chill."

If only it could.

"Mmm." She inhaled the fresh, robust aroma before taking a drink. Her body warmed, but it had more to do with the heat Bodie radiated as he scooted close enough for their hips and legs to touch. She shouldn't allow him the liberty, but strangely she found his closeness comforting.

"Is the home team any good?" he asked.

"I suppose. I don't really follow football."

"What do you follow?"

"My instincts."

"Yeah?" Humor sparkled in his eyes. "What do your instincts say about me?"

She swallowed another mouthful of coffee. "That you're trouble."

"Me?" Bodie's deep, rich laugh rolled through her body like the rumble of distant thunder. "I'm a boy scout."

"I have serious doubts about that."

"I like your smile." His gaze turned molten like liquid gold. "You should wear it more often."

She looked away. "I'll take that under advisement."

"Oh, no." He playfully bumped her. "Don't try to hide it from me now. I'll consider it a challenge to find it again."

Ronni doubted it would be much of one. She found his playfulness more charming than she should, considering the trouble she could soon be facing.

The crowd roared around them.

"First touchdown of the night for the home team." Bodie playfully bumped her shoulder. "We're off to a great start."

"Don't get cocky," Ronni said. "The night is young."

"And chilly." Bodie unrolled his sleeves.

Ronni gulped the last of her coffee and handed him the empty cup so he could have a hot drink.

"Your blanket looks toasty. Do you mind?"

"Tit for tat, huh?"

"Something like that." Smiling, he took the blanket from her lap and wrapped it around their shoulders.

The simple comfort of a warm male body caused her heart to ache. This was so not the time to explore the possibilities.

Dammit, Jeb.

He hadn't shown up yet and already he was screwing up her life.

Laughter rose above the comfortable buzz of patrons inside Dino's Pizzeria. Willow's soft, lilting tone was among them. Bodie couldn't remember the last time he'd seen her so happy, carefree. Maybe never.

"They are good kids, right?" he said.

Ronni's gaze landed on him, only the third time since they'd arrived. "Of course they are." She gave him a questioning look.

"Willow has had a rough time with mean ones. I don't want her getting hurt."

"Alex and Lucas will look after her."

"She seems to be having a good time."

"Hmm." The opening door pulled Ronni's attention again.

"Are you having a good time?" During the football game, he'd sensed Ronni's tension and assumed she was nervous because of his attention. Now he was sure it was something else.

"Yes." She smiled, a perfectly pleasant plastic smile.

"What's wrong?" Bodie decided to tackle the problem head-on.

"I told you earlier, I wouldn't be good company."

"Your company is fine, Ronni. But you jump every time the door opens. Who are you afraid of?"

The warmth drained from her eyes and her smile turned into a brittle frown. "It's nothing."

Bodie didn't push. He wanted Ronni to confide in him but not at the risk of alienating her. He placed his hand over her fingers worrying the paper napkin beside her plate. "If you need someone to talk to..." He shrugged.

"Thanks, but—"

"Ah, don't shoot me down. I'm hoping to strike a bargain." He offered her a smile.

Her reddish-blonde brows arched.

"My wife died in childbirth, so it's always been me and Willow, and my mom." A dull ache rose in his chest. Though he hadn't loved Layla, he had planned a future with her and sometimes he missed what could've been.

"My mother has helped me raise Willow, but some of her ideas are a bit old-fashioned. It would be nice to have someone to talk to." Bodie looked over at Willow, her head bent toward Lucas as he showed her something on his phone. When his gaze returned to Ronni, her eyes had warmed and her expression softened.

Just the response he was aiming for.

"It's hard being a single parent." She blinked away the water in her eyes, then squeezed his fingers. "I lost my husband over a year ago."

"Is this your first date since his death?"

Surprise registered in her expression. "This isn't a date."

"What is it?" Bodie leaned forward, arms resting on the table. He couldn't stop the smile wavering on his lips as a myriad of emotions flickered across Ronni's face.

"We're chaperoning them," she said, more confidently than the doubt that flashed in her eyes suggested.

"Maybe. Willow isn't sixteen yet. And considering the rough time she's had with fake friends, I intend to keep a close eye on her. But Alex—" Bodie glanced at the tall, blond young man with an easy smile and manner. There was a subtle prowess that suggested when he entered adulthood, he would be a force to be reckoned with—if he wasn't already.

"Has been through a lot," Ronni said defensively.

The fierce look in her eyes said she was in protective mama mode and would likely use those pretty white teeth to shred someone to pieces if she felt her son was threatened.

Unbidden affection rushed through Bodie. He could really use an ally as strong as Ronni. All he needed to do was earn her trust and the best way to do that was help her deal with whatever had her so worried. But she was too defensive tonight. He'd have to broach it another time.

"I was nineteen when I lost my father." A bitter lump grew in Bodie's throat. He sucked down his entire glass of water, trying to dilute it.

"Losing a parent at any age is difficult," Ronni said quietly. "Did your mother remarry?"

"No." Bodie knew to tread carefully, but he figured if he spoke to be flattering, the she-wolf would sense the insincerity. "I became her life and now that's a huge complication for us."

He averted his gaze to Willow. His mother wanted to shelter Willow, keep her safe, protected. Caged. More and more, Bodie simply wanted to see his daughter soar.

"She's a lovely girl."

"Thanks." Willow would grow into quite a beauty, like her mother, but she needed a strong feminine role model who would help her discover her own inner strength and develop a stronger spirit than Layla had.

Rather than encourage Willow, his well-meaning mother was more likely to squelch her emerging independence.

"Do you want to get some fresh air in the park?" Bodie could use some.

Ronni's furtive gaze shot to Alex and then to the door. "It's getting late."

"Tomorrow isn't a school day." Bodie stood. "We'll be in full view of the restaurant. The kids will be fine."

He could read the word *no* forming on her tightly pressed lips.

"Unless you're afraid of being alone with me." He held out his hand.

The she-wolf's nostrils flared. Fire sparked in her eyes and pride straightened her shoulders.

Bingo!

He'd pushed the right buttons. His smile grew uncontrollably broader, until she clutched his hand. Electricity shot through his palm as if he'd grabbed an exposed wire juiced with a live current. The powerful charge scrambled his brain and his vision might've gone a little wonky because an overly satisfied gleam lit Ronni's eyes.

She walked over to the kids' table and spoke to them, then sashayed to the door without looking back. He gave Willow a nod. Her smile lit the dining room. Lucas inched closer to her, dropping his arm protectively across the back of her chair. Alex's gaze was fixed on his mother. When she disappeared out the door, his laser-intense eyes swung to Bodie.

The warning was clear. This one would be hell to deal with if crossed.

Bodie turned to follow Ronni outside, willing steel in his legs. He wished the wobble was from something other than the she-wolf's touch, but he'd only drank one beer and Alex's attempt at intimidation had no real effect.

A light breeze nipped Bodie's face as he stepped into the night. Ronni leaned inside her car and pulled out the blanket they'd used at the game. She wrapped it around her shoulders, closed the car door and walked to a nearby park bench. He sat close beside her. Closer than he normally would on a first date but he'd already seen her naked and his instinct pushed him to leave no space between them.

The moment their thighs touched, Bodie's mind flooded with the awareness of her femininity and her vulnerability. All the while, her heat warmed him far deeper than the surface of his skin. If she hadn't been the first to break eye contact, he could've easily drown in the sea of blue her gaze held.

Tilting her head back exposed the creamy expanse of her slender throat. "It is a beautiful night," she said, echoing his earlier sentiment.

"Not compared to you."

Something more than physical attraction awakened in him. Whatever it was, he needed to keep it in check. He couldn't afford to lose his heart or his head when his family's future hung in the balance.

Chapter 7

Tha-dump. Tha-dump. Tha-dump. Tha-dump.

Biting back his annoyance, Bodie pulled to the side of the narrow, two-lane road. The sun had dipped lower than the mountaintops. All he wanted to do was get home, take a hot shower and crash for the next eight to ten hours.

Last night, he'd barely slept. Every time his eyes closed, visions of Ronni's soft-looking lips beckoned him for a kiss while her eyes pooled with depths of emotion he wanted to explore.

I should've kissed her. Long and deep and possessively. Instead, he'd gone with a brush of lips against her cheek to leave her wanting more rather than being presumptuous.

As he walked to the back passenger side of the truck his boots thudded against the gravel. No other sound carried. Right smack-dab in the middle of nowhere was the last place he wanted to be with a flat and no spare.

Correction. He had a spare, but it happened to be in use, as the front left tire.

Severe cutbacks in government spending had every department tightening their budgets. Approval of his request for a set of new wheels was buried somewhere in the pipeline.

Bodie knelt to examine the flat. Nothing protruded from the outer side. His hopes that a simple patch would suffice died when he leaned underneath the vehicle and saw the metal sticking out of the interior sidewall.

Sitting on the ground, he leaned against the vehicle. A few minutes ago, he'd passed the turn to the Brasstown

Bald Visitors Center, but it was nearly five o'clock. By the time he hiked back to the turnoff and up the road toward the summit, anyone who might give him a ride into Maico would likely be gone.

Although he was in excellent physical shape, at the moment, he didn't have the energy to walk several miles of deserted road to get home.

He could shift and fly, but then he'd have to abandon the vehicle, his uniform and his gun. Gathering his strength, he stood, then walked to driver's side of the truck.

Bodie reached inside the vehicle and grabbed his phone. Due to the escalating tensions, a call to his mother wasn't ideal, but it was the only viable option.

"Dammit!" No signal.

He walked nearly fifty feet before the call went through.

"Hi, Daddy." Willow answered the phone and her sweet voice melted his heart. "Are you on your way home?"

"I have a flat. I need *Enisi* to come get me."

Bodie heard footsteps, then a door opened and closed.

"I don't think that's a good idea," Willow said. "She's crankier than usual."

Bodie knew why. His mother didn't exactly approve of him allowing Willow to meet up with Lucas and Alex at last night's football game. Layla's parents had felt the same when she was a teenager. As a result, she'd never learned how to relate to boys, or men, which caused significant difficulties in their brief marriage.

Bodie was determined to raise his daughter differently.

"Alex works at Wyatt's Automotive Service," Willow said. "Want the number?"

"Yeah, give it to me." Bodie had seen the place between Mabel's Diner and The Stitchery. "Maybe I can catch someone before the place closes." Bodie scribbled the number she gave him on the dashboard pad. After they said goodbye, he called the automotive shop.

Silence greeted him after the ringing stopped.

"Hello? Is this Wyatt's Automotive?"

"Who else would it be?" No sarcasm tainted the deep, quiet voice.

"This is Bodie Gryffon. I'm out on 180 with a flat and no spare."

"Whereabouts on 180?"

"A couple of miles northeast of the turnoff to Brasstown Bald Visitors Center."

"On my way."

The call disconnected.

Bodie returned to the driver's seat, cracked the passenger window and locked the doors. Since he was given no ETA, Bodie settled back for a nap.

Tap, tap, tap.

"Gryffon?"

Bodie opened his eyes and looked at a copper-headed man wearing work coveralls standing beside the truck. His name, Rafe, was embroidered on the patch sewn on the upper left chest. His vivid blue eyes were just like Ronni's and Alex's. Neither physically favored the man otherwise, except Alex carried himself in a similar manner. Bodie figured they must be related.

"Are you all right?" Rafe spoke low and soft, yet Bodie had no trouble hearing him.

"Yeah." He opened the door and climbed out. "I didn't get much sleep last night."

The wolfan's eyes slitted just a little. "I heard you were out with Ronni."

Bodie wasn't the type to gossip so he didn't respond.

"She and Alex are family." There was an edge of expectancy in Rafe's tone.

"Ronni and I ran into each other at Mabel's a few days ago," Bodie replied, figuring Rafe was asking out of concern, not simply being nosy. "She was kind enough to let me sit with her at the football game and we took the kids out for pizza afterward. Alex has been a good friend to my daughter. She hasn't been so lucky in the past."

"Ronni has gone through a rough patch, too. She could use a good—" Rafe gave him a look that made Bodie feel as if he were standing on a precarious slope with oil-slick feet "—friend, too. Otherwise, leave her be."

Bodie gave a slight nod and Rafe seemed satisfied.

"I checked your tires while you were sleeping. The thread is worn on all of them. The back right one can't be fixed."

"I've requisitioned replacements, still waiting for approval."

Rafe hoisted the vehicle onto the tow truck. "Are you seeing Ronni again?"

Bodie wanted to say that his plans with Ronni were no one's business, but wolves were pack-oriented. Since Rafe was a male relative, it was very likely that Ronni's personal life was very much his business.

"If she accepts my invitation," Bodie answered honestly.

If Rafe objected, he remained silent on the subject. He hopped into the tow truck and Bodie slid into the passenger seat.

A mile or so down the road, Rafe spoke again. "Do you work up at the Bald?"

"No, I was out at the WMA checking permits and fishing licenses." And scoping out if any of the campers matched the poachers' basic descriptions of three men in a truck. Yeah, that was searching for a needle in a haystack.

"Work alone a lot?" Rafe asked.

"Yep, unless I'm on a coordinated assignment."

"You might want to check in and out with someone local. Cell phones don't always work in these parts," Rafe said. "One day, you might need more than a tow."

Tristan had suggested the same when they'd met for lunch yesterday, but Bodie had been a game warden since before Willow was born. Working alone was part of the job. "I can handle myself."

"We all think that," Rafe said. "Until the moment comes when we can't."

More than capable of taking care of himself, Bodie worried less about working alone than he did about a summons from the Tribunal, which came without warning and usually things did not end well for the one summoned.

If his plan with Ronni worked out, at least Bodie would have an entire wolf pack to guard his back, if and when that moment came.

"We were about to take bets on whether or not you would actually come to our spa day." Nel's voice was light and she smiled sweetly.

"I couldn't wake up Alex. He sleeps like the dead sometimes." Truth be told, Ronni had also overslept after two frustrating nights, dreaming of Bodie.

Why hadn't he kissed her good-night? *On the lips?*

The vibes bouncing between them had been electric. She had desperately needed that kiss, if just for a moment, to block out all thoughts of Jeb and to feel something other than flickers of panic.

Taking her seat at the lavishly decorated table set with antique china and polished silver utensils, Ronni stared at the three human females grinning broadly, their white teeth straight and even, and without the slightest hint of fang. Still, she felt as uncomfortable as a hen in a starving wolf's den. "What's going on?"

"We were hoping you would tell us." Cassie Walker, Brice's mate, tucked a springy red curl behind her ear. The smallest of the group, she looked as fragile as a china doll, but her tenacity and sheer grit were an undeniable force of nature.

"I'm out of the social loop. I don't know what you expect me to say."

"Start with giving us the scoop on the hot guy you were out with Friday night." Folding her arms on the edge of the table, Grace Wyatt leaned forward, her long, blond pony-tail slipping over her shoulder. "Rafe said he hardly got any work done yesterday because of all the people who called or came by the shop to ask about your new boyfriend."

Irritation flashed through Ronni. Since the archaic wolfan law mandated that the eldest male relative of a widowed she-wolf with children was responsible for their welfare, the pack probably assumed she had asked Rafe's permission to start dating. "If anyone wants to know my business, they should ask me."

"That's exactly what Rafe told them." Grace's grin deepened the dimples in her cheeks.

"And why we waited until this morning to ask," Nel said. "Although we were dying to come by yesterday. But we didn't want to intrude, in case the date ran over."

"It wasn't a date and I'm too old for a *boyfriend*." Ronni humphed. "Bodie and I were simply at the same place at the same time."

"Sharing a blanket." A teasing lilt gave Cassie's voice a sing-song quality and she radiated with genuine warmth. Smart, even-tempered and uncannily insightful, she would make a wonderful Alphena when Brice succeeded his father, Gavin, as Alpha.

"He got cold. It would've been rude not to offer." A lame excuse. She-wolves did not arbitrarily share personal items with males. "I was just trying to act like a human."

The brows of all three *human* women arched in unison.

"I wouldn't share a blanket with a man I wasn't interested in getting to know," Nel said.

"I would give him the blanket, but I wouldn't snuggle beneath it with him unless I wanted other things to happen." Grace's green eyes sparkled.

"I thought we were having brunch." Ronni glanced around the restaurant decorated with rich, warm autumn colors. "I don't see a buffet—are we supposed to order from a menu?"

"It's family-style," Cassie said. "The servers will come around with trays filled with each course."

"I hope they start with coffee," Ronni mumbled. "I could use a tankful."

"Me, too, sister." Grace stared longingly into her empty china cup. "Rafe makes me drink the half-caf at home. Sundays are the only days I can indulge in the double-leaded stuff."

"I hope we aren't making you too uncomfortable," Nel said. "All joking aside, we really are interested and concerned about the things that affect you."

"That's a perk of having us as family." Cassie's demure smile was hopeful. Until becoming Brice's mate, Cassie had no family and few friends.

Even though the entire Walker's Run pack had embraced her, there was a small inner circle of absolute trust and Ronni was humbled to be included.

"And we won't stop pestering you until all the deets are spilled." Grace leaned to the side, allowing the beverage server access to her cup. Once the coffee was poured, she lifted the cup to her face and inhaled deeply. "Oh, how I've missed you."

Nel and Cassie were served hot tea.

"I'll have what she's having." Ronni pointed at Grace. "And I'll need a refill in about five minutes."

"Me, too," Grace piped up.

Despite the curls of steam rising from the cup, Ronni lifted it to her lips. The hot liquid sizzled her tongue and slid down her throat, spreading a comforting heat through her body.

The three women continued to look at her but no further teasing ensued. It was up to Ronni to complete the bonding ritual by satisfying their curiosity or shut it down by changing the subject.

If she did the latter, what was the point of coming?

"Bodie's daughter and Alex are friends," she began.

"Bodie and I ran into each other at Mabel's. He's been so busy at work that he hasn't met a lot of people, so he sat by me at the football game."

"Where is he from?" Grace asked.

Ronni shrugged. They hadn't really talked about the past. Hers was too painfully close to catching up with her to mention.

Nel picked up her teacup and blew over the rim. "Tristan said Bodie works out of the DNR office in Gainesville. He moved here a couple of months ago. His daughter and mother came a few weeks later."

"He's a game warden?" Grace peered at Nel above her coffee cup. "Does the pack need to be worried?"

"Well," Cassie began. "When Gavin, more or less, told Bodie to stay out of the Co-op's business, Bodie informed him that the wolf pack falls within the realm of his responsibility. Then, he pointed out that he has law enforcement power and is willing to use it."

Ronni choked on the coffee she'd swallowed. In essence, Bodie had unwittingly threatened the Walker's Run Alpha. It was a very good thing that Bodie wasn't wolfan.

"What did Gavin do?" Nel asked.

"He told Bodie what actually happened and what little the sentinels knew about the three poachers," Cassie said. "Bodie really wants to catch them, too, and suggested working with our security team. Believe it or not, Gavin agreed. He feels that Bodie could become a trusted ally, eventually."

Speculative eyes landed on Ronni again.

"Don't look at me. I barely know the man." Ronni took an unhurried drink of coffee.

"What does your instinct say?" Cassie asked.

At the moment, nothing trustworthy. Ever since Ronni had met Bodie, her instincts were a scrambled jumble of confusion.

"Tristan really likes him," Nel said when Ronni didn't speak up. "Bodie reminds him of Mason." Brice's older brother had been Tristan's best friend until rogue wolfans killed him. Brice had survived the attack because of his brother's sacrifice, and no one in the Walker's Run pack had forgotten the loss.

"Then he must be a good man," Cassie said quietly.

"No pressure or anything," Grace said, "but are you planning to go out with Bodie again?"

"We haven't actually gone out a first time, yet." Friday night was simply a shared outing with their kids. And although she might want Bodie to invite her on a date, she'd rather wait until after the situation with Jeb was settled.

Delicious scents wafted toward Ronni and she watched servers with loaded trays parade from the kitchen. Their table was the first served and a smorgasbord of food was placed before them.

While Nel and Cassie began with fruits and lighter fare, Ronni and Grace dug into the meats and quiches.

"I can see how the football game might've been an accidental meet-up, but grabbing pizza afterward, that was a date." Grace licked the bacon grease from her fingertips.

"The kids were on dates." Ronni speared another sausage link. "Bodie and I were chaperones."

"He kissed you good-night, didn't he?" Grace asked.

"A peck on the cheek is not a kiss." Actually, Ronni wasn't sure what it was. Though Bodie's lips had barely grazed her skin, her face had warmed and the heat had spread through her entire body. He simply stood there, eyes closed, until her tightly coiled breaths synced with his soft, rhythmic puffs and then he'd said good-night and walked away.

"So, it was a non-date date." Cassie nibbled delicately on a banana nut muffin.

"That's how Tristan and I fell in love." Nel stabbed a strawberry using her fork. "We did a lot of things together, but neither of us considered them dates."

Ronni's gaze fell to Nel's baby bump becoming noticeable. What Nel and Tristan had done on their non-dates was fairly obvious, and an accidental claiming had resulted in her pregnancy.

Since Ronni had undergone tubal ligation due to recurrent miscarriages and a problematic, high-risk pregnancy with Alex, an unplanned pregnancy would not be possible. "I'm not looking to fall in love."

"None of us were," Cassie said. "It happened anyway."

The three women were lucky to have met and matched with their true mates, allowing a mate-bond to form. It was something that didn't happen for all wolfans.

Independent of a mate-claim, which was established during sexual intercourse with a bite and bound a couple for life under wolfan law, a mate-bond synced the lovers, body and mind, heart and soul.

Mostly, the bond began forming from the first moment true mates met, but not always. When Zeke had claimed Ronni, to keep her out of Jeb's clutches, she didn't sense a mate-bond. Theirs had developed over time.

So, she'd already had her true mate and lost him.

The argument could be made that she could find another, as Rafe had done. Though his heart had been no less broken, he'd been younger when his first mate died and they didn't have children.

Ronni's situation was different. She was a mother and Alex's needs always came first.

"Bless you," Grace said to the beverage server who refilled her coffee. The young man topped off Ronni's cup, too.

"If you're more comfortable with non-date dates, I'll get Tristan to ask Bodie to join us at Taylor's," Nel said. "We could do a group family night."

"That's a great idea," Grace said.

"No, it isn't," Ronni replied.

"Don't you like him?" Cassie asked.

"I like him just fine, but this isn't the right time for me to start dating."

"That's why this will be a non-date." Nel grinned. "Trust me, Tristan is an expert at setting these up."

"At the very least, it will give Bodie a chance to meet people," Cassie said.

Ronni understood it would also give the upcoming leaders of the pack a chance to assess Bodie for themselves.

"Do whatever you need to do." Ronni waved her hand, as if her heart wasn't picking up speed and her nerves weren't tingling.

Nel leaned toward her. "You will be there, right?"

"I need to check my calendar." Ronni picked up her cup and took a slow sip, watching the three women watching her and hoping they couldn't see the giddiness her brain was doling out.

"If you have any interest in him at all, be there," Grace said. "Now that Bodie has made a public appearance with a woman, all the single ladies will have him on their radar."

Ronni swallowed the silent growl tickling her throat. She might not be sure what to make of Bodie's interest, or her own, but she definitely didn't like the thought of him turning that interest toward someone else.

Chapter 8

"I'll be out in a minute!" Ronni paused the mental replay of her Friday night encounter with Bodie. If not for her busybodied friends probing her for details yesterday, she might've been able to put the non-date date behind her. *Liar!*

Smiling, she finished tacking the hem and smoothed the dress over the mannequin. Everything looked even, but she would inspect the garment more thoroughly later.

Feeling good, she went to greet her customer.

The long-forgotten scent raised her hackles even before the man turned from the storefront window to face her.

"Hello, Veronika." His low, raspy voice caused her stomach to roll over like an armadillo playing dead.

"Jeb." She stood behind the service counter, her palms flat on the glass top. "You shouldn't be here. Gavin is supposed to arrange contact."

"With Alexander." Removing his mirrored sunglasses, he walked confidently toward her. Dressed in snug jeans, a dark blue long-sleeve knit shirt, a black leather jacket and polished shoes, he looked downright civil. "Nothing prevents me from seeing you. And you look..." A smile slithered across his mouth and arrogant possessiveness gleamed in his gray eyes. "Well, I'll give Wyatt my thanks for taking such good care of you."

"Stay away from Rafe."

Jeb tipped his head.

"The Woelfesenat said I had to let you see Alex, but understand this. You will only visit him with Gavin's permission and my supervision, and only so long as he isn't upset by your presence."

"I don't like restrictions, especially those concerning my family."

"We are not your family." Fire flamed in her chest despite the ice crystals in her veins. "We will never be your family."

"Blood is a bond that can't be broken." Jeb's cool demeanor caused chill bumps to pebble her skin. "Everything that belonged to Zeke, I intend to claim as my own. Including you and Alexander."

"Never gonna happen."

His calloused hand firmly captured her wrist. He lifted her hand to his lips and kissed her knuckles. All the while, his calculating gaze froze her breath.

"You should've been mine, Veronika. You were meant to be mine." Turning her wrist, he exposed the tender underside and touched his nose to the delicate skin, dramatically inhaling her scent. "Had any other male been stupid enough to take you from me, I would've ripped out his throat. But Zeke..."

Jeb had loved his brother like no other. Ten years older, Jeb had been the one to raise Zeke after their parents' untimely deaths.

"I left the pack so I wouldn't hurt Zeke. But he's gone now, and I intend to take back what should've been mine."

"I was never yours. I was never going to be yours. There's nothing for you to take back." She yanked free of his clutches.

"I expected resistance." Jeb's jaw pulled tight. "Can't say that I like it."

"Get used to it." Ronni crossed her arms over her chest.

"I should've come for you sooner."

"You shouldn't have come at all."

"Are you going to contradict everything I say?"

"Are you going to listen to reason?"

"This doesn't have to be difficult." Annoyance narrowed his eyes.

"You're right. All you have to do is turn around, walk out that door, leave Walker's Run and never come back."

"I will, as soon as you and Alexander are packed to come with me."

"Alex is happy here. He's safe." She held his gaze. "I'm safe."

"I would have returned to Pine Ridge sooner, had I known the state of the pack." Jeb's fingers curled into his hand. "If Zeke would have told me, he might still be alive."

"We thought you were dead."

"Obviously, you were misinformed." Jeb opened his arms. "I'm very much alive and Zeke damn well knew it."

A vacuum formed in Ronni's chest. The air whooshed out of her lungs and her heart squeezed until she thought it would explode.

Breathe! Just breathe!

"Easy, darlin'." Jeb reached over the counter.

"Don't touch me." Needing to regroup her sensibilities and her composure, Ronni took a step back.

"It seems Zeke was keeping secrets."

"He would *never*!" But the truth of her mate's deception stood before her, full-size, in living color and a very clear and present danger if she didn't get a handle on her emotions.

Forcing a calm she definitely didn't feel, Ronni straightened her spine and lifted her chin. "Zeke knew I was afraid you would return and challenge him."

In her heart, Ronni believed the only reason her mate would have perpetrated a lie was to protect her. Still, pain sliced through her heart and tainted the trust she had afforded him.

"I would never hurt Zeke." Jeb's glacial stare drove an involuntary chill down her spine.

"That's the lie you tell yourself." Ronni blew out a breath.

"You nearly crushed his windpipe when you found out he had claimed me."

"You manipulated him, knowing he was the only one I wouldn't challenge."

"I loved Zeke." And he'd been the one to offer her protection. She didn't need to manipulate him.

"Who's the liar now?" Jeb flattened his palms against the top of the counter. "You never needed to be afraid of me, Veronika."

"You killed your parents!"

"They were bad people. My father beat Zeke unconscious when he was three. I had to make sure that never happened again. And when I joined the service at seventeen, I sent home nearly every penny I earned to help support Zeke. Then I found out our dear mother was drinking and gambling away the money and my baby brother was eating garbage scraps."

Jeb raised his fists to slam the counter, but hesitated. A moment later, he dropped his hands to his sides.

"I'll admit when I came home, I acted rashly. But I was a much better provider for Zeke than she ever was."

"You're not a good man, Jeb."

"I could've been if you'd given me a chance."

"Don't lay that responsibility on me. I am not your keeper."

"You have a fire that I crave and a softness I want to bury myself in," Jeb said as if he hadn't heard her. "I turned my back on you once. I won't do it again."

"For the sake of Zeke's memory, Jeb, you have to leave us alone."

"As the new Alpha of the Pine Ridge pack, I need an Alphena and you're the one I want. Alexander will be my heir. We'll be a family."

"If you want to get acquainted with your nephew, you'll abide by my rules. But purge any thoughts of a relationship with me. You will not become a daily part of our lives. The past is the past, and it's over."

"No, sugar. It's just the beginning."

Feeling too restless for the hour drive down to the DNR office to file paperwork, Bodie turned down Sorghum Avenue toward Maico's town square. Now was as good a time as any to check in with Ronni. He hoped that whatever had preyed on her mind Friday night had resolved over the weekend because he wanted to ask her out again.

She seemed sympathetic to his plight as a single parent and it gave them common ground to explore. Rafe's friendly warning had prompted Bodie to consider a subtler approach rather than the more direct one he'd planned. He didn't want to come on too strong, only to have Ronni shut him down.

His stomach tingled and tightened as he neared Ronni's store. Having had a series of casual relationships and flings, Bodie wasn't the nervous type around women so he wasn't sure what was causing his anxiety. He parked near The Stitchery and strolled to the store, his steps quickening with a bit of pep.

Through the large front window, he saw Ronni with a male customer, her expression hard, angry, determined. Bodie walked inside the store to the jingle of chimes above the door. The tension in the room was as thick as the billowing smoke from a raging forest fire.

The male customer turned, his angry gaze assessing Bodie head to toe and back again.

Although the man didn't appear to be armed with a weapon, he exuded an air of dominance and expectation and appeared to be using his size and formidable appearance to get Ronni to comply with whatever he wanted. Feet apart, hands on her hips and her mouth set in a hard, determined line, Ronni didn't appear intimidated.

That's my girl!

Ronni's gaze targeted him and Bodie could almost see

the wheels turning in her mind. Her expression softened. Then, the rigid tension stiffening her muscles dissolved, somehow making her curves seem curvier and irresistibly enticing.

"Hey, hon." Soft and seductive, her voice was a whisper above a purr and she radiated an incredibly feminine aura that froze him where he stood.

Oh, boy.

She walked toward him. The sexy sway of her hips nearly had him panting.

Bodie's gaze left Ronni's beautiful face for only a split second. Satisfied that the man's position had not changed and that he posed no immediate threat, Bodie returned at least ninety percent of his attention back to her. The other ten remained on the man.

"I missed you." She was really close to him now.

Bodie's nerves began prickling. Anticipation coiled in his stomach and he wondered exactly what she was planning to do.

Whatever it was, he was all in.

Her hands slipped around his neck and behind his head. Lips parting with a soft breath, she leaned intimately against him and slanted her mouth over his in a gentle kiss.

Any rational thoughts he might have had disintegrated in the sweeping heat that stormed his body. His nerves snapped with electricity, super-sensitizing him to her every breath, sigh and moan.

His hands glided over her hips and slid down to squeeze her sweet ass like he'd been aching to do since the full moon.

Bodie saw her eyes fly open and watched the sheer delight, surprise and moment of panic flash across her expressive face. Before she could pull back from the kiss, he drew his hand up her spine and cupped the back of her neck. He cradled her firmly but not so tightly that she would feel trapped or forced. Relaxing in his arms, she opened her mouth for his deepening kiss.

Oh, yeah. This was the kiss he'd wanted to give her Friday night.

Suddenly, an infernal heat flushed his body but he had no interest in cooling down. Something dark and primal began prowling in his mind. Bodie rolled his shoulders, tamping down on the urge to pick up Ronni and fly her somewhere safe and secluded, and spend the afternoon with her naked and sweaty.

Of course, he couldn't. As a man, he would have no trouble lifting her into his arms and carrying her to a bed; however, his raven didn't have the size or strength to fly off into paradise with a woman.

"What the hell is going on?" Ronni's unwanted visitor shouted.

Bodie gentled the kiss, smiling against her mouth because she was so into it that she hadn't even heard the man speak.

"Mmm." Licking her lips, she leisurely opened her eyes. "Veronika!"

She blinked, confusion erasing all the sparkling excitement and interest in her eyes. "Oh!" Slowly, she eased out of Bodie's embrace. However, he maneuvered to place himself between the man and Ronni, in case their situation escalated.

"Who is this guy?" If the man's sharp glare had been a spear, it would have impaled Bodie where he stood.

"I'm her lunch date," he answered, unflustered. "And you are?"

"Jebediah Lyles."

Bodie glanced at Ronni.

"Jeb is my former brother-in-law back from the grave." Ronni's tone suggested she wished he'd stayed dead.

At least now, Bodie had some context. And now that he'd

involved himself in their domestic situation, he wasn't going to allow Jeb to continue harassing her.

"Ronni and I are leaving for lunch. Why don't you schedule a time to catch up when it's more convenient for us?"

Jeb's cold look bordered on lethal. Ronni might've missed the "us" part, but Jeb didn't. "When might that be?"

"Tonight isn't good," Ronni said. "I'm not sure about tomorrow yet."

"I'm only here for a few days, Veronika. Don't make this a wasted trip." Jeb's menacing tone didn't ruffle even one of Bodie's feathers, but Ronni's body went rigid. Instinctively, he cupped her shoulders and pulled her close.

"I want to see Alexander," Jeb said, his scowl deepening. "Make the time, or I will."

He gave Bodie a long, hard look before leaving.

When the door closed completely, Ronni released an audible breath, then thumped Bodie in the chest. "What were you doing?"

"Kissing the daylights out of you while I had the chance." He winked. "And you were so into it."

"No, I wasn't." Ronni crossed her arms. "I was pretending."

"Admit it. It was good. It was real good."

"I admit nothing."

"You're smiling," he teased. "I love it when you smile. Gets me all excited."

Immediately her mouth folded into a frown. "I appreciate that you went along with the act."

"I wasn't acting and you weren't either." An irrepressible smile spread across his face despite Ronni's ferocious look. "Come on. I wasn't kidding about lunch. I'm hungry and you should get out of here for a while to decompress."

"I have a lot of work to do."

"You have to eat." Bodie glanced out the window. Jeb was leaning against a black SUV, talking with another man of equal size and build. "Lock up and we'll have a nice lunch

all the smells circulating in the diner, she was surprised to hone in on just his.

"Hey, what did you say when we came in?"

"My lips are available anytime." The flecks in his eyes were shimmering. "Are you putting in a request for right here, right now? Because I'm good with that."

His smile was outrageously flirty but he made no move to sweep her into his arms, bend her over and plant a big one on her. Despite her reasonable brain's utter dismay, she kind of wished he would have.

"Did you say anything else?"

"No, but tell me what you want to hear and I'll say it." The wiggle of his dark brows made her laugh and he smiled. Without boast or taunt, it was a genuine smile that made her respond in kind.

His gaze settled on her mouth. She knew that was where it landed by the way her lips tingled.

"Hey, you two!" Mabel waved them over to a window booth. "You want the blue plate special? Or order off the menu?"

"The special is fine, and sweet tea," Ronni said, scooting into the booth.

"I'll have the same," Bodie said. "And apple pie for dessert."

"It'll be ready in a few minutes." Mabel stepped away from the table, out of Bodie's line of vision, and gave Ronni an exaggerated wink before heading into the kitchen.

"So supper with Jeb. I'm invited, right?" Fingers laced and arms on the table, Bodie leaned forward. His flirtatious smile returned. "Since we're pretending to be a couple, I could be there."

"We're not pretending to be a couple." She could feel her eyes roll.

"So we're a real couple." He did a little head bob. "Cool."

"We are not." She should've saved the eye roll because was when it was really needed and all she had left in

at Mabel's. You don't have to tell me what's going on with that jerk, but I'm a good listener and no matter what, I'm on your side."

He could only hope when all was said and done, she would be on his side, too.

Chapter 9

From the heat boring into the back of her skull, Ronni figured Jeb's furious gaze tracked her every move down the sidewalk. It didn't help that Bodie reached for her hand, entwining his fingers with hers.

She had no idea why he would go to such lengths to help her. Too proud to admit it, she was extremely glad he did.

They neared Wyatt's Automotive Service and Rafe exited the service bay, cleaning his hands with a blue shop towel. "Ronni. Bodie," he said in greeting. "Everything all right?"

"Jeb showed up. That's him over there." She pointed her head in Jeb's general direction. "He's anxious to meet Alex but I'd prefer for you to be there when he does. If I invite him to the house for supper tomorrow, will you come?"

"I'll check with Grace and let you know." Rafe gave her a slight, assuring nod and she knew he would also inform Gavin. The Alpha wouldn't be pleased with Jeb's attempt to circumvent protocol by not checking in with him before contacting her.

"Thanks," Ronni said, feeling slightly better about the situation. "Bodie and I are going to lunch. I'll stop by later."

"All right." Rafe's gaze slid to Bodie.

"I'm being a good friend." Bodie gave Rafe a thumbs-up.

"What is that supposed to mean?" Ronni asked as they continued their walk.

"I know Rafe is your relative and worries about you," Bodie said easily. "I thought he should know you're in good hands. The best, actually, but I didn't want to brag in case

Rafe thought his were better. They aren't, though. Mine are."

"Oh, really." Although her voice deadpanned, Ronni liked how Bodie's teasing manner put her at ease. He provided moments of levity when she really needed it. And a little clarity.

Since Bodie admitted he was just being a "good friend," that bone-melting kiss was all show, despite their bodies' very real reactions.

They stopped at the corner to wait for a car to go past before crossing the street.

"I should apologize for what happened at the store." She'd outright panicked when Jeb refused to leave and when Bodie walked in, her brain had gone all haywire. Apparently, her body had, too, and she'd be a liar if she denied enjoying the lip-locking show they had given Jeb.

"I'm glad to have been there at the right time."

"Now the shock of seeing him again is over, I'll handle him better next time."

"No worries. My lips are available anytime you need them." Bodie held the door open to a noisy Mabel's Di[ner] for Ronni, then walked in behind her.

"Other things are, too, if you're interested," his v[oice] whispered through her mind. But that wasn't possibl[e.]

Wahyas were telepathic with their own kind wh[ile in] wolfan form but they couldn't communicate with h[umans] in this manner unless they shared a mate-bond. W[hich, of] course, they didn't.

Maybe the loud chattering in the restaurant [made] voice seem like it was inside her head.

"Did you say something?"

Bodie continued looking around the diner a[s if he didn't] hear her.

She tugged on his sleeve and he leaned clo[ser. Warm,] masculine, his scent caused her stomach t[o] this her arsenal of incredulous body language was a flat shake of her head.

"Well, what are we, beautiful? Because something's going on between us."

"Two things you should understand. One, there is nothing going on between us." Yeah, she nearly choked on number one. "Two, my situation with Jeb isn't your problem."

"One." Clearing his throat, Bodie narrowed his eyes at her. "Liar, liar, pants on fire. Need me to pat out those flames with my hands?" He squeezed the air with his hands just like he'd squeezed her butt, which was now warming, again.

"Two, if you're expecting more problems with Jeb, then I'm definitely coming. He's the reason I got to kiss you in the first place and I don't want to miss an opportunity for a repeat."

"I'm not interested in any more of your kisses," she said, although her heart chanted, *yes, I am* with every staccato beat.

Bodie's easy smile turned arrogant and irritating. "Oh, I think you are very interested. Maybe even interested in a little more than a kiss?"

"Keep talking like that and you'll be eating lunch alone."

He chuckled lightheartedly and let the matter drop. That he didn't allow his dominant side to keep pushing her to admit something she didn't want to helped Ronni become even more comfortable in his presence. Fun and playful, he knew how to balance his teasing without crossing the line and disrespecting her boundaries.

"Here ya go." The server smacked two blue plate specials onto the table and slid two large glasses of sweet tea and a big wedge of apple pie in front of them. Dropping the wrapped silverware on table, she said, "Enjoy." But Ronni didn't think she meant it.

"Carla must be having a rough day."

"Must be. She's usually quite flirty."

"You don't say." Ronni watched Bodie unwrap his silverware. If he had a clue that Carla's behavior might be due to jealousy, he didn't show it.

"So what is the blue special?" A knife in one hand, a fork in the other, Bodie peered at her in earnest.

"An open-faced roast beef sandwich with mashed potatoes." Although it was hard to tell since the entire platter was covered in a dark, rich beef gravy. "Haven't you had the special before?"

"Nope." He cut into the sandwich. "I like to live dangerously."

"Is that why you went along with my impromptu charade at the store?" Ronni took a bite of her meal.

"I didn't have a choice. The way you mesmerized me with that sassy little strut, I was completely under your spell." With a daring gleam in his eyes, he held her gaze. "Cast it again. I dare you."

If he only knew how much she would like to do just that. Since Zeke's passing, Ronni had felt nothing but a hollow chill, but something about Bodie warmed her, inside and out.

"What if I don't want to?"

"Oh, you do," Bodie said but didn't push any further.

They began eating in amicable silence and she liked the simple comfort of sharing a meal and enjoying his company again.

"I like you," Bodie said.

She liked him, too. Probably a little more than she should.

"We're both single parents of teenagers," he continued. "We eat the same foods. We have great chemistry, right?"

Bodie's caressing gaze started a chain reaction. Ronni's body heated, her skin prickled, her heart pounded, butterflies danced in her stomach and a jolt of awareness lit up her libido like Fourth of July fireworks.

"Yeah," he said. Though his head bowed over his plate, there was no hiding his bodacious grin. "You know I'm right."

"So what?"

"Let's make a deal." He lifted his gaze. "I'll play your boyfriend until the situation with Jeb is resolved. But whether or not you agree to the deal, if I see that he's harassing you, I will step in to end it. That's nonnegotiable."

"You're a terrible dealmaker. That deal is all one-sided."

"I'm not finished." Bodie pushed aside his empty plate. "You have to give me a real chance at winning you over."

"You can't be serious." Ronni's heart thumped an extra beat.

"See this?" Both of his index fingers pointed at his face. All traces of humor were gone. His dark brows slashed down savagely over eyes now devoid of all humor. The tightness in his jaw sharpened the angles of his cheeks into blades. And determination set his firm, masculine mouth like granite. "This is my serious face."

It certainly was.

"I fully intend for us to explore that spark between us."

"There is no spark." She took a sip of her iced tea and managed to slurp nearly all of it down.

"Then what is it?" A quiver of a smile ghosted his tight lips.

An inferno? "Barely a flicker." She waved her hand dismissively.

Laughter erupted from Bodie's chest. Deep and rich and vibrant, it reverberated through her like a tribal drumbeat.

"Challenge accepted." Locking his gaze on her, Bodie extended his hand. "Do we have a deal?"

"No, we don't have a deal." Ronni tucked her fingers beneath her crossed arms just in case her body had other ideas.

"Chicken." He said the word so softly, she almost missed it.

"Trust me. I am not a chicken."

Bodie actually began clucking.

Well, that was all it took for her wolf instinct to take over and when she regained her senses Bodie was shaking her treacherous hand.

Tugging Ronni to her feet, he kept a firm grip on her hand as they strolled toward Mabel, who was sitting at the cash register, grinning like a fiend.

"Everything was delicious," he told her while paying.

"You two lovebirds come back anytime." Mabel winked.

"Oh, we're not—" Ronni didn't finish that sentence because Bodie pulled her outside. "Look, about our deal."

"Too late to retract it. We shook hands." Mirth danced in Bodie's eyes a half-second before he tangled her in his arms, slanted his mouth over hers and kissed her. Softly at first, waiting for her to open.

Which of course she did because her body happily remembered the last kiss and was eager for more of the same.

His hand trailed down her back to grip her ass, hauling her tight against him. Fingers laced behind his neck, she gave in to his quickening pace. His tongue explored and claimed, branding her with the tastes of sweet tea, apple pie and red-hot desire. Funny how chill bumps began to dot her skin even though she was burning up. She rose on her toes, giving as good as she got.

Suddenly, Bodie tore his mouth away. "And now, we've sealed the deal with a kiss."

"What?" Ronni said, feeling discombobulated and a little unsteady on her feet as the lustful fog began to lift from her brain.

"We don't have to jump into bed together right away."

"Are you insane?" Smacking her palms flat against his chest, she shoved away from him.

"Oh, well if you're all for it, so am I." Playfully, Bodie caught her arm. "How soon can we start?"

A flood of hormones unleashed a very real desire that had nothing to do with the effects of a full moon. Especially since it was still a couple of weeks away.

"Look, I don't need any more complications in my life." Ronni ignored the riotous uproar going on internally.

"Boy likes girl, girl likes boy. Boy and girl have wild,

crazy, sweaty sex." Bodie's ridiculously broad smile was infuriating. "It can't get any more complicated than that."

Oh, yes. Yes, it could.

Waiting in the pickup lane at the high school, Ronni allowed herself a moment to breathe. She liked life simple, uncomplicated. Serene.

Not the hang-and-bang roller coaster ride that Fate had strapped her into today.

The bitch.

Couldn't let Ronni have one amazing thing without it being tied to something shitty. Yin and yang could suck it!

She touched her mouth. Yep. Lips still there, despite Bodie's effort to kiss them right off her face. In full view of everyone inside the diner plastered against the window, watching. The way the tongues wagged around Maico, by sunset, everyone would think she and Bodie were engaged.

The nerve of him!

The tickle in her stomach started up again and in no time, her body was humming.

"For crying out loud," she told her reflection in the rearview mirror. "It was only a kiss."

Yeah, like the Hope Diamond was only a lump of coal.

Teenagers flowed out of the buildings and Ronni grew wistful about not finishing high school. At seventeen, she was married and pregnant and working as a waitress. There had been no time to finish school.

Sadly, she'd miscarried. It had taken a few years of trying to conceive before Alex came along. She would do anything for that boy.

Pride swelled her heart when she saw him walking across the school yard. Tall, handsome, with a confident swagger. A total transformation from the lanky, grieving, uncertain boy she'd brought with her from Pine Ridge.

Someone stopped him.

Jeb!

Ronni's fingers froze on the steering wheel. How dare he show up at the school! What did he hope to accomplish? Alex had never even met him.

She forced herself to breathe. Loosened her hands and prepared to get out of the car.

Alex adjusted the backpack slung across his shoulder and started walking again. Jeb fell into step beside him.

Ronni could see that Alex was tense by his grip on the straps of his backpack, but he didn't seem upset or distressed so she remained in the vehicle.

They crossed the road and walked to the car.

"Hey, Mom." Alex slid into the front passenger seat.

Jeb leaned down to the open driver's window. "I came by to introduce myself."

"How considerate." The snarky tone of her voice should've conveyed how much she thought it wasn't. "But don't do it again. The administration doesn't tolerate unannounced visitors, especially those not on the designated list."

And hell would freeze over, thaw and refreeze a million times before Jebediah Lyles's name would appear on that list.

"And in case you forgot, Gavin Walker is in charge of scheduling your visits," she continued. "I suggest that you don't circumvent him."

Jeb glanced at Alex, earbuds in place and buckling his seat belt. "I have a meeting with Gavin, his son and Rafe this evening to settle the matter of you and Alex returning to Pine Ridge with me. Start packing."

If the matter wasn't so serious, she would've laughed. Gavin had already informed her of his and the pack's support. And Jeb had no idea that not only was Rafe Brice's best friend, but he was also the Alpha's godson. And none of the three wolfans were easily intimidated. So, the meeting Jeb was so cocky about definitely would not go in his favor.

"Mom." Alex tapped the face of his cellphone showing the time. "I'm going to be late." He loved working with Rafe.

His calm, steady, patient mentorship had turned Alex's life around for the better. Jeb's influence would undo all the gains.

"I'll be in touch, sugar."

I'll keep the disinfectant handy.

Jeb stepped away from the car and Ronni rolled up the window.

"He looks like Dad, don't you think?" Pulling out one earbud, Alex watched Jeb stroll across the road like he owned it. He didn't even acknowledge the driver who had slammed on the brakes to avoid hitting him and was now laying on the horn.

Egotistical maniac. If you ever walk in front of my car...

Of course, she would never actually do it, but thinking about it gave her perverse pleasure.

"I see some resemblance," Ronni replied. Except for the eyes. Zeke's hazel eyes had been warm and kind and loving, and the reason Ronni had been able to see past the physical similarities to his brother.

"I don't like that he looks like Dad, because he isn't. And that's kinda creepy."

The creep factor had less to do with Jeb's physical appearance than with his cruel nature.

"What's he like?"

"I really don't know what Jeb is like now. The man I once knew was very different from your father."

She cranked the ignition, then eased the car into traffic. "He shouldn't have come to you without my permission."

"I told him that. He said that I was a mama's boy and that he would toughen me up."

Okay, now she was rethinking her ability to commit vehicular homicide.

Alex laughed. "I told him to piss off."

"Alex!" *That's my boy.*

"He also asked if I knew about your *boyfriend.*"

A growl rumbled in Ronni's throat.

"It's okay, Mom." Alex stared out the window. "I'm cool with him."

"With who?"

"Willow's dad." Swinging his gaze toward her, Alex rolled his eyes.

"Bodie and I—"

"At the football game, he made you smile, Mom. Like Dad did," Alex said. "If you're gonna say Mr. G isn't your boyfriend, then maybe he should be."

The rest of the drive, Alex remained quiet. Ronni wasn't quite sure how to interpret his easy acquiescence toward her dating, but it was one less worry moving forward with Bodie's plan.

Approaching the Sorghum Avenue intersection, she noticed Jeb's SUV several cars back. Before the light changed to red, she turned. At Wyatt's Automotive Services, she parked next to an open bay.

"Later, Mom." Alex jumped out of the car and darted inside to change into his work coveralls.

Rafe strolled into view, wiping his hands on a shop towel. "That was something, outside Mabel's."

"You saw that, huh?" Why couldn't he have had his head stuck under the hood of something at that time?

"I don't think anyone with a view of the diner missed it."

"Bodie." How could she explain? "He's being a good friend."

"Uh-huh."

Jeb's SUV slowly drove by and continued past her store. Breathing easier, she hoped he stayed away for the rest of the day. Rest of her life, actually.

"Jeb said he's meeting with you, Gavin and Brice tonight."

"Yep. Got the call from Gavin about an hour ago." Rafe tucked the shop towel into his pocket. "Gavin is going to establish rules, boundaries and consequences for Jeb."

"Good! I don't appreciate him showing up unannounced at my store or Alex's school."

"I'll make sure Gavin knows. He won't take kindly to Jeb going behind his back, or yours."

"How long is this ordeal going to last?" Not knowing one minute to the next what to expect from Jeb was already wearing on her nerves and he'd been in town less than a day.

"Gavin told Jeb that he could visit with Alex tomorrow night during supper at your house, as you suggested. Then he's expected to leave and not return unless Gavin gives him permission to come back."

"Jeb doesn't like rules and restrictions." He did what he wanted, when he wanted, without regard for what others wanted.

"He doesn't have to like 'em," Rafe said. "But he will have to abide by them. You and Alex are Walker's Run pack now."

Ronni felt a small measure of relief, but until Jeb actually left Walker's Run, she would be on edge. "I'll have supper ready by seven." And, afterward, she hoped never to lay eyes on Jebediah Lyles again.

"Are you coming?"

"Wouldn't miss it," Rafe said.

"I'll invite Bodie, too." Since he mentioned wanting to come, she was at least obligated to ask.

He had a way of putting her at ease and she would definitely need his talent to get through the evening without having a nervous breakdown.

And sharing a lip-numbing good-night kiss with him would be a good way to end an otherwise crappy evening.

Chapter 10

Bodie stared at the grocery list Willow had texted him. Yeah, Anne's Market was technically on his way home from the DNR office but his mother could've used her car to go to the store rather than asking him to pick up what she needed. Since coming to Maico, Mary hadn't driven once at night because she didn't know the roads and said she was too old to learn. However, she was many years away from actually growing old.

He didn't know if her behavior was a protest or if something was wrong, despite her affirmations to the opposite.

Collecting a shopping cart, he glanced out the large storefront window. From this view, he couldn't quite see Ronni's store, but the lights had been on when he'd turned onto the one-way street around the town square and parked at the market.

The trip to his office after lunch to turn in paperwork was nothing more than a blur. His mind had replayed the kiss with Ronni so many times that he'd felt as if they were still lip-locked. If not for his family waiting for him at the camper, Bodie would've forgone the groceries and headed straight to her.

No woman had ever intrigued him the way Ronni did. That she was also a she-wolf was advantageous, but he was also drawn to her as a person.

She responded well to his teasing; not all women did. And he just felt downright comfortable being with her. Sure, she was conflicted about her own feelings toward him but he was going to enjoy winning her over, despite the complication with Jeb.

Friday night, he'd hated when every sudden movement or sound unnerved her. Hated the anticipatory fear that made her hands tremble, especially having been on the receiving end of her gentle kindness.

No one was going to harass Ronni while he was watching over her. Which meant he'd be back on his perch tonight until she was safely locked inside her house.

Bodie reviewed the list again and headed to the fruits and vegetable section. Several women labored over which head of lettuce or bag of oranges to buy. With their human senses less refined, picking produce was more of a guessing game.

Quickly scanning the shelves and bins, he selected optimum bags of potatoes, onions, peppers and Willow's favorite green apples. Ready to head to the next aisle, he watched a cute brunette pick up a cantaloupe, squeeze and sniff it. She hesitated, feeling the others.

"I wouldn't get that one." Bodie pushed his cart alongside hers. "Unless you plan on eating it as soon as you get home. It's already peaked. By tomorrow, it'll be too ripe."

"I need one for Saturday." She gazed at him with big, green eyes. Green-eyed brunettes had been his "type" until he'd encountered a blue-eyed she-wolf. "Which one would you get?"

Bodie quickly located a melon that would ripen sufficiently. "This one."

He held it for her to take.

"Thank you." Her fingers brushed his hands. The innocent graze lacked the sizzling awareness in Ronni's touch.

"You must be Bodie," the woman said before he could walk away. "I heard a game warden moved to town." A coy smile curved her painted lips. "I'm Gillian."

Her gaze drifted to his left hand and lingered. She wasn't the first to check for a ring.

"I hate to meet and run," he said politely, "but I need to finish shopping and get home to my family."

"Oh!" Her eyes widened. "Thanks for helping me pick out a melon. Next time I see you, I'll let you know how it tasted."

"Okay." He angled his cart around hers and resumed shopping.

In the meat section, he made the same mistake and intercepted a woman about to place a nearly rancid package of chicken thighs into her basket. Thankfully, Willow called to check on his progress and he escaped what could've been a lengthy personal interrogation.

After assuring Willow he would be home soon, Bodie gathered the remaining items on the list.

"Excuse me." The woman he was trying not to make eye contact with stepped in front of his cart. "Would you get the jumbo cups down from the top shelf? I can't reach them."

Bodie parked his cart and stepped up to the shelves. "Blue or red?"

"Red," she practically purred in his ear.

"You're a bit close," he said. "I don't want to bump you with my elbow."

"Oops." A throaty laugh filled his ears.

Oh, boy.

Bodie reached up, clasped the bag and turned around. The woman loomed in his personal space again. He held the bag between them. "Anything else?"

"What are you offering?" Her seductive smile muffled a faint growl.

If he were human, Bodie doubted he would've heard it. Since he wasn't, he knew to tread carefully. The last thing he wanted to do was piss off a she-wolf.

"I'm not offering anything other than a helpful hand to reach what you can't."

"Mmm, I have a few places I wouldn't mind your hand reaching. Or scratching." She pulled the bag of cups from his hands, dropped it in the cart behind her and cozied up against him. "Or petting."

"Bodie?" Ronni's voice was a welcome relief until he saw her unamused face. Apparently, he'd been too concerned with pissing off the wrong she-wolf.

"This isn't what it looks like."

"It looks like Delilah is pawing you like a bear after the honey pot."

Okay, that observation was pretty spot-on.

"She asked me to grab her cups."

"I bet she did."

Delilah laughed but Ronni did not.

"Delilah, please excuse us."

"Relax, Ronni. I was just having a little fun at his expense." Delilah stepped away from Bodie and collected her cart, swinging her hips exaggeratedly as she walked.

Ronni cleared her throat.

"I was just thinking." Bodie sidled up to her, his hands naturally gravitating to her waist. "Your strut is much better." He pressed his mouth against the shell of her ear. "So sexy."

"I don't strut." There was a playful undertone to her indignation and he liked that she hadn't automatically assumed that he had been hitting on the other woman, which of course he hadn't been.

He stepped back to give her a little space. "Obviously, you haven't seen yourself from my viewpoint."

"My bathroom mirror is clear enough."

Oh, what he might give to be that mirror one morning. He collected his cart. "So did you follow me in here because you can't stop thinking about that kiss?"

"What kiss?" She gave him a perfectly innocent look.

"I'm more than willing to give you an instant replay. Right here, right now."

Dark pupils in an ocean of blue dilated and her delicate nostrils flared as she wet her lips. "I'll consider a rain check."

"Deal!" He stuck out his hand.

"You aren't going to fool me twice." Despite her dubious expression, a small smile toyed with her lips before she glanced away and he sensed her growing anxiety.

"Hey," he said gently, drawing her close. "Something wrong?"

Shaking her head, she toyed with his open collar and ran her fingers across his Kevlar vest. Her gaze lifted to his face. Uncertainty had replaced the delightedness he'd seen when they parted after lunch. "Were you serious about coming to supper with us and Jeb?"

"Absolutely. Would you mind if I bring Willow and my mom?"

"The more the merrier, I guess. Rafe will be there, too." She let out a weighted breath

"Mom!"

"I'll text you the details," she said, moving out of his arms.

"I got the sandwiches from the deli," Alex called, coming up the aisle.

"Thanks, hon."

"What's up, Mr. G?" Alex stopped beside Ronni. Not even fully grown and he was already half a foot taller than his mother.

"I was talking to your mom about something really spectacular that happened at lunch."

"What was it?"

"Nothing that concerns you." Ronni motioned Alex to start walking. "Good night, Bodie. Nice seeing you again."

Nice? That was as bad as her calling him *cute*.

"Don't forget! Raincheck on that instant replay, right?"

She might've been shaking her head no, but her sassy sashay said bring it on.

* * *

The steady creak of the back porch swing was Ronni's only company, except for the large raven in the tree. The warm glow of his golden eyes and his quiet song, soft like a lullaby, ate away some of her worries.

All things considered, today wasn't quite as bad as it could've been. Jeb's sudden intrusion into her life had been mitigated by Bodie's timely appearance. And his kisses… Well, sometimes a woman got exactly what she longed for and she had been dreaming of kissing Bodie since Friday night.

Unfortunately, she discovered that he wasn't the type of kisser to put fantasies to rest. The reality was that he inspired a whole lot more.

Restless, Ronni needed to stretch her limbs, settle her thoughts about Bodie and mentally prepare for Jeb as a dinner guest in her home.

After leaving the market tonight, she'd talked to Alex about his uncle and the supper invitation she'd extended. Alex had vacillated between curiosity about getting to know his father's brother and frustration at the possibility that Jeb could take them away from all they had grown to love. Ronni had assured Alex that she would absolutely not let that happen.

Come what may, it was a promise she intended to keep.

Placing her cooled cup of tea on the railing, Ronni slipped out of her long-sleeve T-shirt and boy shorts and crouched. Tiny pinches of electricity erupted from her spine and spread along her nerves. Heat flushed her skin an instant before fur covered her morphing body.

Nails clicked across the wooden planks as she padded toward the steps and leaped from the porch. Squawking, the raven hopped from the shadows. In the moonlight, his inky black feathers shimmered with a silvery luminescence. He spread his wings and launched from his perch. High above her, he circled in a dazzling aerial dance. She loped into the woods and he matched her pace, anticipating her every move.

It wasn't quite like running with a wolf, but the raven was company all the same. Weaving in and out of the thicket, he seemed to be playing a game. When his wing grazed her fur, a frisson of awareness electrified her body much like Bodie's touch.

The stress of Jeb's reappearance had definitely screwed with her senses if her instincts confused a bird with a man.

Strange scents drifted on the wind. Apparently, the raven smelled it, too. He cawed and flew ahead.

Ronni slowed her trot to a cautious step. Through the trees, she caught sight of three armed men and froze.

Like the sanctuary, the private forest where most of the pack had built their homes was not a designated hunting area. No Trespassing and No Hunting Allowed signs were posted on all Co-op lands and sentinel patrols routinely canvassed the properties.

If she howled an alarm, the sentinels would come. Of course, the hunters would then know of her presence. If she attempted to race home, the hunters might still see her and shoot, or they might move on and endanger other packmates.

But by tracking them from a safe distance, she could gauge where they were going and alert anyone in their path.

Stepping quietly, Ronni made sure her paws landed softly on the brittle, leaf-covered ground. Any sound could carry on the quiet wind and she couldn't allow a slipup to give away her position.

The hunters didn't seem to follow a particular trail. Rather they meandered along, stopping here and there before starting again.

The raven sat high in the tree, intently watching the scene below. She hoped he stayed quiet and settled, because even one squawk from him would draw the men's attention.

A twig cracked. Ronni hadn't made the sound but she didn't dare look around, fearing to take her eyes off the trio of hunters. One stopped, cocked his head and looked around. Though hidden in the shadows, she still felt the man's gaze rake her fur. Holding her breath, she inched a step back. Her heart pounded to the point of giving away her location. Still his gaze continued to follow her.

The others turned. Whispers wafted toward her in an indistinguishable buzz.

"Run!"

Even as the deep masculine command threaded through Ronni's mind, her paws scrambled to gain the traction needed for an all-out retreat. Shrieking, the raven took flight, rocketing high into the night sky only to dive in a free fall.

The woods filled with shouts and shrieks but Ronni didn't stop. Running full throttle, she zigzagged around the trees.

Boom!

A sound like an exploding cannon ricocheted all around her, making the woods tremble.

Just as she was about to look back for the raven, Ronni sensed the nearness of his presence. Continuing onward, she howled. A chorus of other wolfans answered. The sentinels were close, and they were coming.

Knowing that didn't give her any peace. Wolves were no match against guns.

Near the house, Ronni leaped over a moss-covered log as another shot rang out. The bullet missed, but something sharp sliced through her front paw as it touched the ground. Her leg buckled and she slammed to the ground with a yelp.

"Mom!" Alex's voice screamed through her mind.

Lifting her muzzle, she watched a tawny wolf launch off the porch.

"Alex! No!"

Ignoring her order, he bounded toward her. Another shot blasted.

Ronni's heart failed. Alex zagged but didn't slow down.

A terrible commotion ensued behind her. The raven's shriek rang louder and sharper. Ronni glanced over her shoulder. A flurry of feathers flew around a poacher ducking his head beneath his arms to guard his face from the bird's beak and talons.

Gratitude burst inside her chest. Ronni pushed herself up. Without touching her injured paw to the ground, she dashed toward Alex, placing herself between him and the hunters. When he saw her racing toward him, he slowed, turning to run beside her when she reached him.

Blue and red lights flashed through the trees. A measure of relief flowed through her body. Tristan or one of the new pack deputies had arrived. She and Alex leaped onto the porch and scrambled into the house.

"Mom," Alex called out after he shifted. "Are you okay?"

Hyped on adrenaline, Ronni darted into the master bathroom before shifting. Gulping her breaths, she remained crouched on the floor. *We're safe*, she repeatedly told herself until her body finally believed her and stopped shaking.

"Mom?" Panic raised Alex's voice. "I know you're bleeding!"

"I'm okay—it's just a scratch," she calmly answered, looking at her blood-smeared palm. "Lock the doors and stay away from the windows."

Hearing him walk away, Ronni shut the bathroom door and turned on the faucet, allowing warm water to wash away the blood. After inspecting and thoroughly cleaning the long, shallow wound, she wrapped her hand with a gauze bandage.

Staring at the disheveled woman in the mirror, Ronni watched grateful tears seep from her eyes. Tonight could've ended so differently. She could've lost Alex; he could've lost her. They could've lost each other.

But they didn't. Survival was what they knew best.

Using a wet cloth, she wiped away the dirt, sweat and

tears. Her nerves more settled, she dressed quickly and opened the bathroom door.

"Mom?" Alex stood in the doorway, his eyes wide and skin pale. He might be nearly grown, but he was still her little boy.

"I'm fine." She pulled him into a tight embrace.

He didn't cry, but his shoulders heaved. If she could, Ronni would hold him forever.

More composed, he stepped back. "What the hell was going on out there?" Now that his nerves had settled, Alex's temper began to show.

"It's hunting season," Ronni said.

"But they're trespassing!" Alex stomped behind her into the living room.

"Some people think rules don't apply to them." Like Jeb.

Ronni continued into the kitchen, pulled back the curtain covering the window above the sink and peered outside. Sharpening her wolfan eyesight, she watched several pack deputies fan out to search for the hunters. She checked the sky and trees for signs of her brave little raven, but there were none.

Her heart sank. *Please be okay, little one.*

"Mom," Alex called to her. "Tristan is here."

Ronni dabbed at the sting in her eyes and went to greet him.

"Are you okay?" The gravity in Tristan's voice caused the nervous jumble in her stomach to somersault.

"I sliced my hand on a sharp stick." Ronni lifted her injured palm. "Otherwise, I'm fine."

Relief eased some of the worry in Tristan's face. "The sentinels are tracking the hunters' scents. Did you see what they looked like?"

"I was staring more at their guns than their faces, but there were three of them."

"If you remember anything else, let me know."

"Wait." She called him back. "Have you seen a large raven with gold eyes?"

"Not tonight," Tristan said. "Why?"

"He followed me on my run but didn't come back when I did."

"I wouldn't worry," Tristan said. "We haven't seen any injured or dead animals in the immediate area. More than likely, your raven flew away."

"I hope so." It would hurt Ronni's heart if the raven was injured or killed trying to save her.

Chapter 11

Hands trembling, Bodie dressed quickly and cast his gaze around the woods where he'd hidden his vehicle earlier that evening.

If he hadn't been with Ronni and distracted the hunters, Bodie could've lost her before he really knew her. Just like Layla.

No, not quite.

He and Layla had been married just over a year and he'd never felt an intimate connection to her the way he did to Ronni. When Layla died, Bodie experienced a great shock and mourned her loss but he hadn't felt the cold chill in his core like he did when Ronni had fallen after a shot rang out.

At first, he had attributed his attraction to Ronni to her kindness in the sanctuary when she was naked and he was vulnerable. The gentleness of her touch and the soothing tone of her voice had seeded deep within him. But kissing her had sparked something much more than gratitude.

And when he thought the hunters had stolen her from him, an unexpected tidal wave of dark emotions had flooded his senses. Consumed with an irrational rage, Bodie attacked them in a startling fury of vengeance until he saw Ronni and Alex running toward the house. His sharpened vision had not detected any bloodstains on her lovely tawny fur, but she held up one paw as she ran.

The prompt arrival of the Co-op's security patrol had caused the hunters to flee. Ordinarily, Bodie would have pursued them.

However, right now his instinct was driving him toward

Ronni. It was almost midnight; he couldn't simply show up and casually say, *Hey, beautiful, what's up?*

He reached for his phone. In the middle of typing a text message to Ronni, the device rang with a call from Tristan.

"We've had another run-in with hunters on Co-op property." His solemn voice told Bodie what he already knew.

"Anyone hurt?"

There was a moment of dead silence and Bodie wondered if Ronni had actually been hit but he hadn't seen the wound.

"Nothing serious."

Relief broke the tightness in Bodie's chest. "Tell me you caught them."

"I've got trackers on their trail—if they're still in the area, we'll find them."

Given the state Bodie was in, it would probably be best for the wolves to find the hunters tonight, rather than him. Tomorrow, he might have a calmer perspective but right now, it just wasn't possible.

"Where are you?" Bodie tried to sound casual. "I can help."

"That's why I'm calling." Tristan cleared his throat. "The shooting happened around Ronni's place and she's pretty shaken." There was expectation in his pause.

Bodie didn't need to ponder why Tristan had called him for Ronni. He expected that the rumor mill had gone into full operation after the kiss he gave her outside Mabel's.

"I thought you might like to be with her, but if I've misunderstood what's going on between you and her, I can call Rafe."

"If he needs to know, then call him. I'm already on my way." Bodie tossed the phone on the seat and started the truck. Throwing the transmission into Reverse, he backed out of the hiding spot.

Then, he spun out onto the road and didn't slow down until he reached the hidden turn to Ronni's house. Two

Co-op security vehicles were parked in the driveway, lights still flashing.

Bodie walked to the front of the house and knocked. He heard movement before the door opened.

"Bodie?" Relief and confusion filled Ronni's big blue eyes. "What are you doing here?"

"Tristan called." Bodie stepped inside.

Ronni closed and locked the door behind him. "You didn't have to come."

"Catching poachers is my job." However, the pounding heart and gut-wrenching knots in his stomach were a reminder that this incident was personal. "Are you all right?" The question he'd been dying to ask since watching her go down.

Ronni nodded, her mouth sealed tight, and she hugged herself.

Bodie would've preferred for her to fall into his arms so he could give her some measure of comfort and take some for himself. Instead, he lifted her gauze-bound hand. "What happened?"

"Rammed my palm on a stick. It's nothing serious."

"How is Alex?"

"I'm okay, Mr. Gryffon." Peering down from the second floor, Alex's face was pale, his large blue eyes squinted.

"You can call me Bodie," he said gently. No need for formalities in a time like this.

"Those assholes had no right to be here."

"I'll find them," Bodie promised. "I wanted to be sure you and your mom were safe before I helped with the search."

"You're not going anywhere until I take care of the scratch on your neck," Ronni said. "What got you?"

Bodie swiped his fingers along the inside of his collar and down the corresponding spot on his neck. Something wet and sticky coated his fingertips. He drew back his hand

and stared at the blood. "I'm not sure," he said, instead of telling her that the damn poacher nicked him after all.

"Come with me." Frowning, she turned and walked away with the confident stride of someone who expected to be obeyed.

Bodie glanced up at Alex. The teenager leaned on the bannister.

"No matter what she says—" Alex gave him a sympathetic look "—it will hurt like hell."

Focusing on Bodie's wound would keep Ronni's mind off what could've happened to her and Alex. And what might've happened to her new bird friend. Closing the door behind Bodie, she led him through the bedroom, his gaze lingering on the cozy queen-size bed before she tugged him into the master bathroom, already feeling less anxious with him near.

"Sit." She pointed to the toilet, lid down.

An amused smile hovered on his lips as he followed her instruction.

"Take off your shirt."

"I like the way you take charge." The smile became more prominent. A dark eyebrow lifted, and his gaze slid to the open door with a view of the bed. "Are you going to get rough with me?"

"You're punchy from the blood loss," she said, even though the injury was merely a superficial wound.

"Maybe I should lie down on the bed." Desire darkened his eyes.

The air crackled with anticipation and expectancy. The static charge bouncing between them raised the tiny hairs along her arms. It also resurrected a primal need in her core.

Outside of the biological urge induced by a full moon, she hadn't had a desire for sex since becoming a widow. Until she met Bodie.

Palm up, he beckoned her closer with the curl of his

finger. Feet following her instinct, she ignored the warning flags her brain signaled. As his hand closed around her wrist, sparks nipped her skin.

"There really is something extraordinary happening between us." His gaze roamed her face, feather soft and titillating. "Isn't there?"

Ronni swallowed the breath she held behind a scrunched mouth. "I don't know," she lied. There was definitely something happening. "Between Jeb's arrival and hunters shooting up the neighborhood, I'm a little rattled."

"For the record." Bodie urged her to sit on his lap, and against her better judgment, she did. "I think you're holding up pretty well."

But she was so damn tired of always hanging in there. Sooner or later, something had to give.

Bodie tucked her against his chest. He felt warm and safe and strong, and his clean, male scent held no trace of sickness or disease. Just pure masculine virility.

A distant howl echoed in her mind and the repercussion formed a single chant—*Mine! Mine! Mine!*—that forced Ronni out of the sanctuary of his arms.

"What's wrong?"

"I can't do this right now." Turning away, she hugged her chest to seal in the comforting heat from Bodie's body. Still, her skin cooled and a dull ache began to throb in her heart.

"You can't accept a little reprieve from the craziness happening in your life?"

When he put it like that, it seemed so simple. The reality was that what was happening during the reprieve was much more complicated.

The howling declaration she'd heard—and still heard with every heartbeat—was her wolfan instinct declaring her true mate. It had to be a mistake.

Ronni had known Zeke since childhood. Their mateship began in fear. Eventually, love did come, along with her inner wolf's declaration that he was her true mate. They were lucky. Not all wolfans formed mate-bonds with their life partners.

Still, it had taken years for the ethereal bond to form. She barely knew Bodie. Confused by the stress of everything that had happened, her instinct couldn't be trusted. Immense caution was needed or she would screw up all of their lives.

"I'll catch those bastards." Conflicting emotions flickered across Bodie's face. "Jeb will eventually leave. When the dust settles, I'll still be here."

"One thing at a time." She dampened a washcloth and handed it to him. "First, we tend to that scratch. Now take off your shirt and wash your neck."

She didn't need to look at him to know he was grinning. The image formed clearly and brilliantly in her mind's eye. Prepping a sterile gauze, she gave in to her own smile, knowing that soon the sting of hydrogen peroxide would wipe out all that male smugness.

She turned around and nearly dropped her jaw.

He'd taken his shirt off, all right.

Now, she was used to seeing physically fit males. Among wolfans, nudity was a natural part of life and not reserved merely for sexual activity. And their natural athleticism kept them in prime physical condition.

But holy moly! Bodie was ripped.

As if he was the choicest cut of premium steak, her eyes devoured the richness of his bronze skin pulled taut over impeccably chiseled muscles. His corded neck, shoulders and torso were packed with more hardened bulk than wolfans but his masculine waist and hips were slightly leaner. That by no means diminished the devastatingly erotic ripple effect on his abs when he drew in long, deep breaths and let them go.

"Care to paw my honey pot?" His pecs danced to a silent, though no less hypnotic, beat.

"Um." She had no ability to put together coherent words.

"Should I drop my pants, too?" He stood. "I might have something else that needs doctoring."

There was no *might have*. The outline of his large erection would be visible even to someone with cataracts.

Her mouth went dry because all of the moisture in her body pooled in her sex. Desire spread like a wicked flame through her body, reducing all rational thought to ash.

Consumed by rampant primal instinct, Ronni pounced and Bodie's arms banded around her. He claimed her lips, his tongue searing and branding her mouth with his taste. Abandoning the medicinal gauze in her hand, she drove her fingers through his long black hair and pressed tightly against him, wanting to be completely and utterly possessed. Backing her against the wall, his fingers dug into the fleshy curve of her ass. She locked her legs around his hips and settled so that his long, thick, hard shaft aligned perfectly with her feminine mound.

White-hot kisses dotted the expanse of her neck, drawing out hisses of indulgent pleasure. His hand slipped beneath her shirt, warming and tickling her as he mapped her skin. She wore no bra to impede his roughened fingers from caressing her breasts. He pinched and rolled her sensitive nipples and she saw stars.

She ground her hips against him, cursing the fabric between them but unwilling to stop to remove the barriers and risk breaking the spell. Bodie growled her name and goose bumps ran the gamut of her skin.

Every system in her body focused energy on the tension coiled in her sex. She couldn't breathe, couldn't think. Couldn't feel anything but the powerful ache gnawing at her center.

Bodie shifted his hips and suddenly Ronni exploded. Waves upon waves of pleasure battered her senses until she was drowning in ecstasy.

He stilled and the rhythmic sound of his breathing lured her back to reality. Brushing the hair from her brow, he smiled. Unlike his arrogant, teasing, boastful grins, this one was soft and poignant and filled her heart with so much awe she thought it would burst.

Ronni gave Bodie's lips a soft peck, untangled her fingers from his hair and unlocked her legs to slide down his body until her bare feet touched the cold tile floor. "Well, that was—"

"What you needed."

"I'm not usually like that with men."

"Good." His cocky smile was a little crooked. "I want to be the only man who gets you so hot and bothered that you have to fling yourself at him."

"I didn't fling." *I pounced. Big difference.*

Bodie chuckled.

A dark spot on the floor caught her eye. "What is this?" She picked up two pieces of soft, black fluff.

"Could be bird feathers." He plucked them from her fingers. "A raven swooped over my head when I got out of the truck."

Ronni's breath hitched. "How big was he?"

"Huge. Maybe even giant." Amusement shimmered in his eyes.

"I'm being serious." Ronni bumped him out of her way. "A large raven visits me every night and I couldn't find him after the commotion."

"Well, the one I saw was bigger than any I've seen and had golden eyes."

"That's him!" Relief flooded through Ronni.

"He was squawking and swooping around the front of the house." Bodie handed her the feathers.

"Was he hurt?"

"He looked fine to me." Bodie pulled on his shirt.

"Hey, Bodie!" Alex called from the living room. "Does it hurt yet?"

Bodie glanced at the unrelieved erection pressing against his zipper. "Yeah! Hurts like hell!"

"Told ya!" Alex's laughter sounded strained. Considering the scare they had, Ronni would've worried if he hadn't been affected.

"I bet the raven scratched you on the neck when he flew past you." She picked up the now unusable gauze and tossed it in the garbage can. "I still need to disinfect that scrape."

"Oh, no," he said, scrunching his nose from the lingering smell of antiseptic. "Just a Band-Aid. I've suffered enough tonight."

Guilt pinched her conscience. After taping a bandage over the flesh wound, Ronni cradled his crotch, massaging the large bulge. "I can take care of this, too."

"I came over to take care of you," he said, so soft and sweet that she nearly puddled at his feet. He cupped her arms, holding her upright so she wouldn't.

"Mom! Tristan is here again."

"I'm coming!" She pressed her forehead against Bodie's shoulder.

"No, you aren't," he whispered. "But you certainly were a few minutes ago."

After lightly smacking her backside, he strolled out of the bathroom. Incredulously snapping her jaw shut, Ronni checked her reflection to make sure she looked decent before casually following him out.

Bodie shook Tristan's hand. "I hope you have good news."

Watching his curious gaze flicker back and forth between her and Bodie, she gave Tristan a bland smile so as not to confirm his suspicions about what transpired in the bathroom. It wasn't his business to know that she'd just experienced a rip-roaring orgasm without even having to take off her clothes.

"I don't." Tristan continued the conversation with Bodie. "The sentinels tracked the poachers to an access road where they escaped in a dark-colored truck."

"Plates?" Bodie asked.

Tristan answered with a head shake. "Couldn't get a make or model either. One of our sentinels went down and he became the priority."

"Who?" Ronni's voice shook and tears sprang to her eyes. It didn't matter if the wolfan was someone close or someone she knew casually. This pack was her family.

"Reed." No traces of Tristan's easygoing temperament could be seen in the dark, deadly anger that flashed in his eyes. "Took a bullet to the shoulder and is on the way to the hospital."

"Someone better find those assholes before I do," Alex snarled. Mad, and more than likely still frightened, he visibly shook.

"It's all right to be angry. Hell, I'm as angry as a mockingbird catching a cat near its nest." Bodie moved closer to Alex. "Those assholes could have hurt you and your mother. But if we let their *assery* bring us down to their level, who really wins?"

He cupped Alex's shoulder, and Alex cut his gaze sharply at Bodie but didn't shrug him off.

"I will catch these guys and put them where they can't hurt anyone else, but I need you to give me the time to do it. Okay?"

Alex chewed his words a moment, sizing up Bodie before he gave a nod of consent.

"Good man." Bodie squeezed Alex's shoulder. "I got this, I promise."

Ronni's heart melted and a lump rose in her throat. Watching Bodie handle Alex's fear and frustration like a pro, she knew one thing for sure. Bodie Gryffon was a damn good man, too.

Chapter 12

"Are you going to be in there all night?" Mary's harsh whisper rose above the steady rush of tepid water from the showerhead.

Resigned, Bodie slowly opened his eyes, dismissing the fantasy he hated to abandon. His body still humming from the explosive release of his previously denied orgasm, he unfisted his cock and turned into the water spray.

After rinsing his body, he turned off the water, and exited the tiny stall. Following a quick towel-dry, he pulled on his pajama pants, turned off the light inside the closet-sized bathroom and opened the door.

"We need to talk." His mother turned, walked into the kitchenette and sat at the small table.

Some of the tension the shower had banished returned.

"Willow is asleep," Bodie said softly.

"We won't wake her."

Probably not. His daughter slept like the dead. Still, if abruptly awakened, his sweet little chickadee turned as vicious as a riled red-tailed hawk.

Bodie took the seat across from his mother. A small night-light was the only illumination inside the camper.

"I don't like this," his mother began.

"We'll go house hunting again over the weekend." Bodie rubbed his hand across the sandpapery stubble along his jaw. *Damn.* He'd forgotten to shave. Between Willow getting ready for school and his mother getting dressed, he doubted there would be enough time for him to shave in the morning.

"I meant your obsession with that woman."

"You've told me." Over and over again. Ronni wasn't Tlanuhwa. Or young enough, though Bodie didn't care she was slightly older than him.

And she wasn't pretty enough. Oh, he'd lost his temper with that one. Ronni wasn't an exotic beauty but he could lose himself in the depths of her eyes. Her fine-boned face was more pleasing to him than any other, and her creamy skin and womanly curves made his body burn hotter than a forest fire during a midsummer drought.

"After Layla died, I knew, one day, you would want a mate again. I didn't expect you to take this long, though." Mary patted Bodie's hands, which were folded on the table. "But to go outside our people?" She shook her head.

"The Tribunal made a mistake with me and Layla. We had nothing in common and she didn't like me very much."

"She would have come to love you, in time. As I did with your father." His mother's plastic smile spoke volumes. "The Pairing Ceremony is our way, Bodie."

"Forcing people into relationships that they don't want is wrong. It's the twenty-first century. Ancient superstitions have no place here."

"The Quickening is not a superstition," she said flatly. "It's as real as the Tlanuhwarians themselves."

Growing up, Bodie had learned the stories about his Tlanuhwarian ancestors—giant, unconscionable, bird-like beasts. Vicious and deadly, they terrorized the First Nations people, destroying villages whenever the Quickening awakened them in the spring from a winter-long hibernation to seek a mate. Many people lost their lives during the dark period before the great shift that sparked a sentient change in their development.

"We've evolved, Mom." Modern Tlanuhwas were peaceful people. "We aren't ruled by base instincts."

"Then what draws you to this woman, night after night, if not the Quickening?"

"I like the way I feel when I'm with Ronni." Playful,

passionate, protective. "And we have great chemistry." Explosive, actually.

"That's how it starts." His mother's fearful brown eyes rounded. "An overwhelming physical attraction."

"Lust, Mom. It's called lust. And the overwhelming part happens when a man hits a dry spell." *Going on six and a half months now.* "That doesn't mean I've lost my self-control. And I'm certainly not going to clobber her over the head, drag her up to my nest and eviscerate anything or anyone that comes near her."

"The Quickening is a serious matter," she snapped. "It is a catalyst in awakening the beast."

"Mom, we're not primitives like our ancestors. We have rational minds and the reasoning ability to manage our impulses. The dark ages ended long ago. For the sake of future generations, we must put these superstitions to rest." He glanced toward Willow's bedroom door.

"So you are turning your back on your heritage?"

"No, I'm simply trying to move forward. And I fully intend to keep seeing Ronni." If he hadn't been there tonight, she could've been seriously injured or killed. His mind wouldn't stop replaying the horrific moment when he'd thought she'd been shot.

From a forbidden place within, cold, lethal images formed in his mind. He knew the thoughts were wrong. Still, he felt a sliver of satisfaction envisioning himself plucking out the hunters' eyes and entrails.

"Bodaway!" Mary leaned across the table and clasped his face, pulling down his lower lids. "Your eyes!"

"What are you doing?" he snarled as she jerked his head back and forth, up and down.

"Your eyes are glowing red." Her voice dropped to a whisper. "The beast is beginning to stir. You must be careful!"

"What you saw was the reflection of the night-light on

my retinas." He knocked her hands away. "I'm Tlanuhwa, not a Tlanuhwarian. Those creatures no longer exist."

"You're wrong." Worry wrinkled her brow as she eased into her seat. "One lives inside us all."

"Stop letting your imagination overrule your common sense." Bodie stood, intending to return to the bathroom to shave before he pulled out the couch to sleep. "I don't want you telling Willow any of your fantastical stories. All she needs to hear is that we are Tlanuhwa. We evolved from the Tlanuhwarians. We are a peaceful species now. And she is free to make her own choices."

And so would he.

"This isn't a good time." Ronni glared at Jeb standing at the front door.

"I heard what happened last night." Jeb's low voice rumbled.

"Then you know that Alex and I are fine." She refused to flinch at his intimidating scrutiny. "We're about to leave. Anything you have to say can wait for tonight."

"We got off to a bad start yesterday. I'd like to try again." Jeb's sudden apologetic demeanor raised Ronni's suspicions. The man she once knew was not one who asked for do-overs. He took what he wanted and didn't give a damn about it. "Let me take you and Alex to dinner, just the three of us."

She might've been a high school dropout, but she wasn't stupid.

"If you don't want to come to supper tonight, that's your choice. I won't offer again."

"Rafe said he would be here tonight. I'd prefer just me, you and Alex."

"I'd prefer it if you would leave us alone."

"Now that Zeke is gone, you and Alex are my responsibility."

"I don't need you to be responsible for us. I can support Alex and myself."

"Under wolfan law, I have blood-kin rights."

"You have no rights as far as we are concerned. You were dead to us and we've gotten along just fine without you."

"You know why I had to leave."

"I'm grateful that you did, but you should not have come."

"I've changed, Veronika."

She noticed he didn't say for the better.

"When I heard about Zeke," he went on, "I returned home and cleaned house."

"How is that a change? You were always brawling with someone over something." People in Pine Ridge cowered in fear of Jeb. All breathed a collective sigh of relief when he left.

"I didn't do this for myself. I did it for Zeke. I took care of the sorry bastards who attacked him."

Ronni pressed her hand over her eyes, trying not to see the image forming in her mind of Zeke stumbling into the house. Bleeding and battered and barely clinging to life. Just to tell her how much he loved her and Alex, with his dying breath.

"It wasn't quick. I made them suffer."

She wiped away the tears beginning to fall. "Then you haven't changed."

"I said I did it for Zeke!"

"He's still dead, Jeb. What was the point?"

"I had to make it safe for you and Alex to come home." Jeb's jaw twitched.

"We are home. This is where Zeke wanted us to be. He knew there was something better for us in Walker's Run and we have what he wanted us to have now."

Without taking her eyes off him, she turned her head slightly and called behind her. "Alex, downstairs now! You're going to be late for school."

"We need to come to an understanding."

"No, you need to understand that Alex and I aren't leaving Walker's Run."

"Having me back in your life is a shock. You need some time to adjust."

"All the time in the world isn't enough to change my mind."

Heavy footfalls pounded the stairs.

"Don't make this difficult."

"From my side of things, you're the one making things difficult."

"What are you doing here?" Alex stood next to his mother. Tall, with a quiet assertiveness he'd inherited from his father and Rafe's influence had honed.

"Checking on you and your mama." Jeb studied Alex's face and Ronni knew he was remembering Zeke at that age. "You aren't safe while poachers are a viable threat in the territory."

"Bodie said he'd catch 'em." Alex bumped past Jeb. "Mom, let's go."

Ronni collected her purse and keys from the entryway table and locked the front door. Jeb caught her arm.

"How long have you been seeing that ranger?"

Long enough to fall hard and fast into lust.

"Not your business, Jeb." She pulled free of his loose grip.

"For God's sake, Veronika. He's not even wolfan."

"But he is a good man. And a damn good kisser." Not only had Bodie given her the best kiss she'd had in forever, he'd also pulled all of the tension out of her last night in a long overdue orgasm.

She started toward the car. "Don't come to my store and stay away from Alex's school or I'll tell Gavin that you're stalking us."

"I have a right to see my family."

"Supper is at seven. It's all the time you'll get." She got in the car and closed the door.

"Why are you smiling like that?" Alex gave her a funny look. "I didn't think you liked Uncle Jeb."

"He's not the one I'm smiling about."

Chapter 13

"I appreciate you checking on Ronni and Alex last night after the trouble." Rafe sat on Ronni's cream-colored leather couch, a hand-crocheted throw neatly folded across its back. The man's eyes were intense, never missing a flicker of anything in his surroundings.

Though Rafe was younger than Ronni, she seemed to look to him for support and it wasn't difficult to see the adoration in Alex's eyes whenever their cousin spoke to him. Having no extended family of his own, Bodie found himself a little envious of their close-knit ties.

"Once I knew what was going on, I had to come." Bodie's gaze drifted to the kitchen. Ronni was bent over, pulling something out of the oven. Her jeans hugged curves that he was dying to run his hands over, again.

Rafe didn't seem to mind that Bodie had jumped from being a "good friend" to being in a relationship with Ronni so quickly. Admittedly, the whole thing had happened at a more accelerated rate than he'd planned. But extreme situations called for extreme measures.

If human, he probably would not have involved himself in such a complicated situation. Since he wasn't, Bodie felt confident in his ability to handle himself.

Besides, after last night's scare, his instinct would not allow him to simply walk away from Ronni. Following the plan was no longer an option. He was in this for the long haul because what Bodie wanted for his family was all around him.

Last night, he'd been too hyped up to sense it. But walking through the door tonight and into Ronni's opened-arm greeting, he knew this was where he wanted to roost.

"Tristan said you're helping the Co-op's security team tonight," Rafe said easily.

"I'm doing a fly-over in my Cessna." A licensed pilot, Bodie had offered to provide aerial assistance in the search for the illegal hunters, in the event they were out again tonight.

The doorbell chimed and Bodie walked to the door without giving thought to whether Rafe should've been the one to greet the dinner guest.

"Right on time," Bodie said, rather than offering a welcome because Jeb was definitely not welcomed in Ronni's home.

Jeb's steely eyes peered straight through Bodie. He felt a ruffle beneath his skin but kept his expression neutral.

Nose slightly twitching, Jeb stepped inside the house. His gaze rounded the room before targeting Ronni's cousin.

"Wyatt." Jeb's intimidating stance had no effect on Rafe, who remained watchful and relaxed. Bodie guessed the interaction was some sort of wolfan posturing. Of the two, he would be more concerned with Rafe. Something about him felt more predatory and lethal.

Not to undermine Jeb's strength and determination, because he definitely could pose a threat. However, Rafe's quietness and the slightly feral look in his eyes gave Bodie pause. He hoped it did the same to Jeb.

Jeb looked up at the kids lined on the balcony. Alex, Willow and Lucas peered down, their faces a mix of curiosity and wariness.

Bodie had been surprised to see Lucas, but Ronni said he frequently stayed for supper and overnight. His parents worked at the hospital and sometimes they had overlapping shifts.

"Evenin', Alexander." Jeb stepped toward the staircase. Now Rafe stood, definitely establishing boundaries.

"I prefer Alex," the teenager answered back, narrowing his eyes at his uncle.

"Supper is almost done," Ronni's strained voice called from the kitchen archway. "Kids, come set the table."

Alex led the group downstairs, Willow between the two boys. A warm feeling ebbed inside Bodie at their protectiveness toward his daughter.

From what he'd observed, the Co-op's wolf shifters were definitely family-centric and civic-minded and he wanted his family to be included in their circle of protection.

Once Ronni took the kids into the kitchen, Jeb started in that direction. Rafe moved to block him.

"Have a seat," Bodie said. "If you go into the kitchen, Ronni will put you to work peeling potatoes or washing dishes."

Annoyance curled Jeb's lip but he sat in the chair Bodie had previously occupied. Bodie took the rocking chair, which was more comfortable than it looked, and the crocheted afghan folded across the back held a tinge of Ronni's scent. He found himself turning his head slightly toward it to inhale more of her enticing fragrance.

Rafe wasn't much of a talker with Bodie. He became less of one with Jeb's arrival.

"How long are you in town?" Bodie asked Jeb.

The older man stopped the visual inspection of the room to size up Bodie. His gray eyes were harsh and full of the cold reflections of a man used to hard living; his roughened knuckles had likely paid the way.

"He's leaving in the morning," Rafe said.

The tension in the room skyrocketed, all of it stemming from Jeb, whose light-skinned face darkened, and his hands curled into meaty fists. Rafe merely gave him a mild look.

"Wow, that's a quick turnaround." *And good riddance.* Bodie wanted the man far, far away from Ronni. "Where are you from?"

"Kentucky," Jeb said, glaring at Rafe.

Apparently something had transpired between the two men, or rather wolfans, and Jeb was still sore about it.

"Kentucky, huh." Not nearly far enough away. Bodie had been hoping for something more remote. Like Pluto.

The weighted silence seemed to stretch an eternity.

"Supper is ready," Ronni called from the dining room.

Relieved, the men walked to the table beautifully decorated and loaded with a platter of fried pork chops, mashed potatoes and gravy, green beans, corn on the cob and a squash casserole.

Ronni sat the kids first, Alex on the right side in the middle seat, Willow across from him, with Lucas to Willow's left. Rafe took the right seat from the head of the table. Bodie was directed to the left seat. Jeb clearly wasn't happy to not be seated at the head and grudgingly sat to Alex's right. Ronni sat at the head of the table, as she should in her own house. At the foot of the table, the place reserved for Bodie's mother remained empty. Bodie had passed along an apology that she was having a migraine and unable to attend. Truth be told, she had refused to come.

Dinner was family style. The kids served themselves first and passed the dishes around the table.

Jeb coaxed Alex into conversation. Much like Rafe, Alex provided short answers with little elaboration, although Rafe's tongue loosened a bit when Ronni asked about his twins.

Halfway through the meal, Ronni had eaten very little on her plate. "Excuse me." She stood. "I need to put the dessert in the oven to warm."

When she didn't return, Bodie slipped away to find her.

She stood at the sink, her hands gripped on the edge of the counter and her gaze focused somewhere out the window.

"Hey, beautiful." He eased behind her. "Are you daydreaming about me getting you all hot and bothered?"

She let out a soft but really long sigh. "No."

"Liar," Bodie whispered. "Don't think I didn't watch your sexy little strut to the kitchen. You know what it does to me. Are you angling for a repeat?"

"I did not strut."

"I noticed you didn't deny wanting a repeat." Bodie dotted kisses down the side of her neck and she relaxed against him, which was the response he wanted to elicit. "What are you thinking about?" he asked.

"Every night before bedtime, I sit in the porch swing and think about how lucky we are to be here." The catch in her voice caused his gut to flinch. "I don't want to lose everything."

"I won't let that happen." Bodie's protective instinct surged with a healthy dose of testosterone.

"You barely know me."

"I know you better than you think." He turned her around, backed her against the sink and leaned into her. "I know you are incredibly kind. I know that you love your son more than anything. I don't know what tragedies you've faced but you survived them without them callousing your gentle spirit."

"Wow." She cupped his cheek. "When did you learn all that?"

"When I kissed you." He couldn't very well explain that she had imprinted on him in the woods the night of the full moon. Since then, she was never far from his thoughts; he had a serious craving for her and lately had developed an undeniable impulse to soar high in the sky with her.

It didn't matter that she didn't have wings. There were other ways to fly with her.

Bodie had never experienced this impulse with any other woman. And he wasn't going to let anyone snatch her away from him, especially that arrogant, egotistical wolf sitting at the table.

* * *

"We need to talk," Jeb growled low against Ronni's ear, "privately." He gathered a cup of coffee and a dessert plate from the tray in her hands, continued past her and quietly exited through the back door onto the porch.

Oblivious, the kids turned washing the dishes into a game. There were as many soap bubbles on the kitchen floor as in the sink and their youthful laughter lightened what could've become a somber evening.

Clutching the serving tray, Ronni walked into the living room. Bodie and Rafe were in quiet conversation.

"Is Jeb in the kitchen with the kids?" Bodie's fingers grazed her, accepting his dessert plate. The gentle warmth of his touches had given her boosts all through supper.

"On the porch." Ronni smiled, though she knew it was weak. "He wants to talk to me alone."

"Is that a good idea?" A slight rumble deepened Rafe's voice.

"It's either now, or he'll catch me when I'm alone."

"I'll be watching," Bodie assured her.

Ronni squeezed his shoulder, grateful for his kindness and strength.

"If you need me…" Rafe said. His intense gaze finished his sentence. From the moment he had tracked her down during his pursuit of his blood-kin, his support had been unfailing and unfaltering.

"I know." She handed him an ice-cold glass of milk and a double portion of his favorite dessert, peach cobbler.

"One of Cassie's?" Rafe's eyes glazed.

"She brought it by this afternoon." By far, Cassie was the best baker in town.

With Bodie and Rafe digging into dessert, Ronni slipped into the kitchen and put up the serving tray.

"I'll be on the porch with Jeb for a few minutes," Ronni announced to the kids. "Be careful not to slip on all the water y'all have managed to get on the floor. I expect it to be mopped up when I come back."

Ronni walked outside, leaving behind a chorus of adolescent groans and giggles. The squeak from the porch swing fell silent.

"Supper was delicious," Jeb said. Even in the dark, Ronni could see his eyes narrowed at her. "And the cobbler was excellent."

"I can't take credit for dessert." Ronni sat on the swing but left a space wide enough for another person to sit between her and Jeb. "The Alphena-in-waiting brought it over."

Silence followed the next few uneasy breaths.

Jeb began rocking the swing at a slow, leisurely pace. "When you invited me for a family dinner, I wasn't expecting so many people."

"I told you, I have a new life here. A new family, too." Ronni meant Rafe but she knew Jeb would associate Bodie's family in her reference as well.

When Jeb made no comment, Ronni stopped the swing and turned to face him. "I appreciate you keeping things civil tonight." She hadn't been sure he would.

"I can put on the same airs as everyone else." There was an edge to his voice but no outright anger. "I get that your life has changed and Alex is growing into a fine man."

"I want to keep it that way, Jeb."

"Why do you assume that I would be a bad influence on him? I raised Zeke after Mom died."

"After you killed her."

"I did what I had to do to protect my brother."

"No remorse," Ronni said. "That's why I don't want you influencing Alex. There are alternative ways to handle disputes. Violence shouldn't be your first choice or fifth or tenth."

Jeb leaned forward, his forearms resting on his thighs, his fingers laced. "I don't regret much, but I wish I'd never left Pine Ridge when Zeke was a kid. I could've made things better for him sooner, but I let him down. Then I did it again. When you tricked him into claiming you."

"I didn't trick him. Zeke loved me."

"You didn't love him." Jeb looked sidelong at her.

"I did love Zeke, with every fiber of my being." Maybe not at first, but his kind heart and easy smile and steadfastness won her heart over time. "It's not my fault if you can't accept the truth."

Jeb humphed. "I let Zeke down again when I left Pine Ridge for good. I wanted him to be happy, but I couldn't stand another man touching you. Not even him." Jeb shook his head. "He still ended up dead. For what?"

"For me and Alex. He didn't take sides when our Alpha began to lose power. Zeke just wanted to get us out before the fighting started. It was his idea to relocate to Walker's Run. Rafe was the only family we had left."

"There was me," Jeb growled. "Zeke should have called me."

"We thought you were dead."

Jeb shot her a look that caused her stomach to tighten and roll.

"If Zeke knew you were alive and didn't call you, it means he didn't want you in our lives." Ronni rubbed her hands over her arms trying to stop the heat from leaving her body. "He chose Rafe's help over yours. This is where Zeke wanted us to be, and that is why I will not leave." If she did, Zeke's sacrifice would be in vain.

"You and Alex were his world." Jeb's brow furrowed over his squinted eyes and the air thickened with the weight of his grief. "I won't fail him again." He pushed to his feet. "I have to get back to Pine Ridge." His unreadable gaze seemed to microscopically study her as if memorizing every line and curve of her body. "I'll keep in touch."

It's over? Was he actually going to leave them alone?

He was inside the house before Ronni's muscles unlocked. Unsteady legs carried her into the kitchen in time for her to witness Jeb giving Alex a hug before he left.

She followed him out the front door as he headed to his car. Bodie eased next to her, his arm slipping around her waist and drawing her close to him.

"Is it over?" he whispered in her ear.

"I'm not sure." She gave Jeb a finger wave as he stared at them over the steering wheel. He finally gave a quick nod, then backed out of the driveway.

The air locked in her lungs finally audibly burst free. Maybe Jeb had changed in the years he'd been gone. The man she'd known would never have left quietly or empty-handed.

"What do you think?" Ronni turned to look at Rafe, standing slightly behind her.

"Supper was delicious, the company has been good and today has had enough worries." Rafe shrugged. "He'll do what's in his nature. But so will we."

Chapter 14

Day was just beginning to break and the sky was afire with red and orange streaks that matched the coming season. The buzz of the aircraft engine and whir of the propeller were as comforting as an old friend's voice. Bodie hadn't flown the Cessna, inherited from his father, in weeks and it felt good to get the airplane back into the air.

"No signs of disturbance from our vantage points." Tristan's voice crackled in Bodie's headset.

"All's quiet from my view, too." Flying at night and without lights on the ground, it should have been nearly impossible to see anything, but with Bodie's superior vision, he had no trouble. Unfortunately, there had been nothing to see. The plane's noise likely warned the hunters and they had either left the area or were hunkered down and hiding.

"It was a long shot." Tristan sounded as tired as Bodie felt. "I appreciate your help."

"And I yours," Bodie replied. "Offer still stands if you want to fly shotgun with me."

"Thanks, but I prefer to keep my feet on the ground."

Bodie made one more loop around the Co-op's protected lands. Since he hadn't seen any wolves in the sanctuary other than those with the security teams, he suspected Gavin had warned his pack not to run their beloved woods until the hunters were captured.

Seeing nothing out of the ordinary, Bodie made the turn toward Maico's small municipal airport. Every time he flew, he felt his father's presence and heard his voice patiently coaching him through the take-off and landing.

The wheels touched down smoothly on the runway. "Thanks, Dad."

He taxied to his assigned area, completed the postflight check and climbed out of the plane.

"Did you have a good flight, sir?" Dressed in dark blue coveralls and wearing a ball cap, a young woman, likely only a few years older than Alex, smiled at him.

"Everything was fine, Sarah," Bodie answered the airport line technician. "But I didn't locate what I needed."

"Maybe next time." She slipped past him to the pilot's door he'd left open. "I'll take care of her until you're ready for her again."

"I'm sure you will." Bodie left as Sarah began her tasks of inspecting, refueling and hangaring the plane.

On the drive to the campground, Bodie couldn't stop yawning. Wanting nothing more than a warm, soft bed, he'd have to settle for a small foldout couch.

Tomorrow he would spend the day house hunting with his family. The camper had been comfortable enough for one. His mother and Willow joining him sooner than expected had crimped the space and increased the bickering between his mother and daughter. They needed to find a real home, soon.

As he turned into the campground, a flutter rolled across his shoulders and his gut tightened at the sight of the black SUV stopped in front of his campsite. Bodie parked in his usual spot. Rather than waiting, he stalked toward Jeb, who was exiting the passenger side of the vehicle.

"What the hell are you doing here?"

"Apparently you don't like strangers around your family any more than I like them around mine." An unveiled threat threaded through Jeb's low, quiet voice.

"Ronni and Alex aren't your family," Bodie responded with equal menace. "You've been dead to them for years. Showing up now doesn't change a damn thing. You're nothing more than a poltergeist that needs to be exorcised."

"It'll take more than a priest and holy water to get rid of me." Jeb's humorless smile might've given a lesser man pause.

Bodie stepped closer. "I've taken Ronni and Alex under my wing. They don't need you, they don't want you."

"I will claim what is mine!"

"Stay away from them," Bodie rumbled in a low voice.

"Do you think you can stop me?" Jeb's chilling laughter stirred something deep and primal within Bodie's spirit. "You have no idea what I'm capable of doing."

"I know exactly what you are." Inwardly, a hot tremor shook Bodie though his stance remained rock solid.

The space between him and Jeb crackled with energy. A dark, dangerous entity slithered through Bodie's mind. There was no other way to describe the ominous presence prowling in his consciousness.

Behind his eyes, a searing white-hot pain distorted his vision. Not only did he see Jeb standing before him, Bodie could see the pulse points throbbing at his throat and temples, even at inner wrists not covered by the sleeves rolled to his forearms. He also saw the predatory red glow of Jeb's eyes and something akin to a heat signature radiating from the man's body.

Bodie's fingertips began to sting. He fisted his hands at his sides. "Trust me when I say if you don't leave them alone—" a timbre Bodie had never heard laced his own voice and horrifically satisfying visions of clawing out the man's eyes and stringing out his entrails played in his mind "—you will regret it."

Whatever was happening to him, Bodie had never experienced it before. He wasn't the type of man who derived pleasure from violence. Insomuch as it was possible, he preferred a peaceful path.

"Who do you think you are, telling me to stay away from what belongs to me?" A snarl weighted Jeb's haughty laugh.

"Who I am is a man not to be trifled with," Bodie replied. "Go back to being dead, Jeb. At least to Ronni and Alex."

"If I don't?" The challenge was clear.

"I've already told you."

"Right. I'll regret it." Jeb gave a cold, short laugh. "You've got balls, Gryffon. I'll give you that, but you should focus on taking care of your own family." His gaze lingered on the camper before sliding back to Bodie. "And let me handle mine."

Jeb stepped backward a few paces before he turned and walked to his vehicle.

Stay away from my family, you son of a bitch. That includes Ronni and Alex.

As if he'd heard Bodie's thoughts, Jeb shot him a hard look before getting into the SUV, which promptly sped away.

"Dad?" Willow leaned out of the camper door. "Are you just getting home?"

"Yes, chickadee." Bodie mentally shook off the encounter with Jeb. Maybe his heightened sensory reaction was nothing more than lack of sleep. He moved toward the camper.

"You're bleeding." Willow went inside ahead of him. "*Enisi*, Dad cut his hands."

"I'm fine," Bodie said as his mother came out of the bedroom.

"Let me see." She turned Bodie's hands palms up to inspect the unusual puncture wounds his blunt, square nails had made. "What did this?"

"Some trash I tossed out." More or less the truth.

His mother's gaze lifted slowly to his face and the look she gave him sent a ripple of uneasiness down his back.

"What?"

"Willow, get the first-aid kit," Mary said without taking her eyes off Bodie.

"I can take care of these myself." He broke free of his

mother's grasp to her exaggerated sigh. "Willow, finish your breakfast, then get ready for school."

Without waiting for debate or protest, Bodie went into the bathroom and locked the door. Looking into the small mirror above the sink, he didn't see any changes in his physical appearance other than the dark moons beneath his eyes from lack of sleep. Doubting that he'd snatch more than a couple of hours at a time until the poachers were caught, he turned on the hot water and soaped his hands. Gently, he cleaned and rinsed the shallow wounds.

Then Bodie shucked out of his clothes, turned on the hot water and stepped into the shower to rid himself of the chill from the strange reaction he had to Jeb. However, the heavy weight in the pit of his stomach would likely lurk there until he was satisfied Jeb was no longer a threat.

Chapter 15

"**O**ver there!" Willow pointed to a large round table in the center of a crowded Taylor's Roadhouse buzzing with country-rock music and the chatter of patrons.

Jeb was gone, the weekend was here and Bodie felt as if he'd lived a lifetime in a smattering of days. Tired, but glad to have some down time with family and friends, Bodie shrugged at the hostess and allowed his daughter to tug him to where Ronni was seated. Absolutely stunning, she cradled a copper headed infant in her arms who seemed as captivated by her as Bodie was with watching them.

Mine!

A warm cozy feeling settled in his chest. Everything inside him sighed. Ronni was the one. Absolutely, he had no doubt that she was the reason he'd been drawn to this town.

Typically, he wasn't the type to give credence to fate or destiny but he was fast becoming a believer, considering the irresistible pull he felt toward Ronni.

She glanced up at him and her smile caused a little flutter in his heart. "I saved you the seat next to me." She tipped her head at the empty chair.

"Where are Alex and Lucas?" Willow asked.

"Right there." Ronni pointed at a table of teenagers nearby.

Willow glanced at Bodie with a hopeful expression.

"Go on."

Her smile made his fluttering heart swell.

Before he sat down, Ronni quickly introduced him to

their tablemates. Of course, he knew Tristan, and Bodie was happy to finally meet his friend's girlfriend, Nel.

Rafe, holding his infant daughter Reina, nodded his greeting. Next to him was his perky wife, Grace. Ronni held their twin son, Ryan.

And finally, Brice Walker, who was Gavin's son, sat with his beefy arm draped over his wife Cassie's petite shoulders. Their precocious daughter, Brenna, toddled around the table, giving hugs and kisses to everyone.

After the frenetic pace of the past week, Bodie would've preferred a quiet, cozy dinner with Ronni, but being included among her family and friends meant more than he could express.

Ryan watched him with big, green, curious eyes, his little nose twitching as he chewed his pacifier.

"Where's Mary?" Ronni asked.

"She wanted some time to herself." After spending the entire day listening to his mother and Willow argue about every little thing while house hunting, Bodie had agreed that grandmother and granddaughter needed a break from each other.

"Tiskan!" Brenna lifted up her arms.

Tristan picked up the child, held her for a moment in a giant hug, kissed her cheek, then settled her into his lap. "Brenna is my biggest fan."

"Who dis?" She leaned over and tapped Bodie's arm.

"I'm Bodie," he said, gently shaking her tiny fingers. "Pleasure to meet you."

"Bobee!" The little girl's smile lit her face.

"Close enough." Bodie winked and she giggled. He glanced at Tristan. "How old is she?"

"Eighteen months," Tristan said. "She was an early talker because her mama wouldn't let anyone use baby-talk with her."

"Bobee." Brenna tapped him to get his attention. "I this many." She pointed her index finger at him.

"Me, too." He grinned at her.

She gave him a dubious look, her dark blue eyes searching his face. "Na-uh." Her head of red-gold curls bounced with the shake of her head. "You this many." She held up both hands, stretching out all her fingers.

"Between you and me," Bodie said, "I'm a little older than that, but close enough."

Laughing, Brenna reached for him.

Bodie glanced at Brice and Cassie, who nodded approval, before welcoming the little girl into his arms. He hadn't held a child since Willow was little. Sometimes he missed those days. But having a vasectomy shortly after Layla's death meant the only babies he'd bounce on his knee would not be his own.

Brenna gave him a hug. "You smell funny."

Bodie's heart slammed to a halt. He really didn't want to be outed by a child in a restaurant likely full of wolfans.

"Brenna," Cassie said sharply. "I've told you that isn't polite."

"I showered, I promise," Bodie said to the little girl studying him intently.

"Don't worry," Brice said. "She's obsessed with smells and says that to a lot of people."

Breathing easier, he glanced at Ronni, who seemed oblivious to his close call. Eventually, he would reveal his raven form to her. When she had fewer worries and he had stronger ties to the Co-op.

"Mmm, bye." Brenna wiggled down from Bodie's lap and returned to her parents.

Starting with Brice, the server began taking orders and Bodie hadn't even opened his menu. He leaned toward Ronni. "What do you recommend?"

"The steaks," she answered without hesitation. "Rare."

As the server moved around the table, he noticed that the three women seemed different from Ronni and the three men at the table. It wasn't a specific quirk or identifiable anomaly; something just felt different about them and he began to realize that they were human.

Until meeting Ronni, he'd never picked up on the subtle differences between species. Never needed to really. Tlanuhwas always intrinsically recognized their own kind. Everyone else, he had assumed, was human.

The same could be reasonably true of Wahyas. As long as no one saw him shifting, they would likely continue to believe he was human. And he hoped to keep up the ruse for a good long while.

The server reached them. Duplicating Ronni's order, Bodie pointed to the teenagers' table. "Please put her son and my daughter's orders on my check as well."

"Got it," the server said. "I'll be back with your drinks in a jiffy."

"How do you like Maico so far?" Brice asked, looking at Bodie. As Gavin Walker's son, Brice had the Alpha's ear. Becoming friends with him could increase Bodie's chances of being accepted into the wolf pack. When first setting his sights on Ronni, he hadn't known she was so well connected to the pack's hierarchy.

Even if she wasn't, he doubted it would matter. Spending time with her, Bodie had realized that he simply wanted her, not her connections.

"It's great," he said truthfully. "Maico is a beautiful town. The people are friendly and Willow loves her new school." She had blossomed from a painfully shy girl into an outgoing, more self-assured young lady.

"I love it here, too," Nel said. "I grew up in the city, so I appreciate the coziness and the laid-back lifestyle. Everyone knows everyone so it's like having a big family."

That's what Bodie was counting on.

"How about your mother?" Cassie asked.

"She's not happy we moved, again," Bodie replied. "She doesn't like change."

"I can sympathize," Grace said. "My dad is a military

man, so we moved a lot. Even as an adult, I didn't stay in one place for long. Until I came here." She smiled at Rafe. He put his arm around her shoulders and kissed her cheek.

Bodie noticed wolfans didn't shy away from public affection, but the display wasn't gratuitous or attention-seeking. Their touches, gazes and intimate whispers to their mates seemed natural, nondisruptive and a loving assurance toward one another.

Nonchalantly, he scooted his chair closer to Ronni. She gave him a questioning look, but didn't shoo him away when he casually rested his arm across the back of her chair.

"Willow seems happy," she said, gazing at the table of teenagers.

"She is." That alone made the move worthwhile.

"How's the house hunting?" Tristan asked.

"We looked at a lot of places today. None that my mom and Willow could agree on." Truthfully, Bodie hadn't liked them either. None of them made him feel at *home* the way Ronni's house had.

Willow had echoed his sentiments, stating she wanted a place in the woods. Bodie agreed. It would be easier to shift and fly without worrying about nosy neighbors. At the campground, his mother had to shift inside their camper and fly in and out of a window to avoid prying eyes. He usually drove to a hidden location near Ronni's house.

Throughout the evening, the table conversation was amicable and the food was delicious. The married couples took to the dance floor in shifts so that the twins and Brenna always had appropriate supervision. Bodie admired how the wolf pack looked after one another.

"Come." Taking Ronni's hand, he stood.

"I'm not much of a dancer."

"Neither am I." He gently tugged her to her feet. "Maybe we can fake it."

On the dance floor, her arms slipped around his neck and his slid around her waist.

"Has anyone told you how beautiful you are?"

"Not in a long time." Her soft smile squeezed his heart and he caught a glimmer of vulnerability in her eyes.

"Well, you are." He inched her closer as their movements synchronized. Her heat warmed him as a feeling of contentment wove through his being. For once in his life, everything was beginning to feel just right.

"Liar." Ronni laughed as the music and the line dancers wound down for a break. "You said you couldn't dance."

Bodie had hardly broken a sweat. "I believe you said that you weren't much of a dancer. I merely agreed that I wasn't either."

"Well, you're very light on your feet."

"And you never missed a step." Palm up, he held out his hand.

Their fingertips touched. The air charged and crackled. A zip of electricity shot through her arm and her body prickled with awareness.

The crowd jostled around them. Before Ronni could pull away, Bodie's fingers closed around her hand and gently pulled her toward him. She resisted the urge to snuggle into him until he curled his arm over her shoulder and tucked her against his side.

"That was fun," he said, as they walked toward the kids' table.

"Too bad the others couldn't stay, but I remember the days when Alex's bedtime ruled my schedule. Now he can outlast me."

"You're doing a great job raising him. You have no idea how much it means to me that he befriended Willow."

Ronni felt a rush of pride. Alex was growing into the man she and his father had wanted him to become. Kind, generous, helpful. Those traits were considered weaknesses in their former pack.

"Willow is a sweet girl."

"She gets that from her mother."

"I see you in her, too." Whiskey-colored like her father's, Willow's eyes didn't hold the absolute confidence Bodie's gaze radiated, yet. But the spark was there.

When they reached the table, the kids were absorbed in conversation and oblivious to them.

Bodie laid his hand on Willow's shoulder. "Time to head home, chickadee."

"It's barely past ten," Willow said. "Can't we stay a little longer?"

"Your grandmother has been alone all evening. She's probably ready for us to come home."

"But, Dad."

He held up his free hand, silencing further protests. "I'm working tomorrow."

Disappointment washed the youthful flush from Willow's and Lucas's faces, but Ronni's heart cinched. The poachers were still on the loose and Bodie worked alone.

"Later," Alex said to his girlfriend as he stood.

"Bye." Ella slipped from her seat and rejoined her parents.

"Mom, the keys?" Alex held out his hand.

Ronni dug them from her purse and tossed them to him. "The radio better not be blaring when I get in."

The trio of teens headed out of the restaurant, Ronni and Bodie trailing behind.

"You're doing that sassy strut again," Bodie said as they walked toward her car.

"I don't know what you mean."

Bodie stopped and turned her to face him. "Who's the liar now?" He slanted his mouth over hers, silencing her half-hearted protest.

Inching closer, she draped her arms around his neck to make sure he didn't pull away too quickly and leave her wanting. Bodie's arms tightened around her, assuring her he wouldn't.

She sensed no falsehood in his embrace. He was here because he wanted to be with her, holding her, kissing her.

Maybe something good had come of Jeb's sudden reappearance. After all, she probably wouldn't have given Bodie a chance if her circumstances hadn't warranted it, and she would've missed out on knowing him.

Bodie was a man who spoke his mind, followed his instinct and stood his ground. And Ronni found it incredibly sexy. His essence filtered through her. Strong, masculine and threaded with desire. Her own responded, entwining with his in an ethereal dance.

So tired of always being on the alert, of being overly cautious, she let it all go, completely relaxing her mind. A sentiment that had been buried beneath a mountain of worry began to worm its way through her consciousness and softly thumped in tandem with her heart. *Mine. Mine. Mine.*

Not ready to believe the declaration, Ronni broke the sweet kiss and brushed a piece of invisible lint from his shirt just so she could palm his chest.

"Admit it." His pupils dark and round, Bodie gave her a knowing smile. "Yeah, you can't get enough of me."

"I admit nothing." Except that her entire body prickled with awareness and her judgment was faulty because of the emotional roller coaster she'd ridden the last few days. "It's been a difficult week. I need a little room to breathe." And to let her sensibilities unscramble before she did something stupid, like entertain the thought that they could be true mates.

"That's not part of the deal, beautiful. I'm not going to ignore the pull between us." His voice dropped to a seductive whisper. "And neither are you."

Bodie seemed a hard man to resist for long, though it would be prudent for her to try.

He laced his fingers through hers and they resumed their walk to the car.

Alex was behind the steering wheel with the engine running. Standing beside the vehicle, Lucas placed a chaste kiss on Willow's cheek.

"I have mixed feelings about this moment," Bodie said. "Part of me wants to hide my little girl away from any potential heartbreak. But I'm also happy to see her expressing some independence and experiencing life as a normal teenager."

"Trust me, I completely understand."

"Hey," Bodie growled at the lovebirds, though a smile wavered on his lips. "I saw that!"

Willow's hand flew to her face and the color drained from Lucas's face. Still, the teenager stood tall. "I don't regret a thing." He said good-night to Willow and slid into the back seat of Ronni's car to the peals of Alex's laughter.

"Neither do I," Bodie chuckled in Ronni's ear. "I'll stop by the store for lunch on Monday, but feel free to call, text or even better—sext me anytime."

"I am not sexting you." It was difficult to frown at him with an outrageous smile on her face.

"Admit it." There was a sing-song quality to his voice. "You're thinking about it right now, imagining how much fun it would be."

"What I'm thinking is that I want to go home and go to bed."

"Perfect time to give it a go. Gotta keep up with technology." Mischief danced in his eyes. "What do you say?"

"Some things are better when done the old-fashioned way."

"Duly noted."

They reached Ronni's car.

"Let's go, chickadee." Bodie draped his arm over Willow's shoulder and they began walking toward his truck. Halfway to the vehicle, he turned back. "Lunch on Monday, don't forget!"

Already, Ronni was counting the hours.

She sat in the passenger seat of her car. "One mile over the speed limit and you lose driving privileges for a month."

"At least you let me go the speed limit. Rafe makes me stay five miles an hour under," Alex grumbled, easing out of the parking space.

Lucas sighed. "Will you put in a good word for me with Mr. Gryffon? I don't think he likes me."

"He likes you just fine," Ronni said.

"How can you tell?"

"You're still breathing." Alex laughed.

"I think she's *the one*." Face plastered to the window as they passed Bodie and Willow getting into the truck, Lucas waved at them.

"You're too young for that." Ronni watched Alex check for traffic before driving out of the parking lot and onto the road. "So is she."

"For now." Lucas sat forward. "It's weird how time drags until I see her again but passes in a blink when we're together."

"Is that how it is with you and Bodie?" Alex asked quietly.

"It's a little different for us. I have you, he has Willow. We can't pine away for each other like young fools in love."

"You look at him the way you used to look at Dad."

"Alex, I—" What could she say to make things easier on him?

"Mom." His grip tightened on the steering wheel. "I'm just saying that I'd rather have Bodie around than Jeb."

"So would I, Alex." And with Jeb out of their lives, she couldn't wait to see what developed with Bodie.

Chapter 16

A foul stench slapped Bodie's face. Not exactly the best way to start the new week.

"Damn," Tristan mumbled behind the hand clamped over his nose and mouth.

Trying to breathe as little as possible, Bodie followed him through the somber woods toward the latest poaching site. Brittle pine needles crunched beneath their boots and were the only sounds in the deathly quiet.

In the last few weeks, one Co-op officer had been wounded, and eight deer, two bear, a fox and a dozen black birds had been killed on Co-op property. With their heads, talons and tail feathers removed, the slaughter of the birds had hit Bodie especially hard. He hated violence, particularly violence against animals, who had no defenses against bullets and arrows and coldhearted humans who slaughtered simply for the thrill.

After mentally anchoring himself, he eased around the latest carnage. The deer heads had been taken for their antlers, their bodies left to rot.

"Bastards!" Tristan spat his words. "When I catch these people…" Those responsible, Bodie wouldn't even describe them as people. They were as violent and cruel as his ancestors. He had to stop the senseless slaughter before any more innocent lives were lost. A break, he just needed a break.

So far, only the Walker's Run Cooperative's lands had been targeted. Thankfully, no more incidences had occurred inside the wolf sanctuary or around the members' private residences. But the Co-op owned a lot of undeveloped property. "Ever thought about setting up an electronic or thermal surveillance system?" Bodie asked.

"Gavin and I discussed it. At the time, we weren't having issues with hunters, so he wasn't interested. I intend to bring up the subject again."

"Considering the amount of forested land the Co-op owns, I'm surprised this hasn't been a problem before now."

Tristan's brow wrinkled and he rubbed the back of his neck. "The Co-op is well respected and established in the community. The local hunters are respectful of our preservation efforts, especially since at one time or another, the Co-op has provided assistance to them or a family member."

"You suspect that the poachers are from out of the area?"

"I do."

Despite the symbiotic relationship the Co-op had with the local residents, Bodie wasn't inclined to dismiss the entirety of Maico's population simply based on the idea that the Co-op was too well respected for someone to poach its lands.

In his experience, most illegal hunters lived in the rural areas they hunted and were simply trying to put food on the table. However, whoever was poaching on the Co-op's private lands wasn't doing it because they were hungry. They were collecting trophies.

Using his smartphone camera, Bodie documented the scene and sent the photos to the DNR office.

"Such a goddamn waste," Tristan said.

Both men turned at the sound of someone approaching. Wearing a Walker's Run Cooperative security uniform, a man in his early twenties came into view.

"Shane," Tristan said by way of introduction, "this is Sergeant Bodie Gryffon from DNR. Bodie, this is Shane MacQuarrie. He was with Reed the night he was shot."

"I owe him my life." A lethal glint frosted the young man's gray eyes. "He took the bullet for me."

If Bodie didn't catch the perpetrators before Shane did, another "wild boar" incident might close his poaching investigation, permanently.

"Ronni."

She jumped at Rafe's voice and the straight pin she was pressing through the fabric jabbed her finger.

"Ouch!" She pressed the injured finger to her lips, soothing the sting with the stroke of her tongue. Despite the minuscule amount of blood, the coppery taste filled her mouth.

Wearing jeans instead of his work coveralls, Rafe walked into the sewing room. "You all right?" He hooked his thumbs through the front belt loops.

"I didn't hear you come in. I was in the zone." Only *the zone* wasn't work related. Bodie wouldn't stay off her mind. His scent had imprinted itself in her nose while his flirtatious attention had resurrected her libido, at the most inconvenient time.

Too often, she found herself daydreaming about his kisses, his sensual touch, the lyrical sound of his voice. And his pecs, those bulging, dancing, comically sexy pecs. She fanned herself.

Over the last two weeks, Bodie had stopped by the store to see her nearly every day. A few times they had the opportunity to eat lunch together and had plans to do so again today. And she couldn't wait.

"Gavin wants to see us."

Ronni's indecent thoughts about Bodie train-wrecked. She paused a moment for the debris to settle.

The first worry her mind conjured was about Jeb, but he'd taken up too much residence in her thoughts in the previous weeks and she refused to give him any more space. Besides, she didn't have to worry about any more surprise visits. Gavin had clearly stipulated that Jeb's visitations had to be coordinated through him. She doubted Jeb would be invited back so soon after being sent packing with his tail tucked between his legs.

"Is Alex in trouble?"

"Gavin didn't mention it." And likely, Rafe hadn't asked. When the Alpha or his son called, Rafe merely responded to their requests.

Ronni tamped down her imagination already gearing up for the worst-case scenario. Alex had gone through a rebellious period after they first arrived in Walker's Run, but with Rafe's mentorship, Alex's behavior had gotten back on track. With no reason not to trust that her son was still on the right path, Ronni breathed easier.

Gavin probably wanted to review The Stitchery's I&E ledgers. Last month was the end of her second business quarter.

The Co-op had fronted the start-up money. In return, Ronni paid thirty percent of her earnings to the Co-op. It wasn't a repayment, but something all Co-opers were required to do. All of the money went toward the pack members' housing, healthcare, education and any other expense that would benefit the pack.

Ronni removed the pincushion from her wrist. "I'll get my things."

Stepping back, he allowed her space to leave the sewing room. Ronni removed her purse from the cabinet and slid the thumb drive with her spreadsheets into a side pocket. She turned off the lights, flipped the sign to Closed, then they walked outside for her to lock up the store.

Rafe drove at a leisurely pace toward the resort. Calm, cool, *civil*. That's how most people saw him. And generally, that's exactly what he was.

But if anyone looked close enough, they would see his Wahyarian lurking below the surface. Most Wahyas kept their beastly primitive nature in the deepest, darkest places of their psyche, never acknowledging its existence. An unimaginable circumstance had forced Rafe to unleash his beast and then embrace it.

Rafe said if he hadn't made peace with that part of himself, the creature would've destroyed his humanity. Had that happened, the Woelfesenat would've put him down rather than allow his primal beast to terrorize the public and expose their kind's existence to the human world.

There were valid reasons Wahyas were conditioned to fear the Wahyarian within them, but Rafe was proving the inner beast could be managed. People could claim all they wanted that he skirted the line between civility and barbarity, but as far as she was concerned, Rafe was one of the most decent people she knew.

"Bodie seems like a good family man." Coming from Rafe, who valued family above all else, it was the highest compliment.

"He is." It wasn't difficult to recognize that Bodie's daughter meant the world to him. Pure devotion was readily seen in his eyes whenever Willow was around.

"If Bodie makes you happy, don't dismiss him," Rafe said a few minutes later.

Ronni answered by gazing out the window. She hadn't thought about being happy in a long time. There wasn't room for it when living in survival mode. But that wasn't really living, and since meeting Bodie, Ronni realized that she really did want that kind of happiness again.

Rafe stopped at the valet stand outside the resort.

"Thanks, Jimmy," she said to the young pack member who opened the vehicle door and helped her out.

He grinned. "My pleasure."

The jitters ate at Ronni's stomach as they cut through the lobby to the corridor leading to Gavin's office. Muted voices wafted down the hallway in indistinguishable words.

"Come in." Brice waved them into the room. Gearing up to become the pack's next Alpha, he periodically attended his father's meetings.

Gavin sat comfortably behind his large mahogany desk. His dark blue eyes assessed every move they made entering the office. "Please, have a seat."

Brice sank into the far right captain's chair in front of his father's desk. Rafe waved Ronni to sit in the center chair while he took the one to her left.

"The Stitchery is doing well, I hear," Gavin began.

"It is." Ronni handed him the thumb drive. "I'm grateful for everything the pack has done for us. And their orders keep me busy."

"I'm glad to hear it." Though there was genuine warmth in Gavin's eyes, he did not look glad at all.

"If Alex or I have done something wrong, please tell me." She sat straight, hands folded in her lap.

"You and Alex are not the problem, Ronni."

So, there was a problem. Her stomach sank.

"There's nothing for you to worry about," Brice said. "But—"

There it was, the infamous *but*. It meant, *Forget everything that was just said; here's the real deal and it's probably a doozy.*

"Jeb filed a petition with the Woelfesenat requesting custody of Alex."

Over my dead body.

"On what grounds?" The icy undertone in Rafe's voice raised the hairs on her arms, despite the heat of anger bubbling beneath her skin.

"He claims Walker's Run is unsafe," Gavin answered. "And its leadership—" his face darkened at the pause "—unstable."

A giggle of hysteria rippled through Ronni's mind. For the new Alpha of the most capricious pack in recent years to accuse the renowned and well-connected Alpha of one of the most steadfast Wahyan packs of being unstable was absurdity to the nth degree.

Typical Jeb arrogance.

"He cited our current problem with poachers as his grounds for custody," Gavin continued. "He feels Alex is in danger and wants him returned to Pine Ridge for his own safety."

"Safety?" Ronni's voice hit screech level. They had fled Pine Ridge to escape the violent uprising incited by the Alpha's rogue nephew. Jeb's subsequent takeover was merely a replacement of an egotistical narcissist, not an improvement.

If that bastard thinks that I'll just let my son go...

An arctic chill passed through the marrow of her bones. By hook or by crook, if Jeb did manage to get custody, he knew Ronni would never let Alex go without her.

How dare Jeb use her son to manipulate her?

She felt the heat of Rafe's hand on her shoulder.

"He's not going to take Alex." A glimmer of Rafe's beast blinked in his eyes.

"You will not challenge him," Ronni snapped. Rafe had a mate and two little wolflings to provide for and protect.

In good conscience, she could not allow him to risk a physical confrontation with Jeb. If Jeb proved stronger and got the upper hand, Rafe's Wahyarian would emerge. The Woelfesenat might've given him a free pass when his beast came out to save Grace, but the creature didn't outright murder anyone in the process. If his Wahyarian killed Jeb to keep him from taking Alex, Rafe's reward would be a death sentence.

"No one is challenging anyone." Gavin's authoritative voice broke the battle of wills taking place in the glares she and Rafe exchanged. "This situation has moved from an uncomfortable personal matter to a political pile of shit that I don't want smeared around by either of you."

"I've filed three counterpetitions," Brice said. "One on your behalf, Ronni, one for the pack and one I filed presumptuously for Rafe." Brice looked at his best friend. "I didn't think you would mind."

Rafe tipped his head. "I appreciate it."

"What happens now?" Ronni asked.

"Leave that to me." The pack lawyer and a seasoned arbitrator for the Woelfesenat, Brice was well qualified to handle this nightmare.

Jeb might excel at scaring the little fish, but he'd just jumped out of a puddle and landed in an ocean. Ronni hoped he drowned in it while getting his ass chomped by a shark.

Chapter 17

Beautiful reds and golds dotted the treetops in the distance. Although most Tlanuhwas preferred spring, Bodie loved the crisp, cool air and campfires that embodied fall. And he certainly appreciated seeing the mountains after spending all morning surrounded by the gray walls of his office cubicle.

Unfortunately, the restlessness he'd felt for the last hour or so didn't settle with a change of scenery. He was counting on lunch with Ronni to put him into a better mood.

A dark blue truck crested the hill ahead of him, coming toward him on the deserted highway.

Bodie's gut tightened like it always did whenever he saw dark-colored trucks on the road. So far, none had three men riding in them. Even if he encountered one that did, without actual probable cause, he couldn't stop them.

As the truck drew closer, Bodie sharpened his vision to the single occupant but was unable to get a good look at the driver's face because the man wore his hat pulled down over his brow.

The right blinker came on and the truck slowed, then turned down a side road. As Bodie passed the vehicle, he glanced at the tag number. It matched one he'd seen several times and when he'd run the number through the database, it came back clean.

"Better leave the lights on at night," he told the driver, as the vehicle meandered down the long, narrow road leading to the Thornbriar Lodge.

The dilapidated motel, built in the sixties, was nestled in

a shallow valley and scattered throughout the woods behind the building were a handful of A-frame rental cabins that had weathered far too many seasons without any upgrades.

"No telling what critters might come out of the wood-work after dark." Bodie had checked out the place when his family joined him and immediately marked it off the list of potential residences. He also called the agency that had provided him a list of short-term rental places and advised that the only list on which it should appear was for a demolition crew. In hindsight, he should've mentioned that the photos on the website should be considered criminal misrepresentation of the property.

He shook off the creepy-crawly sensation prickling his neck.

Ten miles later, Bodie drove into Maico's city limits. He slowed approaching the traffic light and turned onto Sorghum Avenue. The two-lane road went right past Wyatt's Automotive Service. At the corner, he turned left and parked behind The Stitchery next to Ronni's car.

He walked along the sidewalk to the front of the store. The chimes jingled as he went inside.

"I'm back here," Ronni's voice rang out. Clear, strong. Strained.

He locked the store's door, flipped the Closed sign, then walked toward the room from where Ronni's voice had drifted. She sat on the floor in front of a mannequin. Long, reddish-blonde hair pulled back in a ponytail, she wore a loose pink sweater over black leggings. Her posture was rigid and her shoulders lifted and dropped in tandem with her short, quick breaths.

"Hey, beautiful, what's wrong?"

"Nothing. Why?" Her harried gaze was quickly blanked. She returned to sticking pins in the garment hanging on the mannequin.

"Well, you didn't fling yourself into my arms, stick your

tongue down my throat and grind against me," he said, intending to break the tension. "I kinda hoped you would."

"I don't fling." Slowly, she stood facing him. Her frown wobbled a bit from the corners trying to turn up. "I pounce."

"Not seeing the difference." He closed the distance between them. "We should reenact the scene, then you can show me how a pounce is different than a fling."

The fire simmering in her gaze heated his skin. Expectancy charged the air. Not wanting to misread the signals, he tuned into her every breath, the rise and fall of her chest, the slight parting of her lips. He even heard the click in her brain when she finally decided to act.

Oh, yeah! It was a pounce. If he hadn't been anchored in a wide stance, his feet spread and his knees flexed to absorb the shock of impact, her momentum might've knocked him to the ground. Automatically, his arms fastened around her, holding her intimately against his body.

Now, this was the way he liked to be welcomed.

Clamping her hand against the back of his head, she pushed his face close enough to hers and claimed his mouth. There was no other way to describe the hard, hurried, hungry kiss. Grabbing the front of his shirt, she urged him toward the nearby cutting table. She perched on the edge, tugging him to stand between her open thighs, then locked her ankles behind his knees.

Before lust clouded his brain, he tipped her chin until she met his gaze. "How far do you want this to go? I need to know if there's a point where I should stop you during this demonstration. You know, in case my manliness is too overwhelming for you."

"Shut up and kiss me." Her sweater flew behind her.

He took that as an all clear. Before yielding to the flood of hormones racing through his bloodstream, Bodie removed his gun belt and stowed it in a safe spot.

Ronni unbuttoned his shirt and tossed it aside. He removed the Kevlar vest, then Ronni yanked off the long-sleeve shirt he wore beneath it.

She playfully pinched and rolled his nipples between her fingers. He made his pecs dance just to watch the fascination on her face.

"That is so—"

"Sexy, right?" He did it again.

"I was going to say 'amazing.'"

"That works, too." He pulled her in for a kiss, unhooking her bra as his hands palmed her back. She peeled away from him long enough to slip the garment off her arms.

Bodie's mouth watered. Visions of her, naked and welcoming, had haunted his dreams. His hands could no longer be still. He reached for her, cupping her face and she nuzzled his palm.

Kissing her gently, he held back the primal drive to take her hard and fast, wanting to savor the sweet moment of her surrender. Since he'd had a vasectomy, pregnancy wasn't a worry, and her scent was deliciously sweet and feminine, untainted by the stench of disease.

He trailed his hands down her neck and over her breasts, which more than filled his hands. Strumming her pale, puckered nipples elicited a deep-throated groan.

Her fingers glided across his shoulders and down his arms. Goose bumps pebbled his skin. His groin grew tight and uncomfortable. As if she knew, Ronni unbuttoned his pants and shoved them down his legs. Already he was hard and wanting. She took him in her hand, stroking the length of his shaft.

"You asked me how far I wanted to go." Sliding off the table, Ronni rose up on her toes. "As far as you can take me."

She shimmied out of her leggings, revealing a red lacy thong.

"I knew you would look good in red, but damn, that's hot." He urged her back onto the cutting table and stood between her open thighs. Then he kissed her deeply, exploring her mouth, wrestling with her tongue, nibbling her lips until they were both panting for air.

Her hands explored the expanse of his chest, squeezing his pecs and sliding down the tightened muscles of his abdomen to the indents just below the hip bones. She cupped his sack, slowly kneading him with one hand while the other gently pumped his shaft.

"Ronni." Her name drifted from his lips on a ragged breath.

Seeming to know he was too close for her to continue, she moved her hands back over his hips and around to his buttocks, pulling him against her so that his cock rested against her lace-clad mound.

Forcing himself to focus, he peppered kisses between the valley of her breasts, sucking one peak and then the other. Every mewl and sigh and groan of pleasure imprinted in his brain, as did the feel of her skin, the shape of her curves and the scent of her desire.

His fingers slid down her abdomen, pushed aside the thong and slipped into her folds, stroking her lightly. Her breath faltered and her hips arched.

He wanted to taste her, to lave her with his tongue until she came in his mouth. But he was too strained with his own needful desire to delay much longer.

He dipped his fingers inside her moist, satiny heat. Her eyes closed and her body trembled as a passionate moan escaped her lips.

Oh, she was close and he had no intention of stopping. He pumped his fingers faster, rubbing his palm against her mound. Her head fell back; her breath turned to pants. Watching shades of ecstasy flicker across her face, he felt the first quiver against his fingers. "Come for me, beautiful."

A soft, mewling growl vibrated in her throat and grew louder as she arched beneath him.

"That's it, baby," he said softly, keeping up the pace as

her walls milked his fingers. God, she was so beautiful in the throes of orgasmic passion.

In that moment, he'd never wanted a woman as much as he wanted her, and though he ached unbearably with restraint, he would not rush her pleasure to achieve his own. Because once inside her, he would come completely undone.

Senses coming back down from the heavenly place Bodie had taken her, Ronni inched off her perch and turned around to bend across the cutting table.

"You have a beautiful ass." Bodie kneaded the fleshy muscles.

"I'm pretty proud of it." She wiggled it for him.

"You're killing me." He slid off her thong and nudged her legs farther apart.

Gasping, she welcomed the push of Bodie's cock as he entered her. It had been so damn long since she'd had human-style sex. She missed the feeling of being filled, missed the pleasure, the release, and the scent of a man hot and ready for her.

He gripped her hips and began thrusting hard and deep. In the mirror in front of them, she saw the intensity etched on his face as he watched the rhythmic joining of their bodies.

She hadn't known it was possible to feel so completely dominated by a human, but Bodie's personality was as strong as any wolfan male. Yet his was a quiet strength. He used his mind to deal with problems, though he certainly had the brawn if he needed to use it.

His gaze lifted to hers watching in the mirror. Something about their reflections magnified their connection, physical and otherwise. Her entire body became sensitized by his touch and his essence invaded despite the defenses she'd tried to set up. The intimacy was overwhelming and she started to panic.

"Stop thinking so much." His hawkish eyes glittered.

"Just breathe." His hand slipped around her and his finger stroked her mound.

A fresh rush of desire shot straight to her sex.

The warmth of his slick skin against hers, the friction of their bodies moving as one, the ebb of his essence entwining with hers were too much to resist.

She closed her eyes, allowing the second deluge of pleasure to wash through her body and soul. Her being splintered within the flood and only Bodie's strong, steady presence kept her tethered and safe.

His body shuddering, a deep, primal male groan emerged from within his chest, then he stilled. Watching in the mirror, she saw his dark lashes flutter. Slowly, his eyelids opened, revealing the satisfied glint in his eyes.

This man, this human man, was as near to perfection as a male could get. His body was sleek and muscular, his face rugged with sharp angles and a masculine jaw. And his heat warmed not only her skin but also the dark places deep within.

Then, there was his chest. She loved his sculptured, muscular chest with dark nipples and dancing pecs that provided her amusement and comfort and assurance.

"I told you." He turned her to face him and pressed against her. "Overwhelmed by my manliness. Yep, I called it."

His playful tease and the bounce in his brow drew laughter from Ronni. God, how long had it been since she'd been able to really laugh? Ages, it seemed.

He tenderly brushed aside the strands of hair that had fallen across her face, then kissed her before moving away to collect their clothes.

"What is the tune you're humming?" The melody and tone were soft and soothing.

Dressing, Bodie gave her a startled look. "I didn't realize I was. I guess I made it up."

"It's beautiful." Ronni focused on smoothing the wrin-

her. "Not my mate. Your grandmother should stick to the facts instead of filling your head with silly notions."

Pushing aside the meat already in the hot skillet, Bodie dumped in the vegetables and stirred.

The door to the camper opened. His mother stood at the bottom of the metal steps, holding a laundry basket. "Something smells delicious."

"Dad is making stir-fry." It had been Willow's favorite meal since learning the dish had been Layla's specialty. Bodie had left out the part that it was all her mother had known how to cook.

"Willow, help *Enisi* with the laundry basket." Bodie's attention returned to the stir-fry.

A moment later, there was a commotion at the door.

"*Enisi*! Are you all right?" Clothes bin hiked on her hip, Willow stood halfway between her grandmother and Bodie.

Mary clung to the metal doorframe, trying to pull herself up.

"Mom?" Abandoning the stove, he bumped Willow aside.

"I'm okay," Mary said.

"Did you fall?" Bodie helped her to the couch.

"No, I tripped," she told him. "Sometimes my foot doesn't clear the threshold when I come in or go out. I'm all right, though."

Willow carted the laundry into the bedroom and Bodie returned to the kitchenette.

"You're here earlier than usual." Mary no longer sounded shaken.

"I'm working a few hours tonight." Lifting the skillet from the stove, Bodie gave the ingredients a toss, then returned the pan to the burner and dialed down the heat.

"Between work and that woman—" Mary huffed "—you're never around. Why did you bring us here?"

"For Willow." He didn't want her restricted to slipping out of an apartment window and sitting in a nearby tree for a few minutes each night when she was born to soar. "The

kles in her sweater. The brush of fabric caused chills to break out, an aftereffect of her skin burnished by Bodie's caresses.

Ronni wondered how long the effect would last because it was distracting. She had a lot of work to do and no time to dwell on how incredible their coupling had been or give thought to how much she wanted it to happen again.

Standing in front of the wall mirror, she checked that her leggings and sweater were on correctly. Nothing looked too rumpled but the band holding her ponytail had disappeared. She ran her fingers through her hair to tame the wildness but she couldn't do anything about the fire in her eyes or the glow of her skin or the healthy flush of a satisfied she-wolf in her cheeks.

Then her brain kicked in. And all the guilt followed. "I need to apologize."

Bodie gave her a dubious look. "No, you don't. You absolutely have nothing to apologize for."

"I do." She sat down on the large round ottoman in the room. "I got some disturbing news earlier."

"Let me guess. Jeb?"

She nodded. "It's being taken care of, so everything will be fine. But I was still hyped up about it when you came in."

"So you used me to get it out of your system. Is that right?" His expression was unreadable.

"Yeah." Albeit unintentionally. And in her defense, yes, his overwhelming manliness really was too much to resist. She snorted.

"Use me anytime, beautiful." Bodie tucked his long-sleeve shirt into his pants. "You won't hear one damn complaint from me."

He finished dressing and walked over to Ronni. "Although, if you feel the need for penance, I have an idea."

Capturing her in his arms, he rubbed his cheek against her jaw. "Run away with me."

"What?" It sounded like the protest her mind put forth, but her body was already cheering at the prospect.

"Our time together has involved chaperoning the kids, deflecting Jeb, some stolen moments in between." He made his serious face, the one that said how much he meant what he was about to say. "I want you all to myself. Let's take a weekend, stop adulting and just have fun."

Ronni had been adulting for most of her life, always in survivor mode from one crisis to another. Just once, she'd like to escape it, even for a few hours.

"Gatlinburg is close. Touristy but we'll have a great time. I promise." In his eyes, she glimpsed his loneliness beckoning her own. "What do you say, beautiful?"

You're acting foolish and getting in way too deep. Say no, say no, say no is what her brain said. However, her mouth had a mind of its own and before she knew what it was doing, the words were already out. "How soon can we leave?"

Chapter 18

"Dad!"

"Hmm?" Bodie finished chopping the onion on the small kitchen counter and glanced over his shoulder at Willow sitting at the table, doing her homework.

"You're humming." She grinned. "I've never heard you hum."

All Tlanuhwa had melodic voices and could hum a tune but few could actually sing.

"Sure you have." Finished with the onions, he began dicing the peppers. "I used to hum you to sleep."

"I don't remember." Willow propped her elbow on the table and rested her chin in her hand.

"You were a baby. After you turned three, you preferred a story at bedtime." Now he was lucky to get a good-night kiss on the cheek.

"*Enisi* said Tlanuhwa hum when they find their m

Maybe in ancient times, but with the Tribunal or trating mateships, the actual instinct had died out a traditional humming song was used during the Ceremony.

"Did you hum when you met my mother?"

"No." Bodie could have lied but that would o up a fantasy in his daughter's mind. "I didn't h held you for the first time."

It had been the happiest moment in his life.

Hours later, he became a twenty-two-year-o with a newborn to raise.

"And you're my daughter." He shook a woo

Walker's Run Cooperative's wolf sanctuary is the perfect place for her Transformation Ceremony and to learn how to fly. And Ronni could help us gain membership into the Co-op, which will give us all access to their protected lands. We'll be safe." Especially from the Tribunal, because Bodie and his family would no longer be without support.

"We can have safety among our own people. Talk to Kane. He will make a way for us to come home."

"Maico is home now," Bodie said, keeping his temper and his tone in check.

After what Kane had done to their family, Bodie wasn't inclined to trust him with anything. Especially their safety.

"Once we find a place and get settled, if you want to return to the flock, I won't stop you. But Willow and I are staying put."

Mary grumbled unintelligible words that could've been curses in the ancient language he had not learned to speak.

"Once the poachers are caught, I'll try to have a more regular routine." Not bothering to look at her, Bodie could imagine the disapproving look on her face, having seen it so often. "But I'm not taking a desk job, so stop suggesting that I do."

His career in wildlife management services included long hours and erratic schedules, but he loved the work. For the most part, the outdoorsmen he encountered were good people. They cared about the environment and weren't intentional lawbreakers. If they got carried away and accidentally went over the allowable limits for fish and game, most cooperated with his investigations and paid their fines without incident.

"What if something happens to you?"

An old argument he was quite tired of rehashing.

"Nothing is going to happen to me." Bodie turned off the burner and removed a pot of rice from the stove. "I take reasonable precautions when I'm working. If something does happen, I have plenty of life insurance."

"She won't care about the money any more than you did."

"Money?" Willow walked out of the bedroom. "What money?"

"Take your homework into your room," Mary snapped.

"I'm not a little girl!" Willow pressed her lips into a defiant frown. "Every time you argue with Dad, I don't need to be sent to my room." She glanced around the camper. "What am I saying? I don't even have my own room." Currently, she shared the one bedroom in the camper with her grandmother.

Willow packed her homework into her newly fashioned study pillow, pointed her chin at Mary and marched outside, slamming the metal door.

Bodie's heart ached. Living in a camper was fine for him but definitely not for his family. He needed to stop worrying about finding the right place and simply find one.

His mother picked up the argument right where they left off.

Sighing beneath the weight he never seemed to get out from under, Bodie opened the cupboard and pulled out three plates. "Once Ronni and I become mates, the Co-op will look out for you and Willow, should something happen to me." He really hoped nothing happened to him. Ronni and Alex had been through a lot. He certainly didn't want any of them to deal with his death.

"Is it time to eat?" Willow called from outside. "I'm starving."

Bodie gave his mother a look to signal their conversation on the matter had ended, for now.

Mary opened the door to let Willow inside. "Your father is stubborn and won't listen to reason."

"You tell me the same thing. Maybe you're the unreasonable one who doesn't listen."

"Willow!" Bodie said sharply.

His daughter spun toward him, her eyes wide and her

shoulders drawing up as if she were trying to shrink. The reprimand withered on his tongue.

"Get the glasses and silverware."

She scurried around him without saying a word.

Bodie placed their filled plates onto the table and everyone sat down to eat in strained silence.

"Lucas asked me to be his girlfriend," Willow practically whispered.

Bodie choked on a bite of food.

"No," Mary said. "You're too young."

And he choked again.

"Dad!" Willow's complaint was clear in her tone and the added syllables she used when saying his name. "He's Alex's best friend. I'm sure Mrs. Lyles will vouch for him. I really like him. *Puh-leeze*, Dad!"

And he kept choking.

Mary began out-talking Willow, and their shrill voices filled the camper.

Bodie slammed his fist on the table and silence fell. Finally, the spasms ceased. He held up his hand to stall any further discussion until he drank some water and calmed the irrational thoughts all fathers had when their daughters began dating.

"I want to know everything. Where you go, what you do. No sneaking around, got it?" He gave his daughter the stink eye.

"Yes, sir." Genuine happiness brightened her eyes that had been clouded with sad resignation only a few months ago.

Coming to Maico had been the right choice for her. And for him. He glanced at his mother's sourpuss expression, wishing he knew what was right for her.

Everyone resumed eating, though the tension in the camper did not dissipate. After supper, Willow went to the bedroom to finish her homework.

"I'm taking Ronni to Gatlinburg," he finally told his

mother, though it might've been smarter to wait until he was on the way out of the door with his overnight bag packed.

"I don't think that is wise." The disapproval on her face increased. "The Tribunal—"

"Has more things to worry about than me taking a woman on a weekend getaway."

"You're being reckless."

"I'm trying to find a way for all of us to be happy." He slammed his dishes into the sink. "Why are you against this?"

"Because this woman has aroused your beast. Every day I see more of its reflection in your eyes and I'm afraid, Bodaway. Afraid of what my son will become."

"There is no beast. It's incongruent with who we've become. But Ronni has awakened something in me," he said, turning toward his mother. "Hope."

And he wasn't going to let anyone keep him from her. Not even his mother.

On Thursday morning, Ronni finished unpacking the special order of fabrics that Nel had requested. The colors and patterns perfectly matched the sketches. Still, Ronni planned to ask Nel to come to the store to inspect the material before starting the project.

The bells over the door jingled and Ronni's body began to tingle. Like a Pavlovian experiment, every time she heard those bells, her hormones went into overdrive, expecting Bodie to walk through that door for a lunchtime rendezvous.

However, it was nine fifteen in the morning. Ooh, maybe he was changing things up before their weekend getaway.

Exiting the sewing room, she had a spring in her step that was nonexistent a few months ago.

"Mary?" She walked into the storefront, masking her disappointment. "What a nice surprise." Although from the dour droop of Mary's face, it might not be a pleasant one. "Are Bodie and Willow okay?"

"Yes." A faint smile eased a little of the sourness in her expression. "You truly care for them, don't you?"

"I do." More every day, it seemed. She loved how Bodie kept in touch throughout the day and into the night. And she looked forward to the impromptu visits when he was nearby.

"He's quite fond of you and your son, too." Something in Mary's tone triggered a gnawing sensation in Ronni's stomach.

"I get the feeling—" Ronni eased onto the stool behind the checkout counter "—you're about to tell me that you disapprove."

"It's not personal."

"How can it not be?" Ronni asked.

"I want what's best for my family and you put them at great risk."

"How?" Jeb was gone; his threats had ceased. Gavin had given assurances that the Woelfesenat continued to deny Jeb's ridiculous petitions, so she had no need to worry.

"Bodie's heritage is one of great traditions. It is the reason we came to this place." Mary smiled as she spoke, though it held no true warmth. "Willow will soon undergo her first ceremony to connect with her ancestors. It's performed in a forest, but it is important that the area is safe from prying eyes and predators."

Ronni could certainly understand Bodie's concern. Poachers were on the loose and he didn't want his daughter accidentally getting shot.

Mary ran her hand across the countertop. "Your Co-op has a sanctuary, doesn't it?"

"A wolf sanctuary, yes."

"Hmm." She gave Ronni a pointed look.

"Bodie hasn't mentioned anything to me." She couldn't grant him or Willow access but she could ask Gavin if the Co-op had a place they could use.

"Our traditions are very private. No one outside of our clan can witness it."

Ronni understood the value of secrecy. It was the reason Wahyas still existed.

"I'm surprised your clan doesn't provide a place for her ceremony." The Walker's Run Cooperative was designed to provide everything the pack needed.

"Bodaway has been angry with our council since his father died. He thinks they will continue to ignore his insolence, but he is mistaken."

"Are you talking about some kind of sanctions, or is Bodie in danger?" Ronni's protective instinct flared. She wouldn't allow anyone to threaten Bodie or Willow, any more than she would stand for someone threatening her son.

"He could be if he doesn't change his ways."

"You mean stop seeing me." Ronni's inner wolf prowled restlessly.

"His sights are blindly set on you—he can't see the truth." A very real fear crept into Mary's eyes.

"What truth?"

"The path he is on will lead him to destruction."

Ronni bit her tongue because she was pretty sure Bodie's mother had accused her of being temptation incarnate with a mind to send Bodie straight to hell.

I'm a she-wolf, not a she-devil!

The tension in the room swelled to an uncomfortable pressure. Mary seemed to be waiting for Ronni to agree to stop seeing Bodie.

The wait would be a long one. Ronni had no intention of breaking away from the intense pull she felt toward Bodie. Like Rafe suggested, she was happy being with him.

Her phone rang, startling both women. Ronni pulled the device from the back pocket of her jeans and answered the call.

"Hey, beautiful." Bodie's clear, strong voice slipped around her like a comforting blanket. He could read the ingredients off the back of a cereal box and the sound of his voice would still soothe her. "What color panties are you wearing? I'm thinking red lace."

"Not even close." She laughed because he always said the most outrageous things whenever she needed a moment of levity. "Try none."

There was a moment of silence. When Bodie spoke again, his voice was low and gravelly. "Keep saying things like that and I might run off the road."

"Don't ask dangerous questions while driving."

"Good plan." He chuckled.

"Um." Ronni noticed Mary watching her intently. "Your mom dropped by for a little visit. I was about to get her a cup of coffee."

Some of the color drained from Mary's face.

"Black, right?" Ronni asked her.

"Yes."

"Have a seat at the table, Mary. I'll be back in a moment." Ronni walked into the small kitchenette.

"What did she say?" Bodie's words were clipped and tight.

"If you keep seeing me, something bad will happen." Ronni's throat tightened, even though she tried not to take Mary's words personally. She was an overprotective mother trying to safeguard her son. Ronni certainly understood the motivation, but she made a mental note to not tell any of Alex's future girlfriends that they were she-devils.

"My mother gets carried away with our traditions and superstitions," Bodie said coolly.

"We've never talked about your heritage, or mine. Maybe we should." Oh, she definitely needed to talk about hers if whatever was between them turned into something serious.

"We will."

The comfortable silence that fell between them was filled with the gentle ebb of Bodie's essence touching hers.

"Why is she worried?"

"Willow is nearly grown," Bodie said. "I'm dating you. I

guess Mom feels left behind. She's clinging to the old ways because they're familiar. While going through this phase, she'll think any woman I date is bad for me."

"Bodie, I've been so focused on my problems that I didn't realize what your family is going through." A sudden move and living in a camper had to be difficult on all of them.

"Willow and I are in a much better place than we were a few months ago." Bodie paused. "My mom will come around. She just needs time."

"I should take the coffee to her." Ronni poured the hot beverage into a large ceramic mug.

"I won't make it for lunch today. I'm catching up on paperwork," he said.

"Should we postpone next weekend's trip? I don't want to upset your mother any more than she is."

"Would you rather upset me?" Bodie's exhausted sigh tweaked her heart. "I want more than a few snatches of your time, Ronni. But if you don't want to go away with me—"

"I do." The words tumbled out.

"Good." Relief rumbled in his voice. "I'll call tonight when I get home."

"Obviously, your mother knows I'm talking to you. Please don't bring this up. I don't want it to cause a wedge in your relationship with her."

"I don't like that she upset you."

"Mary came to me with her concerns and I respect that she did. I can handle this."

"All right," he said after a long pause.

"Don't forget the football game tomorrow night."

"We'll be there."

After disconnecting the call, Ronni served Mary the coffee and sat at the table with her.

"Does that happen a lot?" Mary swallowed her first sip.

"Bodie keeps in touch with me throughout the day." A check-in, of sorts. Since he worked alone in isolated areas, she liked knowing where he was headed or when he was leaving a place.

"I meant, does he always know when you're upset even when you're apart?"

It did seem that Bodie reached out to her whenever she felt overwhelmed. Not that she was stressed every time he called, texted or dropped by to see her, but somehow he always sensed her distress.

She purposely ignored the possibility that it could be a manifestation of a mate-bond developing between them. No matter how she felt about Bodie, Ronni didn't have the strength to bond so intimately with another man. Losing Zeke had nearly killed everything inside her. If not for Alex, it would have. She would never put herself through that again. She simply couldn't.

Chapter 19

What the hell did I get myself into?

Ronni's heart beat louder than the noise from the airplane propeller and faster than the blades turning. Her fingers dug into something on the passenger door that she wasn't quite sure what it was.

If she had known this was how they were traveling to Gatlinburg, Ronni wouldn't have spent the last week wishing for this weekend to hurry up and get here.

Bodie's steady voice crackled through her headset as he talked to the air traffic controller. She tried to calm her nerves, clenching her teeth so she wouldn't cry out. Having never been on board a plane, she wasn't at all confident about leaving behind good, solid ground.

The plane lurched forward, along with her stomach. Swallowing hard to keep down the morning's breakfast, she glanced sidelong at Bodie. His eyes focused forward in complete confidence.

She wished the same for herself but had to settle on simply not becoming a distraction as they hurtled down the runway. When the nose of the plane lifted, Ronni gasped.

"Breathe," Bodie's voice whispered through her headset. A gentle assurance ebbed into her being and the tension in her body lessened. "Now open your eyes."

Ronni pried open her eyelids. Nothing but blue expanse surrounded them. She gulped.

"Have you flown before?"

She shook her head, not trusting her voice.

"I've been flying since I was sixteen," Bodie said.

"Today, the skies are clear, the wind is good and you have nothing to fear."

"I'm not afraid."

Bodie's disbelieving look called her bluff.

"Shouldn't you be watching those gauges and dials?"

"I am, but I'm also keeping an eye on you." He flashed an encouraging smile. "Take a look around—it's beautiful up here."

Ronni wanted to say that she'd take his word for it, but the earnestness in his face touched her. He really seemed to love flying.

She leaned toward the side window and gazed at the hazy mountain range below. Once she got over the initial wave of light-headedness, Ronni drank in the swirl of color, amazed at the majesty of seeing the world from a different perspective.

"Breathtaking, isn't it?"

"Everything looks so peaceful." Considering the chaos she often found herself in, the serenity was astounding.

"I love it up here. When I'm flying, all the weight and stress of the world below slips away."

"You've really been flying since you were a teenager?"

"Yep. My dad was a pilot. Some of my earliest memories are of flying with him. As soon as I was old enough, he signed me up for lessons. I've been flying ever since, so you're in good hands."

Ronni didn't doubt the truth of his words. Exuding confidence and displaying an effortless skill, he was obviously born to fly. She, on the other hand, was a wolfan who preferred to have her feet, and paws, firmly planted on the ground. But since this activity was such an important part of Bodie's life, she needed to at least tolerate it. "Sounds like you were close to your dad."

"I was." Bodie's voice cracked. "He was killed when I was in college. It was so surreal. I had talked to him a few hours before he died."

Ronni's chest tightened in sympathy. "I'm sorry for your loss. I didn't mean to bring up unhappy memories."

"He was a good man and a great father." Bodie glanced at her. "I have no unhappy memories of him, but I miss the memories we could've made. My college graduation, Willow's birth, her first day of school." He shrugged.

"I lost my parents when Alex was a toddler. My dad died from pneumonia. Less than a year later, my mom from a broken heart." Ronni glanced out the window. "After my husband died, I was in a bad place. Then Rafe brought us to Walker's Run and things slowly got better. I like to think that somehow, their spirits were looking out for us."

"I believe you're right." Bodie's soft smile was genuine and warm. And she felt the comforting heat of it all the way to her bones.

"Alex has made good friends and Rafe is a wonderful role model," Ronni continued. "He's done so much for us and Alex adores him."

Bodie remained quiet, his eyes focused ahead.

"Rafe is the only family I have left." She gave a nervous laugh. "At least he was until the twins came along."

"That night at Taylor's." Bodie's voice broke with unspoken emotion. "You had this glow about you while holding his son. Even if that had been the first time I saw you, I would've known that you are a great mother."

"Thank you." She considered Alex her greatest accomplishment.

"There is more to you than being a mother." Bodie glanced her way. "You do know that, don't you?"

"Alex has been a priority for so long, it's hard for me to see myself as anything other than his mother," she said. "Pine Ridge wasn't the safest place for families. With Zeke working long hours at the mill, we decided it was best for me to stay home with Alex. I taught myself to sew and made extra money doing alterations. When he started school, I went back to work, part time as a waitress. Everything was about surviving. It wasn't all bad. Zeke was a good man and he loved us with every ounce of his being."

"Having someone to share the bad times makes it easier to bear," Bodie said.

"When did you lose your wife?" Ronni asked gently.

"Hours after Willow was born. Layla complained of a bad headache. I called for the nurse, but by the time they arrived, Layla was having a convulsive seizure. She lost consciousness, stopped breathing, then she was gone and they couldn't bring her back. Later, the doctor told me she had an aneurysm that had ruptured."

"Oh, Bodie." Emotion swelled Ronni's throat. What should've been the happiest day of his life had turned into a tragic one.

"Life has a way of making amends for losses, don't you think?" He looked at her with genuine affection and his eyes twinkled with possibilities. What else could she do but agree?

"You're doing great." Bodie squeezed Ronni's warm hands as he glided backward on his ice skates, pulling her with him. Though there was no snow outside, the indoor ice rink in Gatlinburg was open year-round.

"I don't know how." She grimaced. "All I can think of is not falling on my ass and breaking my tailbone."

"Trust me, I will not allow that to happen. I'm quite partial to your ass." Besides, from what Bodie had observed, wolfans had a natural athletic ability that gave them a definite edge when it came to anything physical. "Stop thinking of this as a chore to get through. Relax and have fun. Be in the moment."

He let go of one of her hands, turning around to skate beside her while keeping a firm grip on her other hand. "Better?"

"Yes. I'm not worried about you running into anyone now."

Bodie laughed. "That wasn't going to happen."

"You couldn't see what I could."

They completed a few circles around the rink before he let go of her hand. "Ready for a race?"

"Hardly."

He circled around her. "Liar," he said, noting the competitive gleam in her vibrant blue eyes.

"I'll give you an advantage." He began skating backward again. "Ready? Go!"

"Hey!" Ronni pushed forward with the agility and speed Bodie expected from a she-wolf. "Not fair."

Bodie stayed about a foot ahead of her as they glided over the ice. "All's fair in love and ice skating."

"In that case…" Ronni cut sharply to the left. The motion caused her to wobble. She crouched forward and grabbed her knees like he'd taught her to do.

"You'll need to do better than that." His laugh was cut short as he collided with someone behind him and sprawled to the ice.

Smiling, Ronni inched over to him. "So do you."

Bodie looked over at the other skater. "Are you all right?"

The man gave him a pissy face. "Fantastic," he grumbled, got to his feet and skated off.

"How about you? Anything broken?" Clearly amused, she offered him a hand up, which he declined, fearing he'd cause her to topple alongside him.

"I'm good." With one knee planted on the ice, he brought up his other one and pushed to a stand.

"Yeah, you are."

Though falling in front of her tweaked his pride, the teasing affection in her smile soothed his bruised ego. He pulled her close and she planted her hands on his hips, a tactic to steady herself, but he didn't care. He enjoyed the way her heat seeped into his bones.

Leaning into him, Ronni lifted her face to his until her soft lips graced his with a kiss. "Hungry?"

She meant for food, but what he hungered for was something much less tangible. And a lot more complicated. Maybe there was some truth to the Quickening. The more time he spent with Ronni, the stronger whatever it was inside him grew.

Her fear of flying had not escaped his notice. Frankly, he admired that she didn't freak out or refuse to board the plane when he surprised her by driving to the airport instead of the expressway. He was even humbled when she put her faith in him and allowed herself to enjoy the flight.

During the short time they were in the air, he'd learned more about her than in the month he'd known her. Smart, dedicated, courageous. A match with her could turn into something more than he could've ever hoped to have.

"I'm famished," he answered and they skated toward the edge of the rink. "We can stop somewhere on the way back to the hotel."

"How about room service?"

"If that's what you want, that's what we'll get." Bodie helped her step off the ice and they made their way to a bench and sat down.

"I read the resort's menu at the concierge's desk while you checked in. They had a decent selection." Ronni unlaced her skates. "I'd like to unwind a little. We've been going nonstop all day." She looked over at him. "I'm not complaining, though. I can't remember when I've had this much fun."

"Me, either," he said honestly. After dropping off their luggage in their suite, they had gone nonstop, visiting the wax museum, the mirror maze, the pottery gallery and the moonshine distillery, and browsed The Village Shops.

"After Willow was born, everything I've done has been for her. Even when I take her somewhere, I'm focused on whether or not she's enjoying herself without giving thought to if I am."

"This was a great idea." Ronni bumped against his shoulder. "It's nice to feel like a person again. Not just Alex's mother."

After they turned in their skates, they walked outside into the crisp night air. Although it was almost Halloween, holiday lights up and down the main street brightened the darkness.

"I can't believe how busy it is here. I don't think I've ever seen so many people jammed into one place."

"My parents used to bring me here when I was a kid." Bodie tucked his arm around Ronni as they walked. "I used to think this place was magical, like some kind of fairy-tale place."

"It sorta is, isn't it? Look at all the happy people. And the smells, gingerbread and taffy and fudge."

"Careful." Bodie laughed. "It sounds like you're describing the old witch's house in *Hansel and Gretel*."

"Good thing I prefer steak to sweets." Ronni grinned.

"I knew you were my kind of woman," he whispered against her ear before placing a light kiss against her temple.

As they walked hand in hand, Ronni turned toward each display they passed while he watched utter fascination flicker across her lovely face. He wasn't pretending to enjoy her company; he really did. Hope grew that a life mated to this she-wolf would always be this enchanting.

Chapter 20

"**Y**ou're not getting cold feet, are you?" Despite her teasing, Ronni's jumbled nerves converged in the pit of her stomach. She wasn't hesitant about the sleeping arrangements; their trip was the first time she'd left Alex behind. She didn't doubt he would be all right. It simply felt weird to not be in mom mode.

"There isn't one spot on my body that's cold right now." Bodie finally got the card key to work and opened the door.

Their overnight bags tucked in the alcove had remained undisturbed during their absence, despite leaving the balcony French doors slightly ajar to allow the fresh air to draw out the artificial scents from the plug-in fresheners Ronni had pulled out earlier.

The sound of the lock clicking as Bodie secured the room caused a frisson of excitement to course through her body. His molten gaze touched her for a mere moment but it was long enough to melt the bones in her legs. She sank onto the edge of the bed.

"We should order room service before the kitchen closes." Food, sex and then everything else. A male's order of priorities seemed consistent across species.

Bodie picked up the menu on the writing desk. "Burgers, sandwiches, pizza or pasta?"

"Surprise me." She kicked off her shoes and reclined on the bed.

After placing their order, Bodie hung up the phone. "They're busy so it'll be more than an hour before we get supper."

Ronni patted the bed. "Come."

He hesitated.

So cute—he was trying to be a gentleman—but as far as she was concerned, the entire day had been foreplay.

Bodie's clean, masculine scent had teased and tormented her from the moment he'd picked her up from the house this morning. Every time he touched her, she had clenched with need.

Wanting him to soothe the ache before she lost all control, Ronni pulled off her sweater. "I won't offer again."

A lie, and a big fat one, too. Whenever they were in close proximity, Ronni became acutely aware of her feminine essence being drawn to his masculine energy like a supercharged magnet. The irresistible pull was too strong to overcome, even if she wanted to.

Shucking off his shirt, Bodie kicked out of his shoes and stepped out of his pants. Ronni shimmied out of her jeans, but she left on her newest lacy red lingerie. She might be a wolf, but she still liked feeling feminine.

Temptation beckoned from the devilish curve of Bodie's mouth. He didn't say anything, but his eyes worshipped every inch of her before lifting to meet her gaze.

She scooted on the mattress and he followed, stalking up her body, every bit as predatory as a wolfan male. His essence throbbed with strength, virility and possessiveness.

When his body covered the length of hers, he claimed her with a kiss so fierce and full of need it stole her breath. His heat intensified her own and her thoughts scattered. So much for keeping her head this time.

His roughened hands gently stroked her skin, heightening her senses. Each kiss branded her, leaving a blistering trail down her neck, between the valley of her lace-clad breasts, across the plane of her stomach and against her quivering inner thighs as he removed her panties.

Incoherent speech escaped her as his lips pressed against

her folds and teased her with his hot, moist tongue, trapping her somewhere between ecstasy and agony.

The strokes against her sex were whisper-soft and unhurried. All the while, she ached for hard and fast so the pressure building in her core would be released.

She wiggled and sat up. Bodie tilted back his head until his lust-filled gaze met hers. Reaching behind her back, she unfastened her bra and slowly discarded it. "My turn."

Bodie sat up, confusion settling on his features until Ronni urged him down on the mattress and straddled his hips. Kissing him hard as his hands slid over her ribs to cup and knead her breasts, she rubbed her mound against his hard cock. Unintelligible words fell from his lips and an indescribable groan rose from his throat.

"Now you know how I felt."

Bodie's arms tightened around Ronni a split second before she found herself flat on her back against the mattress with him crouched over her again.

He surged inside her. A sigh escaping her lips, she closed her eyes as he filled her body and soul. There was no other way to describe the completeness of Bodie's essence blending with hers.

She danced her fingers over his broad shoulders and down his muscled back. The smooth warmth of his skin made her hands tingle and the slow, steady rhythm of his deep thrusts grounded her. His worship of her body made her feel cherished, comforted and safe.

Bodie's breathing hitched. His thrusts came harder and faster and the gnawing ache in her core intensified until she shattered from the waves of pleasure. Nearly drowning in the sensation, she clutched at his undulating hips until he shuddered with his own release. As he stilled, she buried her face in the curve of his neck.

Loving his masculine scent and the saltiness of his skin against her lips as she nibbled the enticing spot where the neck and shoulder joined. The mate-claim spot where a wolfan male bit a female during sex, marking her as his life-mate. Once the claim was made, it was binding until death. There was no divorce under wolfan law.

Since Bodie wasn't wolfan, if or when the time came, Ronni would have to claim him. Her insides fluttered and she realized she might not be as opposed to the idea as she should be.

Standing on the balcony, Bodie spoke to his daughter on the phone. His words were a bare whisper on the wind, yet Ronni heard his side of the conversation as clearly as if he had whispered in her ear. She loved that he spoke to Willow in the same, soothing parental tone that she used with Alex.

Her heart thudded madly. Bodie was a triple threat: a doting father, loving son and fantastic lover. He was probably as near to perfect as a man could get.

There was a knock on the door. "Room service."

Dressed in the clothes she'd worn earlier, Ronni got up from the small cozy couch in the sitting area to open the door. A resort employee pushed a cart into the room. He set the dishes on the kitchen bar counter and handed Ronni the service ticket for a signature.

"Thanks." Closing the door, she plucked up a quill off the floor. She ran her fingers along the inky black feathers with silvery sheen. If not for the red streak of paint on the quill, Ronni would've thought her raven had followed them.

Maybe there were more of his kind in the area and one had flown in through the balcony doors left ajar while she and Bodie had been out playing tourist. He padded into the room.

"Everything okay at home?"

"Willow and my mother aren't speaking to each other. So everything is normal." The relaxed smile he wore tightened as his gaze fell to her hands. "What is that?"

"I found it on the floor." Handing him the feather, she

studied the tension creeping into his body. "Is something wrong?" She touched his arm.

Startled, he glanced at her. "It reminds me of a story my mother once told me."

"It must not have been a happy one."

"It wasn't." Bodie's displeasure was clearly evident in his furrowed brow and tight jaw. He didn't elaborate and Ronni didn't ask, though she did expect that the time would come for them to discuss their respective heritages. If they were going to move forward in their relationship, everything had to be laid out on the table. Sooner rather than later, before the past uprooted their future.

Chapter 21

The soft, rhythmic sounds of Ronni's peaceful breaths were a lullaby to Bodie's soul. He hated sneaking out on her, but the Tribunal had summoned him with a Tlanuhwa feather, its tip dipped in red paint tainted with blood. Bodie's father had received a similar message before his death.

If Bodie ignored their calling card, the sentries would come for him and might attempt to take Ronni as leverage. If threatened, Bodie had no doubt Ronni would shift into her wolf and expose her species to his people, ignorant of the knowledge other shifters existed. From there, the situation would only spiral into chaos.

Naked, he padded onto the dark balcony, stretched out his arms, triggering a biting current that traveled down his spine and across his shoulders. He launched into the air a raven. The wind filtered through his feathers as he soared upward.

He wasn't alone.

Three ravens surrounded Bodie in a triangular formation. He didn't bother to telepathically communicate with them, nor did they with him during the escort.

They landed deep within the forest, miles from the prying eyes of civilization. Large, golden-eyed, black birds littered the clearing. There was a legitimate reason a gathering of such was called a murder of crows.

Heart pounding, Bodie landed and immediately shifted into his human form to avoid any attempt at caging him and to better defend against a mass assault. "Why have you summoned me?"

The first raven to transform was a man with more silver

than black in the hair that hung down his back. Weariness lidded his dark eyes.

Kane!

Bodie's uneasiness morphed into anger. "Five minutes," he snarled, sitting cross-legged on the leaf-covered ground in front of a fire. "Make this quick and meaningful."

"Leave us!" Kane waved a dismissive hand.

The congregation took flight amid a flutter of wings and squawks of protest. When all were gone, the older man sat down in front of Bodie. "I'm glad you accepted my invitation."

"I've accepted nothing, Kane. The clock is ticking."

"Time hasn't mellowed your temper toward me."

"Neither has it lengthened my patience."

"I seek forgiveness, Bodie."

"That is something I cannot give."

"I can't undo the past."

"I can't forget." Though Bodie had tried to move beyond it. "You were responsible for my father's murder."

"An unintentional consequence. Thaddeus was my friend. I did not wish him harm."

"My father wanted to make things better for us all. He wasn't trying to instigate an insurrection."

"I warned him that the Tribunal was not ready to hear his ideas."

"You did not stand up for him when he was accused of rebellion." The long-simmering anger rooted in the dark recesses of Bodie's heart began to bubble. No matter how often he tried to meditate hoping to expel the corrosive emotion, a piece always remained.

"If I had, his fate would not have changed, but mine would have, and I could not jeopardize my family."

"You coward!" Bodie spat.

"I will carry that shame to the grave."

"My father is already there. Carried on the shoulders of a friend's betrayal."

"In atonement, I have done what I could to protect you and your mother. Including matching you with my daughter." Anguish shimmered in Kane's eyes. "Linking your lineage with mine obliterates the blight. There is no need to continue your self-imposed banishment."

"My father's blood is not a blight. I am proud that it runs through me and my daughter."

"My blood runs through her, too." Kane's straight shoulders sank. "Please, Bodie. Mara died in the spring. I have no other family except Willow."

"How did you know where to find me?"

"I have always known my granddaughter's whereabouts, and yours by extension."

"My mother told you." Bodie's heart broke and froze simultaneously at her betrayal.

"She's concerned about the path you've chosen."

"What has she told you?"

"That you're seeking a mate outside of our people. Mary is afraid of what the Tribunal's response will be to your sacrilege." The grim firm line of Kane's mouth held. "She is right to be worried. The Tribunal overlooked your first offense, when you ended your ability to father children, because I convinced them that you had reacted in grief."

"That wasn't my reason. I didn't want to be forced into another mateship, especially with someone who didn't want to be mine."

"Compatibility takes time."

"No, it doesn't. I've met a woman with whom I connected during our first encounter. It's not hard to communicate with her. She understands me, my humor, what's important to me. We share similar values."

"You are violating the law. The Tribunal will learn of your affair with this human female if you continue down this path."

"Are you threatening to inform the rest of the council if I don't stop seeing her?"

"I'm not threatening, Bodie. Nor would I be the one to expose you. Right now, the Tribunal members are dealing with a growing unrest among your peers who want to challenge the old ways. An unsanctioned mateship with a *human* or even the appearance of such outright disregard for established traditions can put you in a dangerously vicarious position.

"Think of Willow, Bodie. She needs to be safe."

"My daughter's well-being is always my top priority," Bodie snapped. "If you or the Tribunal come near my family—" An excruciating burning sensation erupted in Bodie's fingertips and he saw long, sharp black nails emerging from beneath his natural ones.

"What the hell?" He vigorously shook his hands and the vision dissipated. "Is there a hallucinogen in the fire's smoke?"

"It is as Mary fears," Kane said solemnly. His sorrowful eyes held Bodie's gaze. "The Quickening for this woman has unchained your beast. I am too late to dissuade you from the destructive path you are traveling."

"Destructive for whom?" Bodie focused on the calming breaths he hoped would diffuse his rising temper. "The Tribunal's smothering hold on our people? Well, good riddance. I'm happy with Ronni, truly happy."

"If that which is manifesting inside you continues to gain strength, it will destroy everything, Bodie. Including your happiness with her."

"Now I know where my mother gets her ridiculous ideas. They come from you." Bodie stood. "You and the Tribunal will stay away from my family, and that includes Ronni and her son. If you don't, I will defend them. And if my *peers* decided to use that as a call to arms, so be it."

Whatever hope Kane had for this meeting seemed to fade along with the light in his eyes. He launched into his raven, slicing through the curls of smoke rising from the fire, and disappeared into the night sky.

Bodie had the urge to follow, but the tiny sparks jumping from the fire kept him grounded. The last thing he wanted was to burn down the woods.

Once he put the fire out, he'd return to his beautiful she-wolf and lose himself in the comfort of her softness. Soon, he'd reveal his raven to her and take her as his life-mate.

He doubted the Tribunal would interfere once Kane advised its members to do so; that could make him a martyr and incite the very rebellion they hoped to quell. But if they did come, Bodie intended to greet them with a pack of wolves.

A shrill ringing decimated the silence. Ronni sat up, getting her bearings. "Bodie?"

Neither seeing or sensing him inside the suite, she reached over the empty side of the bed and answered his cell phone. Sobs instantly filled her ear.

"Willow?" Ronni's mothering instinct kicked in. "What's wrong, hon?"

"Enisi," Willow said from between heaved breaths. "She fell on the steps and got hurt. The ambulance just took her to the hospital."

"Where are you?"

"In the camper. They wouldn't let me ride with her."

"Everything is going to be all right, okay?"

There was a muffled sound. "Where's my dad?"

"Um." Glancing around their empty hotel suite, Ronni wondered that as well. For the second time tonight, she had awakened to find him gone. "He stepped out, but I'll have him call you as soon as he gets back."

"Okay." Willow sniffed.

"I'll ask Rafe to come by. You can stay with his family and Alex until we get home."

"Thanks," Willow said quietly.

"Bye, hon." As soon as the line disconnected, Ronni

called Rafe. He didn't hesitate when she asked him to pick up Willow so she wouldn't have to be alone.

The call to the hospital was less than productive. Since Ronni wasn't family, she couldn't get any information on Mary's condition. Anticipating that Bodie would want to leave immediately, Ronni dressed quickly and packed their bags. She padded out to the balcony. The sun had peaked on the horizon and was rapidly laying claim to the day.

Ronni tried, unsuccessfully, not to be annoyed. Bodie had left her alone in the room, *again*, to go off to wherever to do whatever, and now his daughter needed him.

What was he hiding that he didn't want her to know?

Rubbing her arms did nothing to dispel the uncomfortable, itchy feeling prickling her skin.

"Bodie, where the hell are you?"

As clear as if he were standing next to her, Bodie's voice resonated in her mind. *"Right here, beautiful."*

A second later, the door opened and he walked in wearing sneakers, gym shorts and a glistening layer of sweat.

Ronni buried her surprise that Bodie had heard her thoughts and responded in kind. There were reasons it could've happened other than a mate-bond, such as an overactive imagination.

His relaxed grin dissolved and he pulled out his earbuds. "What's wrong?"

"Willow called. Your mother fell and had to be taken to the hospital."

Some of the color drained from Bodie's face. He reached for his phone on the bedside table.

"I asked Rafe to pick her up. She seemed too upset to stay alone."

Phone tucked between his cheek and shoulder, he nodded, but she wasn't sure he actually heard her.

"Hey, chickadee," he said in a soothing father's voice. "Ah, sweetheart. Everything's going to be fine."

How many times had she assured Alex of the same, knowing there was no way to guarantee the promise?

Ronni slipped onto the balcony, lightly closing the door behind her. She inhaled a deep breath of fresh air, allowing it to filter through her entire body before releasing it.

Bodie had simply gone to the resort's gym to work out and her mind had immediately accused him of doing something behind her back.

Just because Zeke had kept a secret throughout their entire mateship that undermined her trust in him didn't mean that Bodie was untrustworthy. Still, it was unsettling to wake up and find his side of the bed vacant and cold, twice in one night.

Shortly after midnight when Ronni had got up to look for him, she had startled him, meditating on the balcony. Unable to sleep, Bodie had said he needed the fresh air.

Ronni sensed something was bothering him but he brushed aside her concern. A little part of her worried that he felt smothered by the amount of time they'd spent together. Maybe all they were good for were the stolen moments.

The balcony door opened.

"Did you call the hospital?" Ronni's grip on the railing tightened.

"Yeah. Mom is going for X-rays, and the doctor wants to do some other tests because she's had a few falls lately." Bodie's chin rested on Ronni's shoulder. Hugging her waist, he sighed. "Thank you for thinking about Willow. She's never had to be alone."

"There's no need to thank me. I'm a mother. I know when my child needs something."

"You think of Willow as your child?" Bodie's tone was perfectly neutral and she began wondering if his feelings ran as deep as hers.

"It's an instinct." She kept all emotion out of her voice, but yes. Willow had become quite special to her.

"Hey." Bodie's hands gripped the railing on either side of her, effectively pinning her between his arms. "Are you upset with me because we have to cut the weekend short?"

"Of course not." Ronni could ignore the feelings creating havoc inside her but that wouldn't do either of them any good. "On the first night we've spent together, you disappear twice. It's unsettling. And you've seemed distant ever since I found you meditating."

"Baby." He turned her around and cupped her face. "When I can't sleep, I meditate and when that doesn't work, I exercise. And I'm not distant. Just tired."

The knot tightening in her spirit made it difficult to believe him.

"I'm going to grab a quick shower and we'll check out." His thumb gingerly caressed her cheek.

"Okay." Ronni nodded.

"We'll have more weekend getaways, I promise." Sighing, he walked inside the room, leaving her on the balcony.

Ronni turned to watch the sunrise painting the sky in vibrant colors behind the hazy mountains.

Her hopes that Bodie's feelings were as real as hers began diminishing. If he didn't trust her enough to share his troubles or worries, maybe they weren't as close as she imagined.

Chapter 22

"Bodaway!"

His head jerked, his eyelids flew open and he found himself awkwardly scrunched in an uncomfortable chair. Restless after the meeting with Kane, Bodie slept very little last night and had planned to spend a lazy Sunday morning making love to Ronni and sharing a leisurely breakfast in bed before coming home.

Instead, his mother's accident had rushed them back to Maico. Ronni and the kids went to her house and he'd come straight to the hospital, only to find the patient peacefully sleeping when he'd entered her room more than an hour ago.

Straightening his back, he wiggled into a better sitting position.

"What are you doing here?" his mother asked. "You didn't need to cut your weekend short."

"Of course we did." At least he and Ronni were able to spend an entire day and night together before having to fly home.

"Ronni probably thinks I did this on purpose."

"Why?" Scooting closer to her hospital bed, he reached for his mother's hand.

"I told her she wasn't the right woman for you."

"She doesn't hold that against you." Bodie smiled. "Ronni said she might feel the same way when Alex gets a serious girlfriend."

"What you're doing with her is unnatural."

"I love her," he said without thinking. But once the words were out, he recognized the truth.

At first, he'd viewed the relationship as an opportunity to gain membership into the Co-op. But that changed so fast and he truly had fallen in love.

"Have you revealed your raven?" A pensive frown tightened his mother's mouth.

"We came home before I had the chance."

"I'm sorry to have ruined your plans." She smoothed the bedsheet over her stomach.

"Then why did you send Kane?" The unexpected encounter had knocked Bodie off-kilter and whatever connection he and Ronni shared had allowed her to sense his conflicted emotions. Just as he had been able to sense hers.

Before she began to suspect that he was harboring a dark secret, he needed to reveal his raven. Once they both came clean about their abilities, they could discuss a future together.

"You spoke with Kane?" Mary's hands stilled.

"He summoned me. And I'm not happy that you have been communicating with him." *Not happy* was so much of an understatement when Bodie couldn't even begin to describe the depths of disappointment, anger and hurt that had twisted his heart.

But he was a parent, too, and intimately understood the drive to protect one's child. Regardless of any true jeopardy.

"I told Kane that Ronni will become my next mate and warned him not to interfere." The ache in his back growing to a burning pain, Bodie stood and stretched. "I'm anxious for Ronni to know I'm the raven who watches over her, but I'm not sure how she'll take the news."

"It shouldn't be too difficult for her to understand, considering she's a wolf."

Fear clanged in Bodie's ears and his entire body chilled.

"Don't look so shocked." Mary used the hand controls to adjust the bed. "I've seen the inside of the Co-op's wolf sanctuary, too."

Fear stabbed Bodie's heart. "Did you tell Kane?"

"No." Mary patted his hand wrapped tightly around the bed's side rail. "That would've been too large of a betrayal for you to forgive."

It absolutely would've been.

"There are whispers of resistance among the Tlanuhwa. If the Tribunal learn we are living among another shifter species, paranoia will cause them to act irrationally. I want Wahyas to be our allies, not our enemies. As a people, we must change but an outright revolt can only end badly for everyone."

Bodie stood, stretched his back and walked to the window to open the blinds. The sun was high above but the sky was overcast and gloomy.

"You knew this time was coming. That is why you brought us here, isn't it?"

"I can't be the only father in my generation to struggle with how the way things are done." Bodie gave a half shrug. "I hoped joining the Co-op would give us a surrogate family, in case things went badly for our people, but I didn't know the wolves were shifters until I met Ronni."

"Will the wolves shelter us if war comes?"

"I believe they protect their own. If Ronni takes me as her mate, I will become a pack member and so will you and Willow."

"But what about our clansmen? We're a peaceful people, Bodie. Many will flee a war."

"I doubt Gavin Walker wants his territory flooded with Tlanuhwa refugees." Bodie crossed his arms and leaned against the wall. "Maybe they have insight on reconciling the old traditions with the new.

"Considering the werewolf legends, I imagine their history isn't unlike our own. If we can learn how they managed to adapt and thrive, maybe there is hope for our species."

"There is more of your father in you than I ever wanted to admit."

"He always wanted me to be happy." The old ache in Bodie's heart throbbed. "Why didn't you?"

"Because I don't want to lose you to the Quickening. Once it fuses your soul to the one it seeks, the Quickening can make you act against your nature and do unimaginable things. I know you, Bodaway. If these things manifest in you, the guilt will destroy you."

"Nothing is going to make me act against my will. True love doesn't do that to a man."

"Fear of losing that love does," Mary said.

Maybe some of that was true. If someone tried to take Ronni from him, Bodie would do everything in his power to keep her safe. But his efforts wouldn't turn him into a monster.

His phone pinged and he pulled the device from his pocket to read the text message.

Hey, hon. How is Mary?

"Ronni wants to know how you're feeling," Bodie told his mother.

"Sore," she answered. "But I'll live."

Bodie replied with only his mother's response but he wanted to say so much more. Like how he wished they could go back to yesterday and do it all again. And that he was growing more restless by the minute because he was here, she was there, and he was damn tired of saying goodbye.

His phone pinged again. This time, Ronni sent a picture of Willow and Alex in her kitchen with the caption:

Having pancakes for brunch. But there's more batter on the counter than on the griddle :)

Bodie's heart smiled because Ronni had thought to include him in their fun. He replied:

Wish I was there.

Me, too.

It wasn't difficult for Bodie to envision laid-back mornings spent with family. A family that had grown from three to five, at least in his heart.

"Willow was right." His mother's voice pulled his attention from the phone. "Ronni genuinely makes you happy."

"That's why I love her." Showing Mary the photo of the kids making more of a mess than brunch, Bodie would've sworn that he could smell the delicious scents of buttery pancakes, maple syrup and sizzling ham.

Someone rapped on the door.

"Mrs. Gryffon?" A tall, fit man, somewhere in his sixties, entered the room. "I'm Doctor Habersham. I'm not your admitting physician but Ronni asked me to check on you."

Studying the man, Bodie stepped forward. When dropping off Ronni and the kids at her house, Ronni had said she would ask Doc—Rafe's adoptive dad, who was also the Co-op's doctor—to stop by. Bodie had assumed the physician would be wolfan; however, nothing in his manner or movements suggested he was anything other than human. "Are you Rafe's father?"

"Yes." Doc's eyes crinkled behind his thick glasses.

"I'm Bodie." He shook the doctor's hand in the customary human greeting.

"Glad to finally meet you, though I wish the circumstances had been better." Doc moved toward Mary's bedside. "How is your pain this morning, Mrs. Gryffon?"

"My right side is sore. If I move my leg, my foot throbs," she replied.

"Any headache?"

"A slight one."

"The good news is that the CT scan doesn't show any cranial trauma incurred during your fall, or any other worrisome process. Bad news is that your X-rays confirm a nondisplaced fracture in your foot.

"Even though they've fitted you with a walking cast, you should avoid weight bearing so it can heal properly. At the very least, you'll need to use crutches. A knee scooter may be better, at least for the first few weeks."

A knee scooter? There was barely enough room to walk around inside the camper.

"And of course," Doc continued. "No driving."

"How long will this take to heal?" Mary frowned.

"A good six to eight weeks, maybe more, depending on how compliant you are with the discharge instructions. You'll need to follow up with your primary care doctor in a week or so."

"I don't have one."

"Then come see me. I'll have my office schedule an appointment for Thursday."

Bodie's shoulders sank and his chest tightened at the added responsibilities his mother's accident would put on him. Already, he was jostling long work days. How would he manage to get Willow to and from school, take his mother to the doctor, do his job and spend time with Ronni?

Simply, he couldn't. Something had to give but he didn't know what.

The pungent antiseptic smell of the hospital burned Ronni's sensitive wolfan nose. She tried to breathe as little of the air, saturated with the scent of sickness and suffering, as possible.

Alex's hand cupped his nose and mouth as they passed a room with an offending odor. "What is that smell?"

"You don't want to know," Ronni answered.

"Gross." Willow pinched her nose.

At the end of the long corridor, she saw Bodie exit a room. He stretched his back and shoulders, then crossed his arms over his chest and leaned against the wall. With his head bowed and chin tucked, he looked like a man deep in prayer.

The weight on her chest seemed heavier with every step. And the jumble of nerves converging in her stomach weren't quite her own. The only explanation was that Bodie's emotions were blending into her own.

Definitely a mate-bond manifestation.

So much for her decision to never allow herself to sync so intimately with another man. And from the way this one acted this morning, he might be having second thoughts about continuing their relationship. "Dad!" Willow called out in a hoarse whisper and she scurried toward him.

Bodie slowly turned his head as if he wasn't quite sure if he was the one being sought. The moment his gaze found Willow, a soft smile lightened his brooding expression.

Ronni could see all the love and adoration Bodie had for Willow in that hug. The father-daughter moment caused emotion to swell in Ronni's throat because she knew the hardest thing he'd ever do would be to let his little girl grow up. Ronni understood the turmoil firsthand. She lived it every day, watching Alex mature.

Bodie's gaze lifted to Ronni. Relief and gratitude shimmered in his eyes. And a rush of masculine energy warmed her, head to toe.

"Hey," Alex said casually as Willow stepped back from her father.

Bodie answered with a nod.

"How's *Enisi*?" Willow asked.

"The nurses are helping her get dressed and then we can take her home." He glanced at the room's closed door. "It might take a while. She's moving fairly slow."

"Why don't you two get a snack from the cafeteria?" Ronni said to Alex and Willow.

"Here." Bodie pulled out his wallet and handed a ten-dollar bill to each of the kids. "It's on me."

"Thanks," Willow and Alex said in unison.

They left in a fast trot, racing to see who got to the cafeteria first.

"Have you eaten?" Ronni asked Bodie.

"Coffee and peanut butter crackers around lunchtime," he said softly.

"Join the kids and get something substantial in your stomach. I'll wait here with your mom."

Slowly, Bodie shook his head as his tired gaze caressed her face.

"Come here," Ronni said, stepping up to him and circling her arms around his neck.

Bodie leaned into her embrace and tucked his face into the curve of her neck. His warm breath tickled her skin.

"I'm glad you're here," his voice whispered through her mind.

Ronni tried not to stiffen. Though she was falling in love, bonding with him could become a dangerous and painful complication if he wasn't falling in love with her.

He pulled back, his brow weighted with concern. "You tensed up. What's wrong?"

"I'm worried about you." It wasn't a lie. "How are you holding up?"

"Nothing I can't handle."

"Just because you can doesn't mean you should." Ronni tugged on the lapels of the denim jacket he wore over a black, long-sleeve T-shirt. "Tell me."

"Mom needs to stay off her foot and won't be able to drive." Bodie tucked his hands into the hip pockets of his jeans. "I'll have to do all the things she normally does until she's healed."

Ronni understood a lot of what that entailed. "I'll pick up Willow for school and bring her home, and take Mary to any follow-up appointments that she has. I'll also pick up items at the market if you give me a list."

"I don't want to burden you."

"You're not. A lot of people gave me a hand when I was

in a bind." She paused. "Let me help, Bodie. I want to do this for you."

Cradling her face in his hands, he lightly stroked his thumbs over her cheeks. "This isn't how I planned to finish our weekend."

"Life gets in the way sometimes." And might have saved Ronni from revealing her wolf, presumptuously. Despite the bond forming between them, he had closed a part of himself to her and she didn't know why.

"I will make this up to you." He brushed his mouth across her lips. Barely a whisper of a kiss, but still the sheer sweetness squeezed her heart. "I really do want more quality time with you."

"Me, too," she murmured, knowing that more did not necessarily imply a lifetime.

Chapter 23

"You aren't an imposition, Mary." Having returned from the first follow-up visit with Doc, Ronni gingerly helped Bodie's mother onto the bed in the first-floor spare bedroom and lifted her soft-casted foot to stuff a pillow beneath her leg.

Sunday evening, watching Bodie struggle to get his mother into the camper, Ronni realized their housing situation was going to be problematic during Mary's recovery. Even Alex had expressed concerns about the less than ideal circumstances.

After they had talked considerably, both agreed they had the means to help, and had invited Bodie's family to move into their home, temporarily.

Stubborn-minded, Bodie had declined the offer, believing that living together with the current predicament would strain rather than strengthen their relationship. Ronni thought this might've been his way of pulling away.

But, yesterday, he changed his mind.

"I feel terrible that you had to close your business to take care of me." Tears welled in Mary's eyes. "Especially after I tried to shoo you away from Bodaway."

"Only the storefront is closed. I worked out of my home before, I can do so again." She had put a sign in the window advising customers to call to schedule appointments. "And I'm not easily shooed."

"You are an angel."

Quite a turn-around from practically being called a she-devil.

"All right, you're all settled." Ronni showed her the little bell on the nightstand. "Ring this if you need anything."

"Thank you." Mary closed her eyes to rest.

Leaving the door slightly ajar, Ronni walked out of the room. Then, she put a teakettle on the stove before going into the formal dining room that had temporarily been transformed into a work area. The most pressing project was almost complete.

Relying on the magazine pictures Willow had shown her, Ronni had fashioned similarly styled curtains and a duvet cover to decorate the girl's new room. Just a few final touches to add, then a quick steam over the fabric, and the bedroom accessories would be finished. By the time Ronni picked the kids up from school, Willow's new room would be all set up.

Nervous, at first, with adding three more people to her household, Ronni now felt having a blended family gave her a greater sense of completeness.

No matter her trust issues, Bodie was a good man, and she was lucky to have him in her life.

The kettle whistled and Ronni returned to the kitchen and poured a cup of tea. Absently, she picked up the ringing phone on the counter. "I was just thinking of you."

"Well, darlin', that's the best news I've heard in a long time."

A chill rippled down her spine and spread into her limbs. "What do you want, Jeb?"

"Thanksgiving is coming. It's a time for family and I want to see mine."

"I'll send a picture."

"I won't tolerate your resistance much longer, Veronika. It's long past the time for you and Alex to come home."

"When will you get it through your thick skull? We are home. And if you show up at my house again, I will shoot your furry ass for trespassing!" She jabbed the button to disconnect the call.

Before she could slam the phone onto the counter, the device rang again. "Don't call me again!"

"Whoa." Bodie's strong, steady voice brought burning tears to her eyes. "Did I do something wrong?"

"No." Ronni swallowed her nerves. "Jeb called. He's coming for Thanksgiving. I really hoped he would stay out of our lives."

"Ronni, I—" The line crackled.

"Bodie?"

"The reception is spotty here."

"Where are you?"

"...at Swallow Cre...checking...and." His words faded completely.

"Bodie?" Ronni sat at the kitchen table, holding the phone to her ear like a lifeline. "Can you hear me?"

Nothing but static answered.

"Bodie?"

The call dropped. Ronni laid down the phone and cradled her head. Jeb wasn't going away like she foolishly hoped.

She wished Bodie was home so she could bury her face in his chest and feel his strong arms holding her tightly.

Warmth rushed through her body and Bodie's distinct, masculine presence filled her mind. The smart thing to do would be to block the budding manifestation of the mate-bond. Right now, she didn't have the strength to resist.

The stress-induced rapid beat of her heart slowed to a calm, comfortable canter.

What she had told Jeb was true. She had a new life and a new family. Come hell or high water, not even Jebediah Lyles himself could drag her away.

Coming home to family was always the best part of Bodie's day. Coming home to his new, blended family for the first time had him bursting at the seams. Although his mother and daughter had spent last night with Ronni and Alex, Bodie had worked with the Co-op's sentinels, flying his plane over their patrols, until nearly morning. So, he'd crashed a few hours at the camper before starting back to work.

Tonight, though, he made sure to get off at a decent hour. He shut off the headlights and climbed out of the truck.

Though Ronni had proposed this temporary solution to deal with the problem of his mother's broken foot, Bodie hoped to make it permanent.

His heart pounded with each step that brought him closer to the front door. Should he ring the doorbell or walk right in?

"Dad!" Willow opened the door before he had a chance to decide.

"Hey, chickadee." He gave her a fatherly hug.

"You have got to see my new room!" Pure joy danced in her eyes and his heart swelled to near bursting.

"I will, but I need to stow my weapon."

"Oh, yeah, I forgot." She strolled into the living room and sat on the floor to finish her homework strewn across the large square coffee table she shared with Alex.

He looked up. "Hey." The boy smiled and his eyes seemed friendly and accepting.

Bodie closed and locked the front door.

"Bodaway, is that you?" his mom called out as he padded down the corridor.

"Hi, Mom." He stood in her doorway. "How are you feeling?"

"Grateful."

Him, too. "Have you had supper?"

"Yes, with the kids. They brought their trays in here and we watched a couple of game shows before they left to finish their homework." She squinted at him. "I think Ronni's waiting to eat with you."

"I shouldn't keep her waiting." Bodie headed into the master bedroom. It looked a little different than he remembered. Now some of his things sat next to Ronni's stuff.

Stepping into the closet, he found his small fireproof safe sitting on a shelf. He unloaded his weapon and inspected it before securing it alongside his ammunition. Then he closed and locked the safe, then placed his utility belt on top. Kicking off his boots, he pulled off his uniform shirt and removed his Kevlar vest. Normally, he would shower as soon as he got in. But all he wanted right now was to see Ronni.

"You're not going to believe what Ronni did." Willow intercepted him. "She's amazing."

"Mom is buttering you up," Alex teasingly called out to Willow. "Wait 'til she grounds you for something."

"I won't do anything that will get me grounded." Willow's ponytail bounced with the bob of her head.

A mischievous gleam that screamed *challenge accepted* lit Alex's eyes.

Bodie warned him with a look of his own and Alex merely laughed.

"Come on, Dad." Willow tugged him toward the stairs. "Sheesh, you're so slow."

Curious, he followed his daughter into her new room.

"What do you think?" She whirled around the space decorated with all sorts of girly stuff.

"Looks nice."

"Are you joking?" Willow gave him an incredulous, bug-eyed look. "This is a-mazing!"

Bodie shrugged. "Okay."

Giving an exasperated sigh that was far weightier than her years should allow, Willow snatched the magazine off the white wooden dresser. "It's exactly like this bedroom."

Bodie looked at the picture, which did not look exactly like the room in which they were standing.

"See the curtains?" Willow pointed at the window.

The soft pastel pattern was nothing like the garish geometrical print on the curtains in the picture, but he did notice the similarities in the design.

"And the duvet is to die for."

"Let's not get carried away." Bodie certainly didn't want his daughter to die over a bedspread.

She flopped on the bed, rubbing her arms against the coordinated coverlet as if making angel wings in the snow. "None of it is store-bought either. Ronni *made* it." She sat up. "Dad, I love *Enisi* and everything, but my room is going to be off-limits. I don't want her making me feel bad because I have a more refined sense of style than she does. And I'm not being frivolous, I'm just tired of being plain all the time."

"*Enisi* means well. Her parents were very strict. She can't help it when those same tendencies surface in her."

"I'm glad you're not that way."

"Me, too, chickadee." He turned to leave.

"Dad?"

Bodie glanced back at his daughter.

"We're staying right?" Willow sat cross-legged on her bed. "In Maico. With Ronni and Alex?"

"That's the plan."

"You're doing this for you, too. Not just me, right?"

"Willow, what are you talking about?"

"One night, I overheard you and *Enisi* talking about the Co-op's sanctuary. You thought it could be a safe place for my Transformation Ceremony." She looked at him with uncertain eyes. "I know only Co-op members are allowed access. Since we aren't members, it's impossible for us to get inside."

"Sweetheart, you don't need to worry about that stuff. That's my job to handle these things."

"But, Dad. I'll eventually grow up, go to college and stuff."

"I'm preparing myself for that time, but that is still a few years ahead of us."

"I don't want you to be with Ronni if you're only doing this for me."

"Again, not your worry."

"Being with her is forever, Dad." Her youthful brow

he needed to apprehend the suspects before the Co-op's security team arrived.

At first, he hadn't found any tracks except those next to the vehicle. After taking his time to survey the area, he'd spotted a telltale sign of recent disturbance, which suggested a likely direction. Every few feet, he stopped to look for the next clue. His enhanced vision enabled him to see the smallest broken twig, unnaturally crumpled leaves, slightly disturbed moss that humans would likely miss.

A doe bleat wafted on the wind.

Auditorily, he pinged the general location and started in that direction. A few minutes later, he noticed a flicker of movement ahead. At first, he saw nothing so he closed his eyes for a few seconds to readjust his sight. Upon opening his eyes, he zeroed in on the ground hunting blind, its camouflage design perfectly blending with the surroundings, hiding in plain sight.

Bodie edged closer and unfastened the strap on his holstered weapon hanging from his utility belt. "I'm Sergeant Gryffon, Georgia DNR. Put down your weapons and come out."

His announcement resulted in a low murmur inside the blind. Finally, the flap opened and two of the men he'd seen shooting at Ronni emerged with their hands free of guns.

A flash of anger clouded Bodie's vision, but he quickly banked it and cleared his thoughts.

The tallest one spoke first. "Is there a problem?"

"Several." Bodie rested his hand on the handle of his holstered gun. "Trespassing on private property, hunting in a legally protected area, hunting without your orange safety vests. And I haven't checked your permits yet. Now tell your friend to come out of the blind. This hunt is over."

The younger man spit tobacco on the ground. "You gonna arrest us?"

"If you don't cooperate," Bodie said.

"You alone?" one of the men asked.

furrowed. "You know she's a wolf shifter, right? Alex and Lucas, too."

Surprise and unease tightened his gut. "I'm aware of what they are. How did you find out?"

"My first day of school, some of the students were really mean and I got so stressed that I had hot flashes up and down my back, and my shoulders prickled." Willow huffed. "I got away from those kids as fast as I could, but I left a trail of feathers."

"Sweetheart, why didn't you tell me?"

"It was embarrassing, Dad. Like starting my period."

Oh, boy.

"Anyway, Lucas followed me to the empty classroom where I hid. He had a bad first day when he came to Maico, too, and said if I wanted a friend, he was there for me. I didn't want to go to class after being humiliated, so we hung out. He asked about my feathers, and I told him. And then I cried because I wasn't supposed to tell him. But he said I wasn't alone, and that he was a wolf shifter!" Willow smiled. "Besides us, I'd never met another shifter."

"Willow." Bodie tried to keep his voice level despite the alarm and anger bubbling. "What you did was wrong on so many levels."

"Maybe for you. But everything changed for me, Dad. For the better. I have friends now, real friends. That might not be important to you, but it is to me. I'm not sorry any of it happened."

"Who else knows?" Bodie's heart thundered in his chest. If Alex knew, had he told Ronni?

Willow's eyes rounded. "No one," she said quickly. "Lucas and I agreed not to tell anyone else, I swear."

"No more secrets, got it?" he warned his daughter as much as himself. Ronni needed to know what he was and he longed to tell her, but having his family move in was a huge adjustment on the heels of her ordeal with Jeb. He wanted to give Ronni some breathing room before changing her world view the way she had changed his.

"Yes, sir."

Bodie hurried down the stairs, knowing Ronni would be on the porch, on the swing. The moment he stepped outside and she gifted him with a smile, all the tension he'd carried throughout the day melted.

"You've been busy." He joined her on the swing, promising himself that he would reveal his raven to Ronni as soon as everyone had settled into their new routines. In case the reveal went badly, he didn't want to ruin their first night as a family.

"I wanted everyone to feel at home." She snuggled close.

"Thank you." He closed his eyes, basking in the warmth of her body and the blanket she shared with him. In that moment, everything was sheer perfection.

Chapter 24

At nearly dusk, Bodie made his way along an overgrown trail, wishing he was home. After a long day of checking licenses and permits, he wanted nothing more than to be with his family. More than a week after moving in, everyone had settled into a comfortable routine and he had decided tonight was the perfect time to reveal his raven.

After supper, he planned to take Ronni for a walk in the woods behind the house, to the spot he'd asked the Co-op's sentinels to stay away from for a few hours, so he could spend some quality time with her.

Bodie ached to get home, to put aside their secrets, and remove all impediments to forming a long and lasting relationship with Ronni. Yet, here he was, still working because a dirt road through one of the Co-op's properties now had fresh tire tracks. Figuring the security team had been in the area, Bodie had driven past. Almost immediately, his instinct began to gnaw his gut until he finally circled back around and drove down the bouncy dirt trail for nearly two miles before he saw a dark blue truck hidden in the brush.

The same dark blue truck he'd seen turning into the Thornbriar Lodge weeks ago. Considering the dried blood in the smelly truck bed, Bodie had been fairly sure the vehicle belonged to the poachers.

Not the type to sit and wait, as Tristan had strongly suggested when Bodie called, he had started tracking the hunters on his own. His badge gave him the right to access public and private property. And, to avoid potential complications,

"No." Not for long, he hoped.

"He's lying," the man inside the hunting blind called out. "I ain't seen no movement since he got here."

"Doesn't mean they aren't there," Bodie replied.

An older, bearded man emerged and pointed his rifle squarely at Bodie.

"Don't—" Pain exploded in his upper chest before the blast deafened his ears. He seemed to fall backward in slow motion. But he hit the ground hard, losing what little breath remained in his lungs.

A deluge of memories of Willow as a baby and now nearly grown flooded his mind. So did images of Ronni and Alex. He couldn't leave them, not like this.

With great effort and pain, he rolled onto his knees and scrambled behind the closest tree. Breathing hard, he drew his weapon.

Raised voices finally penetrated the percussive buzz in his head. Two were panicked. One spoke with deadly calm.

"We do this right and won't nobody know nothing." Heavy footsteps started toward Bodie.

A series of short howls echoed through the woods. Bodie needed to disarm the shooter before the wolves arrived. He gathered his strength and pushed to his feet. "Drop your weapon!" Bodie stepped from behind the tree, his gun raised.

"Not a chance." The man began to lift the rifle at Bodie again.

"I said, drop your weapon!" Movement in Bodie's peripheral vision kept him from pulling the trigger. A dark blur launched at the man at the same time something large and heavy knocked Bodie to the ground. The hunting rifle discharged, striking the tree behind where Bodie had stood.

The man's scream drowned in the commotion of raised voices and barking wolves. Bodie couldn't see what was happening because of the large wolf standing over him.

From the gray-blue color of his eyes, Bodie guessed it was Shane. At Tristan's approach, the wolf moved aside.

Tristan knelt beside Bodie. "I thought you were hit, but I don't see blood."

"He got me dead center in the vest." Bodie glanced at the mark in the tree. "The second might've hit me in the head."

"Glad it didn't." Tristan helped Bodie to his feet and knocked debris from his back. "My team will escort those guys to the sheriff's office. I'll take you to the hospital, just as a precaution."

"Appreciate it." Bodie didn't know how his chest could feel totally numb and burn like a raging fire at the same time. "I doubt I can drive."

"Want me to call Ronni to meet us there?"

"No." Her presence would go a long way in soothing him, but there wasn't anything she could do to help. "I don't want her worrying."

"Word of advice," Tristan said. "Don't leave a woman who cares for you out of the loop. She won't appreciate that you tried to spare her time or worry. Been there, done that. It isn't pretty when it blows up in your face."

"When were you planning to tell me that someone tried to kill you?" Anger and relief wrestled for dominance as Ronni stood in the doorway of the emergency bay, watching Bodie slowly dress. "Or just come home and pretend this didn't happen?"

"Who told you?" Slowly, he turned around. Guileless relief filled his tired eyes when his gaze touched her face. A massive bruise covered his chest, but as far as she could see, he had no bullet wounds.

"Word travels faster than lightnin' around here." Especially for wolfans. Ears particularly honed for her pack's communication system, she'd heard the network of howls. From the first sharp, icy pain that had sliced through her being, she'd known Bodie was the reason for the man-down signal.

"You should've called me." She swallowed the emotion lodged in her throat.

"If it was a serious injury, I would have." He closed the physical distance between them and drew her into his arms, dispersing the emotional vacuum.

Her efforts to constrain the sobs wracking her chest only caused her body to tremble.

"I'm okay," he whispered against her ear.

"You could've died."

"I always wear my vest."

Having lost her first mate to unexpected tragedy, she found no comfort in Bodie's words.

Cradling her face, Bodie kissed her, softly, sweetly and lovingly. The anxious knots in her stomach untangled. Fear subsided but something just as dangerous, just as primal, rose.

She wanted this man. Truly wanted him. Not just for the buffer he had provided against Jeb. She wanted Bodie because he made her feel again. Feel like a woman. A desirable woman. A woman with something to offer.

"Pardon the intrusion." Tristan's voice broke the spell.

Ronni stepped back and pressed her fingers against her tingling lips.

"Doc said you're good to go and I was checking to see if you needed a ride home. But I see you don't." Tristan grinned.

Ronni walked over and gave Tristan a friendly hug. "Thanks for being there."

"Always." He gave Bodie a quick nod. "Take it easy."

Bodie glanced at Ronni. "I'm not sure I can but it'll be fun trying."

With a flash of his trademark smile, Tristan left.

"Let's get you home." She turned to Bodie, who was buttoning his shirt.

"And into bed?" His dark brown eyebrows lifted in a devilish tent. "That's where I should be in my condition."

"No broken bones, no gaping bullet wounds, what condition are you referring to?" Ronni crossed her arms and forced her lips not to smile.

"The one in my pants." He hauled her against him, sealed his mouth over hers and kissed her like the devil was riding his heels.

Desire shot through her, molten and all consuming. In the distance, she heard a lone howl but pushed the noise from her mind.

By the time Bodie broke the kiss, she was panting and so was he.

"You're the only remedy, Ronni." His voice was rich, sultry and sincere.

"Let's go home, sergeant. We've got a lot of curing to do tonight."

Chapter 25

"For a man who had a critical condition in his pants, you're taking a long time with those dishes." Smiling, Ronni leaned against the kitchen counter. Not only had Bodie washed the dishes, he'd helped to make supper because he hadn't wanted his mother or the kids to know that he'd been shot.

"I appreciate you knew which critical condition to tend to first." Bodie towel-dried the pan and tucked it into the bottom cabinet. "It would've been embarrassing if I'd passed out from hunger while you were—" he waggled his brows "—curing me." He laid the dish towel across the empty dish drainer. Then, stepping in front of her, he caged her in his arms. "Thanks."

"For feeding you supper?"

"You feed so much more than my stomach." The emotion in his eyes sparked a warm fuzzy feeling in her belly. More than simple desire, the feeling was tangled with a comfortable sense of completeness. She never expected to feel this level of intimacy with another man, especially a human one.

His kiss was sweet, soft and full of longing, but the possessive grip on her hips assured her that he wasn't a man to be trifled with. Intelligent, strong and with a deep sense of family, he would be a force to be reckoned with if wronged.

With the kids and Mary watching television in the family room, Ronni took Bodie's hand and led him into the bedroom. He pulled his shirt off and dropped it on the floor.

A dark, angry bruise discolored his upper torso. Tears pricked her eyes. "He really tried to kill you."

"But he didn't." Bodie pressed her hand against the left

side of his chest. His skin was warm beneath her palm and she felt the strong, steady drum of his heart even as her hand rose and fell with his breaths.

They took their time undressing each other, stopping for a kiss, a caress, an embrace. He eased her onto the mattress. There was no need for foreplay. He was hard and seeping; she was wet and clenching.

With his knee, he nudged her legs farther apart as he crouched over her. His essence was much more dynamic than she imagined for a human. Bodie radiated a strength and force of will that could rival any wolfan male.

He would make a good mate, someday.

Slowly, he entered her and filled her completely, stretching her inner walls. Their synchronized sighs floated in the silent room.

The rhythm he set was comfortable and satisfying. The way he knew how to comfort and soothe her stirred whispers of things she'd never hoped to have again.

The pesky howl in her mind threatened to become a distraction. She closed herself off to the nagging and focused on how his body joined with hers, the fire smoldering in his eyes and how the masculine strength of his spirit allowed her to let go weighty worries.

Despite recent misgivings, she was still falling in love with him.

"You think too much," he said in a soft, gravelly voice, then kissed her forehead, easing the tension furrowed in her brow.

"Are you asking for my undivided attention?" she teased.

"Absolutely." Trailing kisses down her throat, he found the sweet spot where her neck and shoulder joined. He licked, he sucked, but when he nibbled, electricity charged every nerve in her body. She arched beneath him, her nails scraped down the taut muscles in his back and she clenched his ass, pulling him even deeper inside her.

His thrusts grew harder, faster, and the erotic feel of his

slick skin against hers drove her over the edge. Her body splintered as waves of ultimate pleasure pulsed along each and every cell. Even as she came undone, she felt Bodie's presence gathering every piece of her. He filled her mind, body and soul.

"Mine!" His raspy voice echoed through her mind as he shuddered in release.

Her eyelids would've popped open if she'd had any ounce of her own strength left. But all she felt was Bodie's essence ebbing through her, bolstering her and tethering her. To him.

He nuzzled her cheek and resettled his body on her, not his full weight but enough to know he wasn't ready to withdraw.

"You okay?" His smile was tight but his eyes were warm and tender, and she wanted to curl into his heat.

"Uh-huh" was all she could manage.

Eyes closed, he gently pressed his forehead to hers. She closed her eyes, holding him close. It felt so good to be so connected to another being. She couldn't imagine anything better than this, right now.

When Bodie eased from her, his warmth remained, almost as if he'd left a piece of himself with her.

"I want to show you something." His face set in a serious expression, he scooted to the edge of the bed.

Ronni sat up, pulling the sheet over her chest. "Is it good or bad?"

"That's entirely for you to decide." He stood. "Just remember, whatever you see, it's still me."

"What is that supposed to mean?"

He lifted his arms the way an eagle spreads its wings. Then her heart nearly stopped beating.

"Bodie?" Her voice was shrill because she'd been staring straight into his eyes, and then *poof.* Nothing but air. Something fluttered above her. She looked up and fear clouded her senses. Instinct took over. She rolled off the bed and shifted.

* * *

A frightened she-wolf bearing her pretty, white, sharp teeth in a silent growl wasn't what Bodie had hoped Ronni's reaction would be when he shifted. Maybe he should've waited a few more days after getting shot, but he wanted her to know him completely.

He alighted onto the tall dresser. "Ronni, it's me" is what he tried to say, but likely all she heard was a bird-like cawing.

She lunged but didn't strike. Her low growls sounded ferocious but fear and uncertainty shimmered in her big blue eyes. She truly was brave at heart. A measure of pride welled inside him.

He flew over her head and landed on the bed, then bowed to her the same way he had the night he'd first encountered her in the wolf sanctuary. Her growls softened. She inched closer, her head tilting right, then left as she studied him.

Feeling the imminent danger had passed, Bodie shifted into his human form. "Baby, it's me."

The she-wolf jumped back.

"Don't be afraid." He slowly reached out his hand, beckoning her forward rather than retreating.

She sat on the floor. The faintest shimmer outlined her silhouette before her beautifully naked human body reappeared.

"I'm not afraid," she said with a snarl that rivaled her growl. "Get out!" She pointed at the door.

Bodie shook his head. "I'm not going anywhere."

"You!" She stormed toward him. Her eyes flashing, her hair a tangled mess. "You—"

"I what, exactly? Deceived you?" He sat more comfortably on the bed and patted the space next to him. "Considering you're a wolf shifter, isn't that like the pot calling the kettle black?"

"You've known what I am the whole time?" Her scowl deepened. "You bastard!"

"I wanted to tell you sooner, but first we had to deal with Jeb. Then Mom fell and we moved in. Even if I hadn't got shot, I planned on telling you tonight." He pulled her to him. "I want you to know me. All of me."

"Why?" Suspicion glittered in her eyes.

"I think you're my soulmate."

"You *think*?"

"When I saw your wolf for the first time, there was something about you that intrigued me, but the feeling was stronger than anything I had experienced. There is a connection between us. You feel it, too, don't you?"

"What I feel is hurt." Her voice quieted to a whisper.

He tugged her to sit next to him.

"I had planned to reveal my wolf until I sensed you distancing yourself from me in Gatlinburg."

"I never meant for you to doubt me." Bodie inhaled deeply. He wanted Ronni as a true partner, not just a bed warmer. "The feather you found was a summons from Willow's estranged grandfather. After you went to sleep, I went to see him and we had a heated argument because we don't have the same vision for Willow's future. I didn't tell you because I didn't want you to worry."

"Stop doing that." The blue in her eyes turned a frosty gray. "I'm not fragile, I'm a capable she-wolf and I can handle bad news.

"Zeke knew Jeb was alive and didn't tell me. Now I'm dealing with the consequences of him not wanting to worry me. I'd rather deal with issues head-on, not scrambling to catch up because I didn't know they existed."

"Duly noted!" Playfully, Bodie bumped her shoulder. "Are we good?"

Worry tightened his chest at Ronni's prolonged silence. He'd wanted his revelation to bring them closer together, but what if it drove them apart?

"Even though I proposed a pretend relationship to deter

Jeb, everything that has happened between us is real. At least for me."

"But you're a bird. I'm a wolf."

"So?" Bodie tucked a strand of hair behind her ear. "We have the same family values, we enjoy each other's company and our human forms fit together quite nicely."

"But we aren't human, and I have an Alpha—oh, God." Standing, she hugged her waist. "I have to tell Gavin."

"No." Bodie rose to his feet.

"This is Gavin's territory. And I've only been a pack member for a short time. If he learns that I kept a secret about another type of shifter…" She paused. "Are there more? Do you have a flock or something?"

"I have Willow and my mother. We're the only Tlanuhwa in Walker's Run. I swear."

"But there are others, *tla-noo-wahs*, like yourself?"

He nodded. "Our numbers have dwindled to a few hundred, but I broke with our traditions when Willow was born."

"Why?"

"I promised her mother things would be different for our daughter. To keep our species from dying out, our Tribunal strictly enforces arranged marriages. Young adults are paired based on pedigree, without a chance to know each other. Layla and I had nothing in common. Had she survived—" he swallowed the burn in his throat "—our marriage would have been unhappy and lonely."

"Bodie—"

"I will tell Gavin." He clasped Ronni's arm. "And as for us, I want you as my lifemate but I don't want you to feel pressured. So you set the pace. If you want things to speed up or slow down, say so. I'll follow your lead." A slight ripple rolled across his shoulders. An alpha in his own right, he didn't give up control lightly. "Deal?"

After his heart pounded a dozen times, she answered

with a nod and he could actually breathe again. Everything was coming together and he'd never been happier.

So why did he feel as if Fate was about to drop a ten-ton weight upon his head?

Chapter 26

Bodie's chest rose and fell in rhythm with his shallow, soundless breaths. Ronni couldn't blame her inability to sleep on his snoring. Lying on his back, one arm thrown behind his head, the other hand resting on her hip as she propped on her side watching him, he wasn't making a peep.

Part of her wanted to press against him so that his heat would chase away the hollow uncertainty gnawing her stomach. The other part wanted to roll him off the bed to get some satisfaction in hearing him thud to the floor. A small penance for his deception.

If he hadn't known she was a wolf shifter, Ronni wouldn't have been wounded by his decision to reveal his raven because it would've been a demonstration of trust. Waiting simply reinforced that he didn't trust her. At least not completely.

Muscles growing stiff, Ronni eased from the bed and pulled on the T-shirt she normally slept in and a robe. Barefoot, she padded from the bedroom quietly, pulling the door closed behind her.

In the kitchen, she made a cup of herbal tea. On her way outside to sit on the porch swing, she heard movement upstairs. She left her cup on the counter and climbed the stairs.

Alex's room was dark and he was sleeping soundly so she continued down the hallway.

"Willow?" Propelled by her mothering instinct, Ronni pushed open the door and walked into the dimly lit room. "Are you feeling okay?"

"I guess so." Lying on her stomach, Willow was propped

on her elbows, knees bent with her feet in the air. In front of her was an open photo album and a flashlight.

Ronni sat on the edge of the mattress. "What are you looking at?"

"Pictures of my mom." Sadness tinged Willow's voice.

Ronni's heart ached for the young girl who'd never had a chance to know her mother.

"She was very pretty," Ronni said gently. "You favor her."

"Thanks!" Willow's cheeks momentarily plumped.

"What is she wearing in this picture?" Ronni tapped the photo of a raven-haired beauty looking over her shoulder at the camera, arms outstretched and wearing a cloak made of panels of black material cut and sewn to resemble bird feathers.

"Her transformation robe. She wore it for her first raven shift." Willow's eyes widened and she clamped her hand over her mouth.

"It's okay." Ronni leaned toward her with a smile. "Your dad told me that you are Tlanuhwa."

"Oh, good." Willow rolled her shoulders. "I thought I had messed up."

"How old is your mother in the picture?"

"Sixteen." Willow traced the outline of her mother's cloak with her finger. "I'll be sixteen next month."

Understanding dawning, Ronni felt her heart sink. Mary had mentioned Bodie's interest in the Co-op sanctuary as a place for the traditional ceremony performed at that age.

If Bodie had asked Gavin about access to the land, he would've explained that only Co-op members were allowed inside the protected area. Membership was exclusive to the pack. Generally, humans were only admitted to the Walker's Run pack if they were mated to a pack member.

The prickly feeling in Ronni's stomach made her nauseous. Had she been duped? Was Bodie's attention simply a ruse to gain access to the Co-op's sanctuary for his daughter's first shift?

"I wish I could wear my mom's robe for my transformation." Sadness had quieted Willow's voice more than usual.

Ronni's heart swelled and broke at the same time. She couldn't fault Bodie's drive to do whatever it took to protect his daughter. She had the same instinct for Alex. The situation with Jeb had prompted her to accept Bodie's interest. The big difference was that he had outright known her situation yet remained silent about his own agenda.

Regardless, she would make sure his daughter had a safe place to undergo her ceremony. Even if Bodie was simply using Ronni for access to the sanctuary, she would not put Willow at risk by backing out of the relationship now.

Compartmentalizing the turbulent emotions Bodie had uncapped, Ronni focused on the young girl who ached for her mother. "What happened to her robe?"

"It burned up." Willow gave her a matter-of-fact look. "Dad says anything touching our skin when we shift turns to ash."

Apparently, there were commonalities among the two shifter species.

"*Enisi* said there's no reason to spend a lot of money on something that's going to disintegrate after one use." Willow's sigh sounded near tragic. "I'm supposed to wear that." Her gaze slid to the flowery housecoat folded over the edge of the dresser.

"No matter what you wear, I'm sure it will be an exciting day for you."

"You'll be there, won't you?" Willow looked at Ronni with eyes so much like her father's, set in a delicate feminine face, and her fragility tugged at Ronni's motherly instincts.

"That's up to your father, hon."

"Oh, he'll want you to come." Willow's smile erased the worried expression she wore when Ronni had come into the room. "I know it."

Ronni wasn't as convinced. "Well, you have school tomorrow." She stood. "It's past time for you to be asleep."

Willow slipped the photo album under her bed, scrambled underneath the comforter Ronni had made, and wiggled into a comfortable spot. "Thank you for everything."

"You're welcome, sweetie." Ronni turned off the flashlight and laid it on the nightstand, then pulled the door closed.

Coming down the stairs, she watched Bodie shuffling into the living room, bare-chested and wearing his plaid pajama pants.

"Everything okay?" he asked.

Not by a long shot.

He gazed at her with such expectancy and sincerity that Ronni was tempted to confront him about his ultimate agenda. But it was late and she really didn't want to fight. Bodie had been good to her and Alex. She sensed that he did care about them and he was putting forth a real effort to make things work, just as she had done in the beginning of her mateship with Zeke.

"Couldn't sleep." She closed the distance between them. "I was going to sit on the porch but I saw Willow was up. She's all tucked in now."

"Are you ready to be tucked in?" His warm fingers laced through hers and led her into the bedroom. "Are we good?" he asked, climbing into bed after her. "Something feels out of sync." He scooted closer to her, draping his arm over her hip as she turned to face him.

"You're tired and overthinking." She kissed his forehead. "We're fine."

"Good." The muscles in his face relaxed and a soft smile touched his lips. His eyelids lowered until they closed. "You're the best thing that's happened to me in a long time."

Although Ronni sensed sincerity in his words, she wasn't sure if he was referring to their relationship or the fact that she was the key to helping his family.

In the end, she figured it didn't really matter. He would get access to the sanctuary; Jeb's harassment had stopped. All in all, a pretty fair bargain. Still, she couldn't help but wish it could've been more.

The next day, Ronni found herself knocking on Gavin's partially opened door. Having no intention of betraying Bodie, she was still obligated to inform the Alpha of what she had done. "Got a few minutes?" she said, slipping inside his office.

"Of course." Gavin pushed aside the survey map on his desk and waved his hand toward the chairs in front of his desk.

She eased down into the chair, perching on the edge. "I showed Bodie my wolf."

Gavin's thoughts did not register on his face. "Have you claimed him?"

"No." She had intended to do so, but her emotions were still reeling from last's nights ups and downs. "We're still figuring out that part."

"You know the law."

A Wahya could only reveal his or her wolf to a human if the person was the wolfan's mate. Or if the human was in peril.

"I trust Bodie and his family," Ronni said. "I wouldn't have moved them into my home if I didn't." It wasn't a lie. Even though she felt betrayed by Bodie's ultimate agenda, she did trust him with the Co-op's secret because he was a shifter, too.

"A slumber party is not a mateship." Though Gavin's tone was civil, there was an irritable growl in his voice. "This doesn't simplify the situation with Jeb."

"I thought the matter had been settled." She hadn't heard from him in several weeks.

"Brice and I have been handling his ridiculous petitions so you wouldn't have to deal with him." Gavin leaned forward, resting his arms on top of the desk. "He still insists on you and Alex returning to Pine Ridge. Things would be much simpler if you were in a mateship."

"I shouldn't have to claim a mate to be safe from a predator like him. I should have control over my own life and my son's until he comes of age."

"The law is the law."

"It's archaic and demeaning. Human laws, as poorly written as they may be, are at least inching forward."

"Brice is working to modernize the Woelfesenat's mindset and outdated laws."

"And what are you doing?" Ronni challenged. "As long as the Alphas keep practicing the old ways, progress will remain an elusive, unrequited dream."

Gavin's face darkened and he seemed to chew his words before he spoke. "Do you love Bodie?"

"That isn't the point. For you to ask is a cop-out."

"As Alpha, it is my job to protect and guide this pack." Gavin's voice was level but strained. "You and Alex are not impacted by Jeb's actions in isolation. As I've said before, the most expedient way to minimize his disruptiveness to you and this pack is to eliminate his only advantage by circumventing him with a mateship."

Gavin stood and walked to the window looking out into the woods behind the resort. "Bodie is a good man. He risked his life apprehending those poachers. That alone is enough to bring him into the pack, so revealing your wolf to him isn't a significant concern to me."

"But you are concerned about something."

Gavin took his time gathering his thoughts. When he turned back to Ronni, his face was grim. "In the past, when our species was threatened with extinction, there was a practice that when a she-wolf's mate died, his closest male relation claimed her as his own."

"What?" Making it to her feet while her head was exploding was a miracle in itself. "That's ridiculous."

"We thought so, too, until Brice had a conference with our councilman. It appears Jeb's claim may be valid."

"This can't be happening." Ronni's stomach churned and her knees weakened. "Why does he have all the rights and I have none?"

Gavin gently clasped her arm and helped her to sit down. "Brice is challenging the custom. And it is just a custom, not a law."

"Why can't the Woelfesenat simply tell Jeb no? Why does this claim have to be challenged?"

"The practice began during a time of widespread upheaval and fighting among the packs. Since you and Alex fled Pine Ridge during a violent transition, Jeb asserts that the custom continues to be relevant.

"The Woelfesenat is obligated to at least consider his petition because you remain unmated. That is why I asked if you love Bodie. If you do, a mateship is a simple solution. The council will not rule against an established mate-claim."

I just can't shake the bad luck that's been following me.

Over the last year and a half, she'd lost a husband and fled her birth pack to save her son. The few possessions she and Alex brought with them to Walker's Run were lost in a fire a few months later. Just when her life seemed to have righted, Jeb had to show up and turn everything upside down again.

She was so sick and tired of being tossed around by situations beyond her control. Would she ever be able to make a decision that wasn't a knee-jerk reaction to the chaos?

"Regardless of what happens in your relationship with Bodie, the pack will stand with you against Jeb." Gavin squeezed her shoulder. His assurance only increased the knots in her stomach.

No matter the obstacles, Jeb was a man determined to get what he wanted. Unchecked, he would continue to escalate until violence erupted. Ronni wouldn't endanger packmates who had been so good to her and Alex.

"I'll talk to Bodie."

There was a quick rap on the partially open door before Bodie himself walked into the room. "Talk to me about what?" He brushed a kiss against Ronni's cheek before sitting in the chair next to her.

"What are you doing here?"

"I called him before you stopped in." Having returned to his desk, Gavin shuffled papers into a folder and dropped them into the desk drawer.

"I thought I was meeting with you, Brice and Tristan."

"They will be here shortly."

"I hope so. Ronni and I have plans for a late breakfast." Eyes trained on Gavin, Bodie casually draped his arm across the top of Ronni's chair and she looked at him. Really looked, long and hard, at him.

Not an ounce of trepidation or fear oozed from Bodie's relaxed posture. Cool, collected, fearless, Bodie demonstrated no concern that he was in the presence of a wolfan Alpha who wielded the ultimate power in pack-related matters.

Her lovesick heart thumped happily while her rational brain crossly detailed the reasons why it shouldn't.

"Everything okay, beautiful?" Bodie brushed aside her hair and kneaded her shoulder. "You seem tense."

"It's probably nerves." Gavin shifted his gaze to Ronni. "She just informed me of showing her wolf to you, which under ordinary circumstances is a significant violation of our law."

Now the tension creeped into Bodie's body. His hand on her back withdrew. He sat a little taller in his seat and his shoulders broadened and his back stiffened. "If you're about to tell me she's getting punished, then you and I are going to have a big problem."

"Not at all." An infinitesimal smile played on Gavin's lips. Maybe he thought it amusing that Bodie had threatened him.

Ronni did not. Her stomach clenched so hard she forgot to breathe.

"I find her unsolicited confession quite timely and appreciated," Gavin said. "It makes the discussion about last night's incident easier."

"I appreciate the assist from Tristan and his team. Things would have ended differently if they hadn't arrived."

"If not for your efforts, the poachers would still be at large."

"They went after Ronni, wounded one of your men, and ruthlessly killed nearly two dozen animals and birds. I had to bring them to justice."

Resting his arms on the desktop, Gavin steepled his fingers. "Which brings me to the reason why I invited you here. On our first meeting, I told you that membership was exclusive, but on rare occasion a select few outside our congregation have earned their place because of special service to the Co-op."

"Joining the Co-op was never a factor in apprehending the poachers."

Bodie's dedication and commitment to do the right thing could've cost him his life, but he didn't back down. Pride pearled in Ronni's chest.

"I didn't believe it was." Gavin leaned back in his chair with his hands folded over his silver belt buckle. "When we met, I said you might be a kindred spirit. Your actions last night proved you are. And since Ronni has shared her wolf with you, I'm sure you understand that the Co-operative is how the Walker's Run wolfan pack hides among humans."

Bodie nodded.

"If you accept membership into the Walker's Run pack, you and your family will have a one-year probationary period to learn our ways and customs."

"Great." Bodie leaned forward, mirroring Gavin's posture. "I'm particularly interested in why a reasonable Alpha, like yourself, allowed Jeb the freedom to harass Ronni within your territory."

"Bodie," Ronni whispered urgently, shaking her head no, because he had practically issued a challenge in his ignorance of wolfan etiquette.

However, the gleam in his eyes when he gave her a soft smile suggested he knew exactly what he was doing.

"That is a complicated subject requiring more time than I've allotted today," Gavin said mildly. "Brice will answer any questions regarding our laws."

Realizing her Alpha had not taken offense, Ronni released an audible breath.

"However," Gavin continued, "Ronni and I were discussing a permanent solution to Jeb's intrusive meddling."

"What is it?" Bodie reached for Ronni's hand and she swallowed to keep her throat from closing.

"Ronni could claim you as her mate. A mateship supersedes any rights Jeb thinks he has and will effectively end his ability to interfere in Ronni's and Alex's lives. Do you find that agreeable?"

"Absolutely, I'm agreeable. What do we need to do, and how soon can we do it?" Excitement flushed Bodie's face.

All the while, Ronni's heart began a slow descent into her stomach. Bodie had said she could set the pace in their relationship, but at the first opportunity, he'd gone back on his word. Now she couldn't help wondering if all of his promises would be so easily broken.

Chapter 27

The full moon dappled the woods with muted light. In her wolfan form, Ronni loped behind Bodie flying slightly ahead of her. Days had passed since Gavin had invited Bodie to join the pack and put the idea of a wolfan mateship into his head. The sooner the better, Gavin had said.

Bodie had let Ronni decide when, and knowing Gavin was anxious to settle the negotiations with Jeb, she had selected tonight.

Bodie veered to the right and she followed, keeping pace as if her paws weren't weighted with doubt.

Zeke had claimed her when she needed protection from Jeb and, although she had believed Jeb had died a short time later, he had been a specter haunting their mateship. She didn't want that to happen with Bodie.

He changed direction again.

"How much farther?" The question drifted from Ronni's mind.

"Just ahead of us," Bodie answered.

"I'm glad you can hear me in this form." Although they had shared thoughts while both were in their human bodies, she wasn't sure the telepathic communication was possible while she was a wolf and Bodie was a raven.

He gave her a quick glance. *"I can now, but not when you didn't know I was a shifter."*

Maybe it was another manifestation of the mate-bond, or it could be simple intent. When she'd thought Bodie was just a human, she hadn't tried to communicate telepathically with him.

They neared a dense area of trees and a jutting of large boulders near the water sparkling with moonlight. Bodie alighted on the ground and transformed into his human form. Ronni did the same.

Still crouched from the shift, she looked around. "This is where we met."

"My life changed that night." Moonlight glanced off Bodie's long, dark hair and rained down his muscular frame, bathing him in a silvery glow.

Ronni's body tingled as he helped her stand. His hand stroked the hair from her face. "I couldn't think of a more perfect place."

He drew her into his arms. She loved how her softer, curvy body molded against his hard, sculptured physique. Her fingers waltzed along his broad shoulders and slipped through his long, dark hair. Beneath the slashes of his brows, intense desire glittered in his eyes and pressed against her stomach, his hardening shaft lengthened and thickened.

Lifting her chin and tipping back her head, he claimed her lips with a fierce, demanding kiss that left no doubt in her mind about what he wanted.

She yielded her body, but wanting to remain focused on only the physical connection with him, Ronni broke the kiss before his essence reached into her being. Smiling, she drew her palms down the chiseled plains of his chest and knelt, lightly gripping the base of his cock. Then, she kissed and licked the slit before taking his length into her mouth.

He sharply sucked in his breath. Watching from beneath hooded eyes, he twisted his fingers in her hair.

Moving to his sack, she teased the seam with her tongue and gently nibbled. Deep guttural groans rumbled in his throat. Taking his tip into her mouth again, she sucked hard while her hand milked his length. Unintelligible words tumbled from his lips. The sheer look of indulgence on the face of the strong, towering man before her shot a surge of feminine power and satisfaction throughout her body.

Through slitted eyes, he watched as she worked her mouth and tongue down his shaft. He held his hips still, though she saw the strain in his clenched muscles.

"If you keep going, I won't last." From the fierce look on his face, she knew he wasn't ready to end this so soon.

She allowed him to slip from her mouth and he knelt beside her. Hand cupping her head, he kissed her hard while easing her down to the moss-and-leaf-covered ground. The earthy smells of the forest mixed with his male musk and her own scent heightened her expectation.

He stretched beside her, his fingers sliding over her hip as he trailed kisses down her neck to the valley between her breasts. Despite the slight nip in the autumn air, her body burned and tingled beneath his touch as he took her breast into his warm, moist mouth, his tongue teasing her peaks into maddeningly tight buds.

His fingers slid through her wet tender folds, teasing her opening and heightening the anticipation curled in her belly. Barely dipping his finger inside her caused a needful clench in her sex. She ached to the point of breathlessness, wanting to be filled, possessed. Completely joined with him.

Kissing her slowly, deeply, stealing her breath and sharing his own, he taunted her, rubbing his plump cock against her opening but not entering.

Full of need and want, she grabbed his shoulders and rolled him onto his back. His laughter was deep and soft, and only added to her frustration.

Straddling him, she slid down his shaft with a long, deep, heavenly sigh. Her eyes opened and she laid siege to his mouth, thrusting her tongue inside and dueling with his in a furious mating ritual.

He palmed her back down to her butt to knead the fleshy muscles there as her sex gripped his shaft in a hard, fast ride until the clenching ache built into maddening pressure. Hovering on the brink, she held her breath in anticipation of welcomed relief.

Bodie's fingers dug into her hips and lifted her from his body. Before the protest formed on her lips, he rolled her beneath him and surged inside her. Hard, deep thrusts quickly drove her back to the point of ecstasy.

She pressed her face against his throat and kissed where his neck and shoulder met. The place he expected her to bite.

The taste of his skin, salty, musky and deliciously male, caused her canines to prick the inside of her mouth.

This time, there was no hovering on the verge; he drove her right over the edge. Her head tilted back as her body came undone from the tremors of pleasure pulsing through her. With his own release, Bodie's essence flooded her being. She opened her mouth, pressed her teeth against his skin and froze.

Growing still, he slowly opened his eyes and adjusted his body so his weight wouldn't become uncomfortable for her. He brushed the errant strands of her hair from her face.

"I'm sorry." Tears stung her eyes. Even though Bodie had consented to Ronni claiming him, it just didn't feel right tonight. If they were to become mates, Ronni wanted the foundation of their relationship to be love, not desperation.

"Hey, beautiful," he said gently. "It's not your fault that my sexual prowess so completely overwhelmed you with pleasure that every thought went right out of your head except how good I was making you feel."

The tension inside her broke and she laughed. "I was not overwhelmed by your sexual prowess."

"Are you sure?" Amusement sparkled in his eyes. "'Cause from my viewpoint, you looked pretty damn into me."

"How do you know? You had your eyes closed and couldn't see anything." Smiling, she rolled toward him on her side, loving how he could tease away her worries.

Propped on his elbow, Bodie rested his other arm comfortably on her hip.

"Don't overthink it." He pressed soft kisses on her neck

and shoulder, causing chill bumps to spread across her skin despite his heat. "I don't need a bite to prove what I already know. You're mine, Ronni. And I'm yours."

"Maybe once my problem with Jeb gets settled, I'll be ready."

"Our problem." Shadows cast by filtered moonlight sharpened his features and he watched her intensely. "You are not in this alone."

Bodie's essence saturated her being, except the little part of her that wished Jeb dead, likely the only way to be rid of him for good. Because if and when Ronni did decide to claim Bodie, she didn't want their future haunted by the likes of Jebediah Lyles.

Bodie heaved a relieved breath, pulling into the drop-off lane at the high school. He hadn't expected traffic to be so heavy on the last day before the Thanksgiving break and wondered if it was always this hectic.

"Bye, Dad!" Willow opened the front passenger side door, and slipped out of her grandmother's car.

"Bye, chickadee."

Bodie was grateful Ronni had slept in, finally giving him the chance to take the kids to school and run some errands. He loved Ronni's doting ways, but some days, she ran herself ragged trying to take care of everyone.

It also gave him time to think.

On the last full moon, he and Ronni had agreed to make their relationship permanent, at least in terms of the wolfan laws. But, when the moment came, she had hesitated.

What he'd told her that night was true; he didn't need a mate-claim to prove a mateship. In his heart, they were already mates.

And he completely understood her need for closure regarding the situation with Jeb. Even though it made Bodie a little sad and more than a little frustrated knowing the simplest and fastest way to get that closure would be establishing a mate-claim.

"Later...Bodie." Alex gave a slight wave, his expression unreadable. The kid didn't seem to mind the new family dynamic, but it was hard to tell, since he never said much.

Ronni had told Bodie not to worry. Alex took after Rafe—a deep thinker but a man of few words. Bodie wasn't sure that trait in a teenager was a good thing.

Willow and Alex made their way to the school entrance. Of course, Lucas joined them and Bodie didn't appreciate the arm the boy snaked across Willow's shoulders.

Nothing personal against Lucas; he seemed to be a good kid. In all likelihood, Bodie would be disgruntled by any young man showing an interest in his daughter. After all, Willow was still his little girl.

After breaking free of the traffic in front of the school, Bodie headed to Wyatt's Automotive Service. Despite the early morning hour, several cars were already waiting. He parked, then walked into the service area.

Wearing jeans and a button-down instead of his usual work coveralls, Rafe strolled toward him.

"It looks like a guy has to get up before the roosters to be first in line here."

"Pretty much." Rafe cracked a rare smile. "I'm tight with the boss, though. I'll get him to squeeze you in."

"Thanks. My mom's car needs an oil change and tire check."

Rafe whistled over one of the service technicians and Bodie handed her the keys.

"I'm meeting Tristan at Mabel's for breakfast," Rafe said. "Care to join us?"

"Sounds good. I only had time for coffee this morning." Bodie fell into step with Rafe as they walked toward the diner across the street. "I took the kids to school so Ronni could sleep in. She's been taking care of my mom and working like crazy from home." Not to mention the multiple times they'd coupled last night. "I figured she needed a break."

"You're a good man."

"I'm trying."

Mabel's Diner was already bustling with activity when Bodie and Rafe walked inside. The delicious breakfast scents of fresh cooked eggs, sizzling bacon and cinnamon rolls made Bodie's mouth water and his stomach growl.

They didn't have to wait to be seated; Tristan had already claimed a booth. He stood as they approached. His rumpled uniform was a sign that he had just got off duty.

"Hope you don't mind me crashing the party," Bodie said.

"Not at all." Tristan clasped Bodie's hand in a firm shake. "I was going to call you later."

They took their seats, Bodie and Rafe on one side of the booth, Tristan on the other.

"The check is on me." Bodie handed out the plastic menus tucked behind the condiments. "This guy..." Bodie tipped his head toward Rafe. "He pulled some strings to get my mom's car at the head of the line for an oil change. And you," he said to Tristan, "I owe you a lot more than I can repay for the assist you and your team gave me with the poachers."

"I'm more than happy that we were actually there in time." Tristan reached his hand toward Bodie. "Oh, I hear congratulations are in order."

Puzzled, Bodie accepted the handshake. "For what?"

"Didn't Ronni claim you?" Rafe asked.

It seemed news spread fast among the wolves.

"Not yet."

"Why not?" Rafe gave him a hard, dark look.

"Ronni didn't feel it was the right time and that's okay. Mate-claim or not, I plan to spend the rest of my life with her."

"Well, all right then," Rafe said.

The server took their orders, then delivered their break-fast platters while conversation easily flowed between the three men. Bodie knew he needed to tell his friends about his shifting ability but wasn't sure a public diner was the place to do it. He would talk to Ronni later. Maybe they could plan a dinner party for the occasion.

"Will you be at the Co-op's festival on Thanksgiving?" Tristan asked.

Bodie unwrapped his silverware. "That holiday doesn't quite mean the same thing to my family as it does to most Americans."

"We simply celebrate our family and friends on that day. And reflect on the losses and additions to our pack over the past year." Rafe gave Bodie a sincere, accepting look. "There won't be anything there that disparages your heri-tage. You have my word."

"I'll think about it." Willow had already said she wanted to attend when Ronni mentioned the get-together. On the other hand, his mother had adamantly refused.

"Jeb is still planning to come," Rafe said quietly. "Just thought you should know, in case you didn't."

Still coming?

Bodie's heart sank that Ronni hadn't told him Jeb was coming in the first place. If she had confided in him, he could've allayed her fears and given her more assurances about his desire to do everything possible to safeguard her and Alex. "No, I didn't know."

When he explained his family's reluctance to celebrate Thanksgiving, instead of telling him the truth, Ronni had suggested that they spend the day at home, creating their own family traditions.

"Ronni is very sensitive to others," Tristan said. "If she knows you had concerns about attending the festival, she wouldn't put you in a compromising position where you had to choose between her family and yours."

"Here's the thing." Bodie swallowed the lump in his throat. "As far as I'm concerned, it's *our* family." And he was going to make damn sure Jeb Lyles knew it.

Chapter 28

Standing on the ladder and hanging the last of the seasonal decorations, Ronni caught herself humming the tune she'd heard so often from Bodie. She smiled, then laughed because she couldn't remember the last time she felt so... *happy*?

True to his word, Bodie had not pressured her about a mate-claim. He understood and supported her decision to wait, while Jeb still lurked in their lives.

His compassionate reaction strengthened her belief that one day, she would feel confident in claiming him. Until then, she had relaxed in the knowledge that he actually cared for her, and Alex.

"The house looks perfect," Mary said. "Like it popped out of the pages of a storybook."

Ronni's heart tweaked. The little A-frame she and Alex lived in upon moving to Maico had truly been a fairy-tale cottage. Her plans to spruce it up and revitalize its original charm had gone up in flames, literally. And their new home was a mansion compared to the little shack they'd owned in Pine Ridge.

She and Alex owed so much to Rafe and the Walker's Run pack for their support and encouragement. Every day, she was thankful for their new life. Without them, she wouldn't have her home, her business and she wouldn't have been in Walker's Run to meet Bodie. His presence in her life had banished the loneliness and gave her a new sense of herself that she hadn't known was lacking.

"I wish I could've helped more." Because of her foot,

Mary mostly sat in the recliner, advising Ronni where to put things.

"You saved me from going up and down the ladder a hundred times to check if something was crooked."

From the purr of the car engine coming up the drive, Ronni knew Bodie was home from his errands. A little thrill revved her heart.

"I'm going to sit on the porch swing for a while," Mary said.

"Do you need help?"

"No, no." Using her knee scooter, Mary hobbled toward the kitchen door.

"I'll be fine."

Ronni fussed with the garland draped over the large entertainment center. One little piece simply did not want to bend in the right direction.

The front door opened and closed.

"Need help with the groceries?"

Bodie's palm cupped the back of her calf and her skin tingled. "I didn't go to the store."

"Did you forget the list?" She glanced down.

Bodie's jaw was clenched and his gaze was cold and hard. Her mind filled with the worst-case scenarios a parent could imagine.

"What happened?" In her haste to climb down the ladder, Ronni's foot slipped.

"Slow down." Bodie's strong hands gripped her waist and kept her from falling. "The kids are fine."

Taking a deep breath, she stepped off the ladder. "Why do you look worried?"

"Because I am, and a little pissed, too." He rubbed his jaw. "Scratch that, I'm a lot pissed."

"Why?"

"When were you going to tell me about Jeb?"

"Um, I did tell you. He's the reason we got together in the first place."

"Ronni."

She found the warning growl in his voice utterly sexy.

"I know Jeb is coming to the Co-op's fall festival."

"You should, I told you."

"When?"

"Right after he told me. You called after I hung up on him." She could almost see the wheels turning in his mind as he tried to remember. "I had taken your mom to her first doctor's appointment and you were calling to check on her."

Bodie blew a long breath. "We must've had a bad connection and I didn't hear you. Why didn't you bring it up later?"

"Well, I didn't know that you hadn't heard me. And I really don't want to talk about Jeb more than necessary."

"Is he the reason you decided not to attend the festival?" Bodie asked flatly.

Acid crept up from her stomach and scratched her throat.

At her silence, Bodie anchored his hands on his hips and he seemed to loom over her. Ronni wasn't afraid, but knew she'd disappointed him.

"I shared with you that Thanksgiving is a time of mourning and remembrance for my people because of the exploitation our clans suffered when our lands were settled by foreigners. How dare you use something so personal to me as an excuse to avoid a situation that needs to be resolved before it escalates any further?"

"It wasn't intentional," she said quietly. "You didn't want to go. And honestly, I don't want our first holiday together to be ruined because of Jeb."

"You do realize that he will show up here if you and Alex aren't at the festival."

"No, he won't. I warned Jeb that I would shoot him for trespassing if he comes here again."

"You don't own a gun."

"You do," Ronni said, deadly serious.

Bodie stifled a laugh and the tension in his body eased. "From now on, I'll deal with Jeb." He clasped Ronni's hands and held them against his chest. "I want us to be a family, a real family. What concerns you and Alex affects me. Put your trust in me. I won't let you down. Deal?"

"Deal!" Ronni slipped her arms around his neck, and his essence folded around her like a warm security blanket.

"The house looks amazing," he whispered in her ear.

"With all that male pissiness in your eyes when you came home, I'm surprised you noticed."

"Well, I did." He nuzzled her neck. "And I've noticed all the things you've done for Willow. You understand her and she's blossomed because of you."

"Well, I am a pretty good mother," Ronni teased.

"You are so much more." Bodie placed tiny kisses along her jaw.

The kitchen door opened and closed. "All right, love-birds. I'm coming through. Make sure you're decent."

Ronni muffled a laugh behind her hand.

A crooked smile appeared on Bodie's face. "The coast is clear, Mom."

Mary paused entering the family room.

"The Quickening is growing stronger." Grimly, Mary looked at Bodie. "It will consume you if you don't find a way to quench it."

When she disappeared down the hall, Ronni asked, "What's the Quickening?"

"A Tlanuhwa myth. According to legend, the Quickening awoke my ancestors from periods of hibernation and drove them to search for their mates. They were danger-ous, primitive creatures, probably not unlike werewolves."

"We don't like the term 'werewolf.'" Ronni crossed her arms.

"I suppose not, since Wahyas have evolved well beyond their primordial origins. As did we." Bodie tugged her el-bows until she opened her arms and he slipped his hands around her waist.

"Is the Quickening like the Wahyas mate-bond?" Ronni

and Bodie had discussed wolfan courtships, mate-claims and mate-bonds after Gavin had strongly encouraged them to form a mateship.

"Other than stories, I'm not sure anyone knows exactly what the Quickening is or how it manifests. Typically, our mateships are arranged by our Tribunal so modern-day Tlanuhwas don't need the Quickening to find their mates."

"Is Mary worried because our relationship wasn't arranged by your Tribunal?"

"Mom is very traditional, but that doesn't mean she doesn't like you. Or that she doesn't approve of us. So don't start worrying." Bodie kissed Ronni lightly on the nose. "I think we should start our own traditions. And we'll start by going to the Co-op's festival next week rather than staying home."

Ronni's eyes lit up and Bodie could see how much the gathering meant to her.

"Are you sure?" She cupped his face and he nuzzled her hand.

"Absolutely. I want Jeb to see once and for all that you and Alex are my family and I'm not about to let you go."

The crisp, fresh mountain air carried the scents of delicious food, and the chatter of hundreds of people spread through the Co-op's private grounds couldn't drown out the harsh thud of Bodie's heart against his ribs. It was only midmorning on Thanksgiving Day and these were the early birds. More were expected by the afternoon.

Ronni had mentioned that the Walker's Run pack was one among many throughout the world. But there would be more people at their Co-op's festival than the population of his entire species.

How had Wahyas learned to not only survive but thrive?

If Bodie found out how they did it, maybe the information could revolutionize his people's way of life and effectively bring the Tlanuhwa mindset into the twenty-first century.

"Are you all right?" Ronni squeezed his fingers laced with hers.

"I wasn't expecting a crowd this size."

"I was a little overwhelmed at first, too. But after a while, you get to know everyone."

"When Gavin said the Co-op operated as a municipality, I didn't realize the magnitude," Bodie said as they walked through the large, private community park. "Are other wolfan packs this organized?"

"Hardly," Ronni said tightly and her entire body tensed. They had talked about her former pack and her past troubles with Jeb. Afterward, Bodie had wanted to do the man bodily harm. But the past was the past, as Ronni had said. And he didn't want to embark on a future with her by acting impulsively against his nature.

"Hi, Willow! Hi, Alex!" Lucas rushed toward them. "The band from Taylor's is setting up for a concert. Want to watch them with me?"

Willow flashed Bodie her *please-Dad-I-must-do-this-or-I-will-die* look and Alex glanced at his mother for approval.

"What are the three rules?" Ronni said.

"Answer your calls by the third ring, don't do anything stupid and don't get into trouble," Alex replied.

"I'm adding a fourth," Bodie said. "Don't let Willow out of your sight."

"Dad!" She drew out his name into at least three syllables, but her face radiated with happiness.

Lucas took Willow's hand. "I won't, Mr. Gryffon."

"Meet us at the tents before lunchtime," Ronni called after them.

Alex turned and waved in acknowledgment.

"Is it all right for them to go off alone?" Mary asked, sitting in the motorized scooter Gavin had arranged for her to use for the day.

"They'll be fine," Ronni said, although there was a slight uncertainty in her voice.

Bodie draped his arm across her shoulders for encouragement. She had wanted so much to enjoy their first holiday together and, despite her nerves, was putting up a brave front.

They approached several large open tents with tables of people engaged in various conversations.

"All those questions you've been asking me about wolfan laws and government, Brice can answer far better than me." Ronni waved at him sitting at a table in the center tent. "He'll probably tell you more than you ever wanted to know about how the Woelfesenat works."

"I doubt that," Mary said. "'Why' was Bodie's favorite word as a child."

Ronni gave Bodie a peck on the cheek. "I'll get us some drinks."

As she walked away, Bodie admired the confident, sexy sway of her hips, even though he knew she was a bundle of nerves.

So far, there was no sign of Jeb. While Bodie thought the man simply hadn't arrived yet, Ronni's mind had probably conjured scenarios of her former brother-in-law taking off with Alex before anyone knew he was missing.

Among this family-oriented pack, Bodie simply could not see that happening. All of the sentinels were on duty, so there were plenty of eyes and ears on everyone.

Bodie and his mother entered the large tent where Ronni's family and friends sat at a big round table. As Bodie introduced his mother, an older woman with an elegant bearing stopped at the table.

"Hello," she addressed Bodie and Mary. "I'm Abby Walker. Gavin's wife." She warmly shook Bodie's hand. "I'm glad you joined us today. I've heard much about you."

"We're happy to be here."

"Mary." Abby shook his mother's hand. "Would you care

to join me? I'd love to introduce you to some more wonderful people."

"Thank you." His mother didn't seem to give Bodie a
second thought as she followed Abby to a nearby table.

"Don't worry," Brice said. "My mom will take good care
of her."

Bodie sat down, enjoying the positive energy buzzing
around him.

"How are you adapting to your new reality?" Brice asked.

"Pretty well, I think." Being a member of the Walker's
Run Cooperative, and thereby a member of their wolfan
pack, was more than he could've hoped for. "I have so many
questions, like how the Woelfesenat works and how Wahyas
have managed to thrive and survive globally without being
exposed to the majority of the human public."

"Well." Rubbing his hands, Brice leaned toward Bodie,
excitement bringing out the striking difference in the color
of his eyes.

"No shop talk," Cassie said flatly. "We're here to have
fun and celebrate all the good things that have happened in
the pack over the last year. You can schedule a wolfan civ-
ics lesson for next week."

"Sorry, man." Brice shrugged. "We'll get together later.
I promise."

Bodie was only slightly disappointed because he admired
how the wolfans believed in the importance of quality time
with family and friends. And he was honored to be among
them. Tristan and Nel walked up.

"You're playing horseshoes with us, right?" Smiling,
Tristan gave Bodie a friendly pat on the shoulder.

"I'd love to, but…" He paused, searching for Ronni and
found her talking to his mother at the table where Abby had
taken her. Ronni handed Mary a cup of coffee and kissed
her cheek.

A warm sensation ebbed through Bodie. Ronni's genuine kindness toward his family touched him deeper than anything ever had. "I, um."

"It's okay, man." Tristan chuckled, helping Nel into her seat. "We've all been there."

Ronni returned, her fragile smile in place as she said hello to everyone. "I figured you would rather have this than coffee." She handed him a chilled bottle of water.

He stood, thanking her with a sweet, tender kiss, hoping it conveyed how deeply he appreciated everything she did.

"How about those horseshoes?" Brice stood, as did Rafe.

Ronni's golden-red eyebrows arched in a delicate curve. "Were you buttering me up so you could play with your friends?"

"Um." Bodie wished he could sense if she wanted him to stay with her or if she was teasing.

"Go on." Smiling, she playfully tugged on the leather vest he wore over his button-down shirt. "Jeb is with Gavin and Abby said the sentinels are watching him like a hawk, so go have a good time. I'll be fine."

This time when he kissed her, it was long and deep and possessive. When they broke apart, Bodie's brain was hazy and his body burned.

"I'll meet you for lunch," he said, taking a few steps backward as the three other men started out of the tent.

"I'll be here." There was a wistfulness in Ronni's eyes and Bodie made a mental note to ask her what it meant when they got home later.

He caught up to the others, although they hadn't walked too far ahead due to Brice's slight limp. Bodie figured there must be an interesting story as to how he'd injured the leg, but it could wait for another time.

"Before we get to the horseshoe pits," Bodie said. "I need to confess something." Although he and Ronni had talked about inviting everyone to supper, Bodie didn't want to keep harboring his secret any longer.

The men stopped, giving him their undivided attention.

Like ripping off a Band-Aid, the best way to tell them was to get it over quickly. "I'm a raven shifter."

The men stared mildly at him as if still waiting for him to speak.

"You did hear me, right?"

"We did," Brice replied. "But we already knew."

Bodie's surprise was overcome by disappointment. "Ronni told you." Even though he'd asked her not to do so.

"No," Rafe said. "But wolfan custom dictates that she should have told me."

"I asked her not to tell anyone." And Ronni had chosen to honor his wishes rather than follow protocol. Bodie's heart was already full, but it grew some more. A few months ago, he wouldn't have believed that he could fall in love. But he had fallen madly, deeply in love.

"If you all know what I am, have you told the pack, or your wolf council?"

"No," Brice said. "My dad wanted to see how first contact evolved with you."

Bodie gave a laugh. "I'm not typical of my people."

"Your people are the Tlanuhwa, aren't they?" Tristan asked.

"Yes. You know the legends?"

"I do."

"Well, we've evolved beyond raiding villages and eating the villagers. We're a peaceful people now."

"Good to know," Brice said. "Now, can we get moving? If we're late, we'll have to forfeit the game and I do not want to lose to Reed and Shane again this year."

They started walking toward the horseshoe pits.

"If Ronni didn't tell you, how did you find out?"

"After a full moon, the sentinels found unusual black feathers inside the sanctuary and tracked them to Ronni's house," Tristan said. "Later, she mentioned that a rather large raven was roosting in her backyard at night.

"The night I called to tell you Ronni had been shot at,

I asked you to come over. The speed at which you arrived suggested that you were close by. Then when I saw you with Ronni, my instinct made the connection. So, I had sentinels watching Ronni's house and after you moved in, the raven stopped showing up."

"That's pretty thin evidence." Bodie chuckled.

"Yeah, it was. Until you gave me the evidence yourself."

"I didn't give you anything."

"After you were shot, I saw a few feathers sticking out of your hair and collar. You didn't notice when I swiped them. Then, I matched them to the ones found the night the poachers were after Ronni. I never could catch you shifting, so all I had was a really strong hunch."

"Wolfans always trust their instincts," Brice said.

"Were you ever going to tell me that you knew?"

"We believed you were man enough to tell us when you were ready," Rafe said. "Now that you have, you've earned our trust and loyalty."

Brice gave Bodie a friendly slap on the back. "Welcome to the Walker's Run wolf pack."

"We'll always have your back," Tristan said.

Bodie was glad to hear it. Because if Kane's suspicions about an uprising among the Tlanuhwa came to fruition, Bodie would likely be the Tribunal's first target when putting down the rebellion.

Chapter 29

"Oh, no," Grace said right before the bloodcurdling wailing began.

It started with Reina waking up from a nap and looking around for her daddy, followed by the protruding bottom lip, glossy from slobber due to teething. Next came the sniffs and the big blue blinking eyes that squeezed out rather large tears.

Grace lifted Reina out of her mobile swing, held the baby against her shoulder and patted her back. "Shh, shh," she cooed softly to comfort the child.

Ryan watched his twin, his eyes large and green. His russet brows rose in sympathy or concern. Usually the quiet one, he scrunched his face and let loose a wail to rival his sister before Ronni could get to him.

"There, there." She picked up Ryan and held him close, remembering when Alex was that age.

Sometimes she missed those days.

Nel dug into a diaper bag. "Here." She gave Grace a burp cloth, likely with Rafe's scent on it.

"Thanks." Grace placed the cloth on her shoulder and beneath Reina's cheek. "Such a daddy's girl, this one."

Reina quieted. Ryan didn't.

"He's not one to cry a lot," Grace said, worry evident in her face. "Did something bite him?"

Ronni checked his arms and legs for insect bites. "I don't see anything."

"Take him to see Brenna," Cassie said. "She's with Abby. I've noticed he gets fussy if he loses track of her."

Ronni rubbed Ryan's back, his cries turning into soft heaves. "Oh, little one," she cooed against his head. "You're much too young to set your heart on a little girl." She walked him around the tent before meeting up with Abby and Brenna.

"Goodness," Abby said to Ryan. "What upset you, little man?"

"Reina realized Rafe had left. When she started crying, so did he."

"Why-un." Standing next to Abby, Brenna looked up at the baby. He twisted in Ronni's arms to see her.

His breathing eased and he babbled and laughed as Brenna chattered to him.

"They're a handful at this age," Abby said. "But when they're all grown up, you can't help wishing for one more of those early days."

"I know," Ronni said quietly. "Sometimes when I'm with the twins, I see the same expressions Alex had at their age." It made her heart feel full and hurt at the same time.

She could not have any more children, and neither could Bodie. Naturally, both agreed Alex and Willow were enough for them. Still, Ronni wondered what it would've been like to conceive a child with Bodie.

"Hello, my love." Gavin kissed Abby sweetly.

"Papaw!" Brenna raised her arms for him to pick her up, which he did.

"How's my grandson this morning?" Ryan and Ronni both turned their heads toward Doc.

"He got upset when Reina started crying but he's better now," Ronni said, freezing the smile on her face as Jeb walked up with Cooter.

"Come to grandpa, little fella." Doc held out his hands and Ryan practically leaped into his arms.

"Gavin, thank you for the tour of the grounds," Jeb said. "If you don't mind, I'd like a few minutes with Ronni."

Ronni bit her tongue. The one Jeb should be asking permission from was Ronni. By the same token, she, not Gavin, should be the one to grant or deny his request.

"No more than five minutes," Gavin told Jeb. "I don't want either of you missing the festivities."

"Neither do I." Jeb nodded and she hoped he understood that if he didn't return her in the allotted time, the sentinels would.

Still, a sliver of alarm ran through Ronni as Jeb's fingers curled around her elbow. After steering Ronni out of the tent, he unexpectedly dropped his grip on her arm and strolled beside her with his hands clasped behind his back.

"You looked good with that baby in your arms." Jeb's voice was tight and he looked straight ahead instead of at Ronni. "I wish..." His voice trailed off.

"If you're entertaining ideas about me and you and a baby to boot, stop. My baby is almost grown. I'm not having another one."

"You're still of childbearing age."

"Not the point. But then, when have you ever cared about anything other than what *you* want?"

"Why is it wrong for me to want what Zeke had? To want what I saw at your house the night I came to supper?"

"What did you see, Jeb?"

"A family. People who cared."

"There's nothing wrong with wanting a family or people who care for you. It's wrong to force your way in and take what isn't offered."

"Gryffon took what was mine," Jeb growled. "Do you know how hard it was for me to sit at your table and be civil to the man who stole you from me?"

"Bodie didn't steal anything from you. Alex and I aren't yours. We never were." Ronni stopped walking. "We never will be."

"You're wrong, Veronika." Jeb faced her. "I will claim what is mine."

"I'm not available to be claimed."

"Have you done something foolish?" Jeb's fingers clutched her upper arms.

"What I do is not your business."

"The Woelfesenat might not agree. My arbitrator files complaints with them daily, expressing the dangers you and Alex face in Walker's Run."

"You are the only danger to us."

"Are you forgetting what happened with the poachers?"

"Bodie caught them."

"Yeah, an unfortunate ending to a well-laid plan. I really wanted them to put a bullet in him."

"They tried." Ronni struggled to break Jeb's hold. "What did you mean by 'well-laid plan'? Did you have something to do with those poachers?"

"Feisty *and* smart." Jeb actually smiled, broad and wide, flashing a mouth full of straight white teeth. "You'll make me a fine Alphena."

"You're wolfan. Why would you have anything to do with poachers?"

"I had to do something to shake up the Woelfesenat's perception of Gavin's perfect little pack. Unfortunately, that plan didn't get me what I wanted. But the second one will."

"What are you planning, Jeb?"

"To rescue my family and bring them home." He checked his watch. "We need to go." Jeb jerked Ronni alongside as he began walking at a fast pace.

"No!" She dug her heels in the soft ground, but Jeb continued to pull her with him as his speed increased to a near run.

"Let. Me. Go!"

"You might want to cover your ears, sugar."

"Don't call me—" The rest of Ronni's words were drowned out by a loud explosion.

Smoke and debris engulfed the outdoor stadium where the band had been playing. Screams and frantic howls rose among the chaos of people scrambling away from the disaster.

Ronni's heart froze. "Alex!" She started to run but Jeb grabbed her by the waist and spun her around.

"You're still fast." Jeb laughed.

Ronni rammed her elbow into his ribs. He let out a string of curses but didn't let her go. "What is wrong with you?" She struggled to get free. "Alex is in that stadium!"

"Calm down. Alex is fine," Jeb snapped. "I had him taken to the SUV before the explosion."

"Why?" Ronni shrieked. "What's going on, Jeb?"

"You forced me to take drastic measures, Veronika. If you would've come back to Pine Ridge when I asked nicely, none of this would've happened." He grabbed her face and jerked her head toward the commotion. "This is all your fault."

"Are you insane? Children were at that concert! Alex's friends were with him! Where are Willow and Lucas?"

"Don't know, don't care. You and Alex are my only concern."

Ronni's stomach rolled. "Oh, God." Her hands shook as she took her phone from her back pocket. She dialed Bodie's number, but Jeb jerked the phone from her hands and smashed it on the ground.

"Listen carefully, Veronika. I'm not going to repeat myself. You and Alex are leaving with me. When we get to Pine Ridge, I will claim you as my mate. You aren't going to fight me or resist in any way. If you do, I will hunt down and kill Gryffon and his family, and I won't stop until I've put down Wyatt, his mate and those little wolflings of his. Do you understand?"

Oh, she understood all right. Numb, Ronni nodded.

"Then let's go home, sugar."

"Willow!" Bodie fought his way through masses of crying kids and hysterical parents. "Alex! Lucas!"

He would've shifted into his bird form to search for them, but the billows of thick black smoke obscured the sky.

The panicked howls added to Bodie's own inner chaos. Finally, he saw Rafe's red head bobbing through the exodus of people exiting the outdoor stadium. The stoic look he normally wore was twisted with anguish. "I didn't find them!"

"Neither did I." Bodie's throat tightened around his words.

His phone rang with an unknown number. "Hello?"

"Dad!" Willow's anxious voice sliced right through his heart.

"Where are you? Are you safe?"

His daughter's sobs filled his ears, shredding everything inside him.

"Sweetheart, calm down and tell me where you are."

The only words Bodie made out were *concession stand*. He repeated them to Rafe, who took off. Bodie trailed slightly behind him, grateful Rafe knew where to head. Once they broke free of the stampeding crowd, they ran toward the concession stand, which appeared to be undamaged.

"Dad!" Willow darted from behind the counter with Lucas running after her.

Bodie scooped his daughter into his arms, holding her tight. "You're okay," he kept repeating to soothe her as well as himself.

"Where's Alex?" Rafe's usually clear, steady voice cracked.

"We don't know," Lucas said, putting on a brave front though his eyes reflected his panic. "He went to get us something to drink but was taking a really long time. When he didn't answer his phone, we decided to look for him. But he wasn't here. I even checked the bathroom. Then the outdoor stage blew up."

"It's all right, Lucas." Rafe gently squeezed the teenager's shoulder. "We'll find him."

Bodie called Ronni again. He shook his head at Rafe. "She's still not answering."

"Take them to the tents. I'll keep looking." Without waiting for discussion, Rafe took off.

"Come on." Even though Willow was nearly sixteen, Bodie clutched her hand. "You need to steer us in the right direction," he said, draping his other arm around Lucas's shoulders. "I don't know the layout of the park."

"That way." Lucas pointed and they began walking away from the heart of the commotion.

"What caused the explosion?" Lucas asked.

"I don't know," Bodie answered. "I'm sure Tristan will find out."

"Do you think Alex is okay?" Willow blinked back more tears.

"I'm sure he is, sweetheart. Maybe he made it back to the tents."

Lucas didn't look at Bodie but his jaw clenched as he stared straight ahead.

The walk across the grounds took only a few minutes but each step dragged as if Bodie had concrete blocks for feet. Grateful that Willow and Lucas were safe, Bodie wouldn't feel relief until Alex was back with them.

Nearing the tents, Bodie focused his vision and scanned the occupants. He saw Cassie, hugging children as they filtered into the tent and then pointing them toward a designated area where an adult would safeguard them until their parents were located.

Grace and Nel were at a table, caring for the babies.

Where the hell is Ronni? And where's my mother?

Believing them to be safe, Bodie had focused his worry and attention on finding the kids. Finally stepping inside the tent and not seeing the rest of his family drove his anxiety beyond panic mode.

He tried reaching out to Ronni through the mate-bond, but he couldn't sense anything but his own jumble of emotions. There was no way to contact his mother either. In their human form, Tlanuhwa could only receive visions of what another Tlanuhwa in raven form was seeing.

"Thank God you're all right." Cassie squeezed Lucas. His eyes watered and his pressed lips formed a grim line. "Your mom is over there with Abby and your dad is with the sentinels."

"Thanks," Lucas said quietly. He turned to Willow. "Tell Alex to call me."

Willow nodded.

Lucas started to walk away, turned back and gave Willow a quick, tight hug before going to find his mother.

"Come here." Cassie motioned to Willow.

She let go of Bodie's hand and went to Cassie who wrapped her in a big hug. "I'm so glad you're all right." Cassie's eyes lifted to Bodie and he knew she was asking about Alex.

Bodie shrugged and shook his head.

"Why don't you help Nel and Grace take care of the babies."

Willow looked to Bodie.

"Go ahead, sweetheart."

Willow hugged him again before leaving.

"Where is Ronni?" Bodie scanned the faces of those inside the tent again. "And my mother?"

The calm, reassuring expression Cassie had shown the kids faltered. "Ronni left with Jeb before the explosion."

"What?" All of Bodie's jumbled emotions came out in the single word.

Cassie's eyes widened for a split second, then her delicate brows arched in a quiet command for him to step back and take a breath. A true alpha female, despite her petite frame.

"I didn't mean to yell at you," he said, mindful of his tone.

"We're all a bit stressed right now." Cassie touched his arm. "Alex is missing. Ronni is missing. And Jeb is here. Do you think that's a coincidence? Because I don't." Bodie laced his hands behind his head and squeezed, hoping to stall the massive headache pounding inside his skull.

"Jeb is here under treaty and Gavin assigned extra sentinels to keep an eye on him."

"Sentinels who are now helping with the aftermath of the explosion." Bodie took out his phone and called Ronni again. "No answer," he spat.

"That's not the only way to communicate with her," Cassie said. "Calm your mind and reach out to her."

"I've tried. It's not working."

"Block out what's going on around you. Focus on her," Cassie said. "Only her."

Closing his eyes, Bodie recalled their last kiss, how soft her lips were, the warmth of her skin. The way she tugged his leather vest to pull him closer. How happy he was coming home to her every night and talking about their day. And that he loved her, much more than he ever thought possible.

A feminine presence fluttered inside him.

"Ronni?"

He felt wrapped in a tight hug. *Thank God!*

"Alex and I are leaving with Jeb."

"Like hell you are!"

"Don't follow us. It's for the best."

"Dammit, Ronni! Where are you?"

Silence followed with a bone-chilling emptiness.

"Jeb has them," he snarled.

"Where is he taking them?"

"She didn't say. And now I can't sense her. All I feel is the deathly cold in my bones." At least until his frustration and fear turned into raging fury.

A volcanic heat erupted behind his eyes, temporarily blinding him. "Oh, God!" He grabbed his head, pressing his palms against his eyes.

"You need to sit down." Cassie's hands gripped his arm. In his mind's eye, he saw blue skies above him, felt the rushing of wind against his face and beneath his wings; only he wasn't the one in the air.

There was a sudden dive and Bodie swayed with the drop. When the descent leveled, a road came into view below.

"Bodie? What's happening?"

"I see a deserted four-lane highway. There's a black SUV ahead. It's Jeb's vehicle, I'm sure of it."

"Where is the highway, Bodie? Can you see any landmarks?"

"Just miles of road." He needed to think. He'd scoured the entire area endless times when searching for the poachers. Something should look familiar. "Wait!"

To the left, he saw trees scorched by a late summer brush fire. "It's the old Shewbird Highway."

In his mind, he heard a familiar caw. "Mom?"

His vision returned to normal.

Cassie's gaze locked on Bodie while she spoke to someone on the phone. "Yes, I'll tell him," she said, disconnecting the call. "Tristan is calling Sheriff Locke to set up a road block. He says they'll have Ronni and Alex home soon, so sit tight."

"Like hell I will." Bodie stretched out his arms. "Keep an eye on Willow. I'm going to get the rest of my family and bring them home."

Chapter 30

"**Y**ou better not have hurt my friends." Alex punched the seat in front of him. Jeb's driver glanced into the rearview mirror at them, but didn't slow down.

"Blame your mother," Jeb said calmly, as if he hadn't committed an act of war against the Walker's Run pack as a diversion to kidnap Ronni and her son. "If she would've come home when I asked, I wouldn't have had to use a bomb to get her attention." Hand resting on Ronni's leg, Jeb squeezed her thigh.

She swallowed the bile rising in her throat.

"Once we get to Pine Ridge, we'll put this mess behind us and you can make new friends."

"I don't want new friends, you asshole!"

"Alex! Control yourself." Even though he was nearly grown, Ronni reached for him and drew his head against her shoulder. She lowered her voice to an airy whisper. "When you get the chance, run! As fast as you can and don't look back. I'll be right behind you." She bit her lip at the lie.

The only way to stop Jeb from coming after them again was to put him down or die trying.

Alex responded with a nearly imperceptible nod. She kissed his head, imbuing him with all the love her mother's heart held, then released him.

"You coddle him too much," Jeb scoffed. "I'll have to teach him to toughen up."

"You've already taught him plenty," Ronni snapped.

"Aw, sugar. Don't be cross. I'm doing what's best for our family."

"So am I." Ronni launched from her seat between Alex and Jeb, dove between the two front seats and jerked the steering wheel hard.

The vehicle swerved sharply to the right. The driver battled to regain control but Ronni's grip had cemented and she wouldn't let go. Cursing, Jeb grabbed her waist in an attempt to pull her free.

"Mom! What are you doing?"

She jerked the wheel again and clamped her teeth into the driver's arm.

"Crazy bitch!" He stomped the brakes.

Ronni would've smashed into the dashboard and likely gone through the windshield if Jeb hadn't yanked her into the back seat.

The vehicle crashed into the embankment. Steam rolled from beneath the crumpled hood.

"Goddammit, Veronika! You could've killed us!" Jeb growled.

"I'm not finished yet." She drew her arm back and slammed it into Jeb's nose. "Alex, run!"

His door flew open and he leaped from the car, shifting into his wolf. Paws touching the ground, Alex did exactly as Ronni instructed and bolted down the highway.

Rafe was the fastest runner in the pack, Alex a close second. Jeb and his henchman would never catch him.

Ronni scrambled to get out of the vehicle. Jeb snatched her back inside.

"Carl! Get Alex and bring him back," Jeb snarled.

"I hope you handle the pack better than you're handling them," Carl growled. "If not, you won't be Alpha for long." He exited the SUV, shifted and darted after Alex.

Jeb grabbed Ronni's jaw. "If you were any other woman, you would be dead now."

She spit in his face and punched him hard in the crotch. Reflexively, he doubled over. Ronni launched out the open door and shifted as Alex had done.

Amped on adrenaline and fury, Ronni practically flew down the road. Gaining on Carl, she saw a dark shadow emerging from behind the hill Alex was cresting.

"Alex! Don't stop! Keep running!"

He didn't listen; he skidded to a stop and simply stood frozen, except for his nose lifting in the air as the shadow grew. Carl's pace increased, closing the distance. Ronni's mind screamed for her son to run, but he didn't move.

A deafening screech sliced through the sky, followed by a thunderous swoosh of giant wings belonging to the horrific creature rising over the hill where Alex stood.

"Run! Dammit, run!"

The giant bird-like monster swooped over him, but its fiery gaze focused on a different target. Screeching again, the creature grabbed Carl with large, orange arms ending in three sharp talons rather than hands and soared upward into the bright blue sky with its whip-like tail snapping the air.

Before relief settled, Jeb's wolf slammed into Ronni. The force knocked her several feet and she hit the ground, losing her breath.

"What the hell was that thing?" He stood over her.

"Bodie." It had to be Bodie. Wahyas had their primitive Wahyarian, lurking inside them, so it would make sense that Bodie's kind did, too.

Love and gratitude rushed her heart and she nearly choked on the emotion. He had come for her and Alex, even though she had blocked the mate-bond communication to keep him from following.

"Isn't that interesting." A toothy grin spread across Jeb's muzzle. *"I could use a creature like that in Pine Ridge. Too bad I'll have to kill him."* Jeb's sadistic laugh raised Ronni's hackles. *"Reckon his daughter will have to do."*

"Stay away from them!"

"This is what is gonna happen, sugar. I'm gonna kill the bird man and take his daughter. Then, we're all going back to Pine Ridge. You're not going to run again and you better

not fight me when I claim you. If you do, I'll take my anger out on the girl. Do you understand?"

A screech overhead disrupted Ronni's response. With a wingspan of at least twenty feet, the bird creature swooped low, swatting Jeb with his wing hard enough to send the wolfan male tumbling down the side of the road.

More than ten feet in length, the creature landed on muscular hind legs that looked like they belonged on an overgrown black panther rather than a bird. Folding its wings on his back, he padded toward her on paws and talons as his tail snapped the air behind him. Slowly reaching toward her with his talon arm, he gently grazed the fur beneath her chin.

"Are you all right?" Bodie's voice threaded through her mind and his masculine essence invaded her senses.

"I think so." She stared at the golden speckles within his dark red eyes. *"How did you find us?"*

"My mother followed you and showed me where you were. When she saw me coming, she returned to be with Willow."

"Willow and Lucas are safe?"

"Yes." Bodie stretched out his giant wings. *"Take care of Alex while I deal with Jeb."* He lifted off the ground. *"No matter what happens, don't interfere. The sheriff is on his way."* With that, he zoomed overhead and darted after Jeb.

"Mom!" Alex was bounding toward her.

"I'm all right." She stood, a little wobbly at first.

He slid next to her and affectionately rubbed his muzzle beneath her chin.

"Everything is going to be fine." She licked his face.

"Was that Bodie?"

"Yes."

"That is so cool!"

No, it isn't. She hid her thoughts from Alex.

Though Ronni loved Bodie for coming after them, she was also deathly afraid for him. If his beast was as dangerous and primitive as a wolfan's Wahyarian, the creature's violent tendencies could destroy the kind-hearted, generous man she'd grown to love.

A cold, deadly rage slithered through Bodie.

Clutching Jeb's fur at the base of his neck, Bodie flew him away from Ronni and Alex and dropped him into the woods, close enough to the ground to not cause harm, although it was a struggle not to tear him to pieces. The wolfan rolled to his feet.

"I'm gonna kill you!" Jeb's thoughts screamed through Bodie's mind, startling him. He'd assumed the mate-bond had allowed him to hear Ronni's thoughts when she was a wolf. But hearing Jeb's voice in his head, Bodie now considered that a telepathic link while in their alternate forms might be intrinsic to both shifter species.

"Considering I outweigh you, I doubt it."

"I'm a wolf, you're a mutant bird. And I'm going to devour you like a roasted turkey on Thanksgiving." Jeb laughed. *"Ironic, isn't it, since that's today."*

Using his wing as a shield, Bodie blocked Jeb's attack. His claws ripped through Bodie's outer feathers but failed to connect with flesh. He slung the wolfan to the ground.

Bodie had never used his Tlanuhwarian form in a fight. Actually, he hadn't believed he could.

His mother had been right, all along. The darkness he'd felt stirring inside him was the beast waiting to manifest and when the opportunity presented, it had wasted no time seizing its freedom.

After the vision his mother had shared, Bodie launched into the sky, intent on getting back his mate and her son. Fire had erupted in his veins. At least, it felt like fire. A white-hot heat had flashed through his body. On its heels followed an excruciating pain that sliced down his spine and along every nerve.

He'd choked on air and damn near thought his lungs

would explode. A flash of light blinded him and then, it all stopped. The pain was gone, he could breathe again and everything he saw was tinted red until he reached Ronni, who was engulfed in a beautifully brilliant silver glow.

"Ronni belongs to me!" Jeb growled.

"She's mine!" Bodie had never been more sure of anything than he was of Ronni being his fated mate.

His body flashed with burning heat, again. And the urge to shred the wolfan's flesh from his bone caused Bodie's talons to flex and his tail to crack the air like a whip.

"You stole her from me," Jeb snarled. *"But I will reclaim what is mine!"*

"Never!" Gaining control of his irrational impulses to paint the woods with Jeb's blood, Bodie swung his wing, knocking Jeb to the ground.

He needed to apprehend, not kill. If the legends were true and Bodie gave in to the murderous instinct, he would lose his humanity and very likely the woman he loved.

Jeb pushed to his feet and pounced, only to have Bodie knock him down again.

"I can do this all day, or at least until the sheriff arrives. It's not too hard to figure out that you were responsible for the explosion. I might not know how wolfan justice works, but I do know you will never see Ronni or Alex again."

Jeb shifted into his human form, shaking with rage. "Nothing will keep me away from what is mine!"

Suddenly, a wretched scream tore from his throat. Jeb dropped to the ground, writhing in apparent pain.

Bodie jumped back, unsure of what was happening.

Bones cracked and reformed beneath Jeb's skin, which turned a putrid gray. His torso twisted, his head elongated, and his jaw snapped and dangled loosely before his entire body erupted in light.

When the brightness faded, there was nothing left of man or wolf. Bodie's heart thundered as the mutant creature, covered in stiff, bristly hair, rose on freakish gangly legs ending in paw-like feet that spread into four individual toes with long curved nails. More than seven feet tall, the beast threw back his large, flat wolfish head with a wailing howl, then charged, gnashing his huge, razor-like teeth.

Horrified at what Jeb had become, a sense of panic flooded Bodie's senses. He was all that stood between the hideous beast and Ronni and Alex.

The creature swung at him with paw-like hands, the long, black nails tearing through Bodie's feathers and scoring down to the muscle. Bodie swung his tail, smacking Jeb upside the head.

The werewolfish creature stumbled backward, snarled and charged. Bodie lifted into the air before the tackle, but Jeb grabbed his tail and gave a good, hard yank.

Bodie slammed to the ground. Jeb attacked, slashing at Bodie's wings and down his back. Gritting against the pain, Bodie pushed up and used all his strength to buck Jeb off.

The scent of his own blood and sweat caused something to click in his brain. He was the one getting torn to shreds while Jeb barely had a scratch. If Bodie didn't start fighting back, Jeb might get lucky enough to strike a fatal blow.

The gleam in the werewolf's black eyes said he knew it, too. Charging again, his shoulder rammed Bodie's chest and the force of the collision threw them both to the ground. Razor-like teeth mowed through the feathers on Bodie's chest. Using his feet, he kicked hard and Jeb flew at least twelve feet before hitting the ground.

This time when he got up, Jeb didn't run toward Bodie. He ran in the direction Ronni and Alex were waiting.

Flying over Jeb, Bodie landed several yards ahead. He stretched his wings, creating a barrier between Jeb and the ones he loved.

Howling, Jeb picked up speed with deadly intent.

Bodie let go of the last shreds of humanity that had kept the violence inside restrained. The primal force that rose within came from a time when his ancestors terrorized the earth, feasted on their enemies, and anyone else who crossed their paths.

He flew into Jeb's creature, pecking at the rage-filled eyes. Bodie's mind barely registered the pain of dangerously sharp teeth and claws sinking into and slicing through his muscles. The taste of bloody fur coated his tongue, the scent of battle filled his nostrils. Bits of the beast's flesh hung from Bodie's beak and stuck in his talons.

A ferocious howl shook the trees. Bodie responded with his own war cry.

Leaping with claws opened wide and lethally sharp, Jeb swiped Bodie's throat and Bodie stumbled backward. Something warm and sticky flowed down his neck and chest.

He lifted off the ground, slapping Jeb in the face. In a diving swoop, Bodie used his talons to knock the werewolf off his feet. Then, landing on his chest, Bodie plucked out one of Jeb's eyes to the sound of his rage-filled cry of pain.

A large hand slammed against Bodie's face, knocking him over. Quickly hopping up, he barely avoided Jeb's deadly retaliatory pounce. In turn, Bodie struck him from behind, scraping talons down his back and leaving a trail of gaping wounds. Another howl of pain filled the woods.

Jeb started running at an incredible speed. If Bodie didn't end this, the next time Jeb ran, he might make it out of the woods.

He took flight and swooped over Jeb. Digging his talons into Jeb's shoulders, Bodie soared upward. In his beast form, Jeb was quite a bit heavier than the wolf Bodie had carted away. He tightened his grip to keep from dropping him.

Jeb growled and struggled as they ascended higher. Just as Bodie cleared the tops of the trees, excruciating pain ravaged his chest. Reflexively, his talons opened and Jeb slipped from his grasp.

Bodie dove after him, but Jeb swung at him with his claws. Circling back around, he caught Jeb's leg with his talons, only to have Jeb grab him by the throat.

He batted his wings in a desperate attempt to dislodge Jeb's hand. They were falling faster than he could compensate. As his vision grew dark, Bodie used his talons to score Jeb's exposed abdomen until the werewolf let go.

Stretching his wings to reestablish equilibrium and halt his descent, he heard Jeb's ear-piercing howl, a ground-shuddering thud, and then there was silence.

Bodie dove along the path Jeb had fallen and landed a short distance from his broken body. Unsympathetic, he watched as the pitiful creature morphed back into its human form.

Stretching out his wings, Bodie lifted his beak to the sun filtering through the trees. Fire crackled along his nerves. An incredible pressure built behind his eyes until the pain forced them to close. He didn't open them until he felt the soft, damp ground against the flat soles of his feet. He staggered over to Jeb and dropped to his knees.

Jeb glared at him with his remaining eye. Blood oozed from his nose and mouth and behind his head. "Thief," he wheezed. His gaze turned inward and he mumbled to the phantom in his mind. "Ve-ron-i-ka, *mine!*" His final breath whined from his chest and the sentient light in his eye went dark.

"May your next life be a peaceful one." Bodie laid his hand over Jeb's face, closing his eyelid.

Sitting on his haunches, he stared in horror at the blood streaking his body and the lifeless man before him. Filled with disgust and shame, Bodie gripped his head in his hands.

"What the hell have I done?"

Chapter 31

Silently screaming, Ronni stared at the spot where she last saw Bodie, falling from the sky before he disappeared behind the treetops in the distance.

With Zeke's death, she'd felt a sharp pain stab her heart as a crushing weight stole her breath. Right now, other than sheer shock, she felt absolutely nothing. Not even the warmth of her son's wolfan body pressed against her as they crouched in the shallow roadside ditch, waiting.

"Mom!" Alex's ears twitched. *"I hear a siren!"*

Thankfully, he'd kept his head down and hadn't seen Bodie falling, likely to his death.

"Please," she begged Bodie, while shielding her thoughts from Alex. *"Please let me know you're all right! I love you!"*

Flashing lights crested the hill.

"It's the sheriff!" Alex stood on all four paws.

"Stay down until I tell you to come out." No matter her personal turmoil, Ronni's priority had to be her son's safety.

She climbed out of the shallow ditch and padded to the edge of the road.

The speeding car began to slow its approach, finally stopping about five feet from where Ronni waited in her wolf form, crouched and ready to react if needed.

A rotund man climbed out of the car and peered at her over the hood. "Are you Ronni?"

Cautiously, she nodded.

"Is Alex with you?"

She answered with another nod.

"Wait right there. I have something for you." Sheriff Locke walked to the back of the car and opened the trunk.

Ronni's heart pounded while visions of rifles and other weaponry danced in her head. When he shut the trunk, it sounded like a shot fired.

"Mom! Run!" Alex launched out of the ditch and darted toward the sheriff.

"Alex, stop!"

"Whoa! Whoa!" the sheriff called out. "It's only blankets!"

Alex skidded to a stop barely a foot away from the uniformed man. He sat, his ears folded flat against his head.

"It's all right, son." Locke dropped a saddle blanket in front of Alex. "I know you were just trying to protect your mama."

Locke walked to Ronni and laid a blanket beside her as well. She shifted and quickly wrapped it around her body. Alex followed her lead.

"Thank you, sheriff."

"After I learned about the Wahyas here, I figured these would come in handy." He returned to the car, then came back with two bottles of water. "Drink it slow and easy," he said. "I'm not good with people throwing up."

He helped Ronni stand, then gave her the water. Alex approached cautiously for his.

"Why don't you sit in the squad car?" Locke said to Alex. "I want to talk to your mama and you'll be safe in there."

Alex watched Ronni for her nod of assurance before going to the car.

"Where's the fellow who took you?"

Dead, she hoped.

An involuntary shudder of rage rolled through Ronni. Bodie was likely dead because of Jeb. If the son of a bitch was still alive, he wouldn't be when she got through with him.

"Bodie chased Jeb into the woods. I couldn't see much

of what happened after that." Except Bodie falling fast out of the sky.

Tipping her head back, Ronni drank a long sip of water to cool the burn in her throat and squinted from the sting in her eyes.

"Is Bodie like you?"

"Not exactly," she said, nearly choking on emotion.

"I don't see how there could be any gray area. Either you're a Wahya or you aren't."

A growing rustle in the woods drew Ronni's attention. Trepidatious, her heart missed a beat.

Dear God, please let that be Bodie.

"Get in the car." The sheriff's hand went to the gun holstered at his side.

Heart pounding against her chest, Ronni couldn't get her legs to move.

"I said, get in the car!"

Naked and bloody, a man stumbled into the clearing and collapsed, facedown.

A rush of adrenaline lightened Ronni's feet. Running, she didn't care if Jeb was still in the woods or that the sheriff was yelling for her to come back. She needed to get to Bodie. Needed to make sure he was safe. Most of all, she needed to tell him that she loved him.

"Bodie?" Sliding to the ground next to him, Ronni gently rolled him onto his back. "Can you hear me?"

One of his eyes slid open. "Jeb is dead," he choked out the words.

"I don't care." Right now, all that mattered to her was Bodie.

"Really?" He slowly pushed himself up and rolled into a sitting position. "Well, I killed him because of *you*!" He shot her an angry, accusatory look that stabbed her heart. "And you don't give a damn about that? How do you think that makes me feel?"

"That's not what I meant." A different kind of unease settled into her bones.

"What did you mean, hmm? Are you happy he's dead?" Shoving away from her, Bodie climbed to his feet, seemingly unaware of the bleeding cuts and deep scratches on his body.

"Yes, dammit. I am." Angry they were fighting over Jeb, Ronni tightened the blanket around her and stood. "He was a bad man. A threat to me and my family. And I won't shed one tear over his furry ass."

Bodie's face darkened. "You *used me* to get rid of *him!*" He shook his finger in her face.

Ronni's temper flared. "We used each other!" Not what her heart wanted to say, but pride got in the way. "You were the one who suggested a pretend relationship when we had lunch at Mabel's." She jabbed him in the chest. "You were the one who later said you were not pretending. You said your feelings were real but all you really wanted was entry into the Co-op's sanctuary for Willow's Transformation Ceremony. So, congratulations, bird-man. You got what you wanted."

"So did you, she-wolf." The contempt in Bodie's gaze felt like a stake through her heart. Her blood chilled and her body shook from the cold despite the warmth of the blanket.

"Our deal is done," Bodie snarled. "Stay out of my life and I'll stay out of yours." He stretched out his arms and darted into the sky.

Her whole body shaking, Ronni's knees gave out and she crumpled to the ground. Hot tears seared her cheeks.

"I'm getting too old for this shit," the sheriff grumbled, walking up behind her.

"Me, too," she whispered. Bodie had shattered her heart and she didn't have the strength to pick up the pieces. Not only had she lost him, but Willow and Mary, too.

"I don't know what he said to you, hon. But people often

say things they don't mean in the heat of a high-stress situation. He'll come around."

Ronni shook her head because as Bodie flew away she'd felt the violent separation of their essences.

"You and Alex can't be here when the deputies arrive." Arm around her shoulders, Sheriff Locke helped Ronni to her feet. "Come on, let's get you home."

"The last place I want to be is home." With her family torn apart, Ronni doubted the house would ever feel like home again.

Nearly two days' worth of Willow's torrential tears drove Bodie outside for the umpteenth time.

Following the fatal fight with Jeb and a visit to the emergency clinic for stitches, Bodie had picked up his mother and daughter, gathered their clothes and personal items from Ronni's house, and returned to the camper.

Willow had not yet forgiven him.

Bodie considered the real possibility that she might never get the collapse of her new family.

Truth be told, neither would he.

Sitting in one of the three lawn chairs in the small square patch of grass outside the camper, he desperately tried to remember how to breathe. An invisible band had clamped around his chest, squeezing every bit of air from his lungs and squashing what was left of his heart.

"Bodie." His mother hobbled out of the door.

"Be careful." He jumped up, ignoring the pain in his legs, and limped over to help her down the steps.

"You be careful," she responded. "Reopen those stitches and you'll be back in the ER."

Unless dying, he had no desire to return there. Twice in a matter of weeks was more than enough for him.

Not long after they had returned to the camper, Tristan had stopped by to officially give him the news.

Several people had died in the explosion, more were injured. Jeb's dead body had been found and the sentinels had located his driver stuck up the tree where Bodie had left him.

The man had filled them in on Jeb's involvement with the poachers and the explosion. His intention had been to make the Woelfesenat believe that Ronni and Alex would be safer with him in Pine Ridge.

When that didn't work, Jeb had worked out a plan to force them to return with him.

It had nearly worked.

Probably would've worked if Bodie hadn't...

Bodie couldn't allow his thoughts to dwell in that dark place. It was too dangerous.

"I know coming back here is a serious inconvenience," he said, helping his mother into one of the lawn chairs. "I'll find a real home as soon as I can." He'd have the time, now that his new injuries had put him back on medical leave.

"According to Willow, we have a home and I'm inclined to agree."

"Moving in with Ronni and Alex was a mistake." Thankfully, they weren't home when Bodie and his family stopped by to collect their things.

"When your tempers cool, you'll both see things differently."

"No, I won't." Bodie sat in the chair opposite his mother. "I killed a man. How could Ronni be so cavalier about it?"

"You tried to catch him."

"I'm still responsible for a man's death."

"A bad man," his mother scolded. "Think of the people killed and injured in the explosion. Willow could've been among them."

The truth didn't ease the turmoil within.

"Ronni knew it would come to this."

"Oh, she's a seer, is she?"

Bodie rubbed his temples. Why didn't the damn pain

meds obliterate his pulsating headache or the crushing pain in his heart?

"I saw her leave the tent with him. She was afraid, but strong."

"Mom—"

"You need to hear this." She wagged her finger at him. "I went to the ladies' room to shift."

"You could've got hurt."

"I have a broken foot, not a broken wing. Now let me finish." She frowned. "Ronni fought with him after the explosion. I can only imagine that he laid the blame on her. Maybe he threatened more violence because she simply gave up and went with him. She's a mother and a she-wolf. It's her nature to do whatever it takes to protect her family."

"Apparently, it's my nature, too. And right now, I'm protecting my family by cutting Ronni out of our lives." Bodie limped to his truck.

"Bodaway, you're making a mistake."

"No, you were right all along. My mistake was getting involved with a she-wolf in the first place."

The squeak of the porch swing was not the solace it once was. Now Ronni rather detested it. She made a mental note to pick up a can of WD-40 from the hardware store when it opened tomorrow morning after the Thanksgiving weekend. Maybe she'd get a saw, too, and cut down the empty tree branch where Bodie, in his raven form, used to sit and keep her company.

For the last three nights, she waited and watched for him to return to his perch, only to go to bed disappointed and even more heartbroken. Tonight would be no different.

"The house is too empty." Alex let the door bang behind him. He plopped next to her. "I don't like it."

Bodie's family had only been with them a short time but their absence had left a giant void in Alex's and Ronni's hearts.

"I don't get why they had to leave." Alex's frustration caused a growl to rumble in his throat. "Jeb's dead. Everything should be all right, but it isn't."

"Life doesn't always go the way we think it should."

Alex laid his head against her shoulder, something he hadn't done in a long time. "You love Bodie, don't you?"

"I do, but sometimes things happen that hurt our hearts and we can't get past them."

"But he came for us."

"He did, but Bodie is a man of peace. He wasn't prepared to kill Jeb." And he'd laid all the blame on her for involving him in a situation that turned deadly. Even though he'd been the one to jump into the thicket without looking.

"The whole thing sucks, Mom. I like Bodie, and Willow is my friend."

"Just because Bodie and I aren't seeing each other doesn't mean you can't be friends with Willow, and you don't have to stop liking Bodie either. He's still a good man."

Alex got up from the swing. "A good man doesn't abandon his family."

The kitchen door shut a little harder than usual as Alex went inside. Ronni continued to swing in silence.

She still believed Bodie was a good man. He simply valued his lofty ideals more than her. And that was something she didn't know how to combat, or if she should even try.

Chapter 32

Excited chatter filled the air as students finishing their first week back to school after the Thanksgiving break poured out of the buildings, filtered across the campus and made their way toward the cars and buses lined up to take them home.

Movement in the rearview mirror caught Bodie's attention. He watched a car ease into the parallel parking spot behind him and stop. The driver wasn't Ronni and the little flutter in his heart returned to the dull, endless ache.

He missed her tremendously but he couldn't get past that he'd killed a man, something that was deeply ingrained in him to never do. Or how much it hurt when she flippantly disregarded how conflicted he was over what he'd done.

And the scariest thing about his actions was that he knew unequivocally that he would do it again without a second thought, if she were in danger. That was the truth he simply couldn't bear. Despite the ages of evolution, he was just as dangerous as his ancestors.

Better to keep the truth hidden than to risk unleashing a monster again. Next time, he might not have the strength to resist the craving to kill without mercy.

Knock! Knock! Knock!

Startled by the unexpected noise, Bodie squinted at the tall, young man standing outside the truck door. The ache in his heart tripled.

He rolled down the window.

"You're an ass!" Though Alex's voice was angry, hurt shimmered in his eyes. "You have no idea what Jeb said he'd do to you, to Mary. To *Willow*! If Mom hadn't agreed to go with him, there would be a lot more people dead."

"Alex—"

"My dad was a good man. Mom says you're a good man, too, but you aren't." His body trembled with emotion and restraint. "You did what Jeb tried to do. You broke up our family. That doesn't make you a good man. It makes you just like him."

"Alex, wait!" His heart breaking, Bodie jumped out of the truck, but Alex had darted through the traffic and down the block.

"Dammit!" Bodie kicked the loose gravel, climbed back into the truck and slammed the door.

"Dad?" Willow stood at the open passenger door. Her eyes were large and round and she wore an expression of awkward surprise.

Bodie swallowed his frustration and his guilt.

"Is everything okay?" She slid into the passenger seat and quietly closed the door.

"Of course it is, chickadee."

"I saw you talking to Alex." She buckled her seat belt and Bodie did the same.

"Well, he did all the talking. He's quite upset with me."

"Yeah, I know." As she stared out the window, her reflection showed the sad resignation he'd seen so often on her face before moving to Maico.

"Alex hasn't been harassing you, has he?"

She swung her head toward Bodie. Her eyes, so much like his own, narrowed. "He's mad at you, not me."

Bodie turned on the engine and eased out of the pickup lane. "I found a nice apartment today. I think you'll like it. You'll have your own room and bathroom. And the complex has a swimming pool."

Willow's excitement was nonexistent. Had he really expected her to be happy with the news when he himself wasn't?

Ten minutes of stops and starts and they were finally clear of the school traffic. He turned down Main Street. Every damn day this week, he got stuck at the red light at the Sorghum Avenue intersection. The first day, they'd been close enough to see Ronni's store a few blocks down and Willow had burst into tears. The next couple of days, she'd heaved soul-wrenching sighs that stabbed his hurting heart over and over again until Bodie thought he might die from it.

Tense, he watched the green light turn yellow while they were several blocks away. Even if he stomped on the accelerator, he wouldn't make it to the line before the light turned red. He eased off the gas.

Willow sat a little straighter, knowing the intersection was ahead. He slowed to a stop, preparing himself for his daughter's daily emotional release.

"I miss Ronni." Willow's soft statement affected him as much as her tears and sighs.

"So do I." The words scraped his throat.

"Why don't you fix it?"

"I don't know if this is something that should be fixed, sweetheart." He didn't want to give the monster inside a foothold. The only way he could ensure it didn't take hold was to stay away from the one woman he would do anything to protect.

The light changed and Bodie continued through town, turning at the last intersection and heading to the KOA campground. "Hey, you haven't told me what you want for your birthday or Christmas yet."

Bodie hoped the thought of presents would lighten her mood.

"I want us all back together, Dad." She stared out her window. "Otherwise, what's the point?"

"Ronni? Are you here?" Nel called out from the front of the store.

"I'm in the sewing room!" Ronni stuck a straight pin

through the black fabric. After two weeks of rushing to the front every time the bells jingled, hoping to see Bodie, she began forcing herself to count to fifty before walking out to greet customers.

Nel's footsteps fell silent at the doorway. "Oh, wow! What is that?"

Ronni stepped back from her latest creation. "It's a cloak for Willow to wear on her birthday when she shifts for the first time. I know I promised to finish your projects, but I needed to get this done." It was her way of saying goodbye to Willow and sending her love.

"It's lovely." Nel stepped closer to see the garment from the back. She gasped. "You've sewn the panels so that they look like feathers."

"I tried to replicate the one Willow's mother wore for her first shift."

"It's a shame she'll only wear it once."

"I'm hoping it will last so she can give it to her daughter one day."

"Tristan said shift energy disintegrates anything that it touches during transformations."

"Anything but silver." Ronni opened one of the storage cabinets and pulled out the material she would use to line the interior of the cloak. "This is silver fabric."

"As in *real* silver?" Nel rubbed a corner of material between her fingers.

"Yep. The cloth is actually cotton but it has been immersed in a silver solution and put through a curing process so that it sticks."

"I've never heard of such a thing."

"Silver textiles have actually been around for a while. Pretty cool, though." Ronni returned the fabric to the cabinet.

"This is amazing, Ronni. Willow means a lot to you, doesn't she?"

"I know it's crazy." Tears stung Ronni's eyes. "Bodie and

I weren't together long and they were only at the house for a short time, but I feel like a huge part of me is missing."

"I felt the same way when Tristan and I were separated." Nel hugged her. "That big hole in your heart and soul means Bodie is your true mate. You have to keep feeding the mate-bond if you want him to come back.

"After I returned to Atlanta without Tristan, every night before I went to sleep, every morning I woke up, and at random moments throughout the day, I would think of him and send him all the love I had. I didn't even know it was working until he showed up at the art gallery the night of my first showing."

"It was different for you. Tristan loves you."

"Do you honestly think that Bodie doesn't love you?"

Yes, she actually did believe that. Bodie had never professed his love, and his abrupt abandonment was proof that Ronni had been mistaken about the connection she thought they had shared.

"Well, maybe this will change your mind." Nel handed Ronni a large package wrapped in brown. "Open it up. It's yours."

Ronni carefully unwrapped the present. Her breath caught in her throat as her eyes roamed the painted canvas depicting Ronni in a red, flowing gown and Bodie dressed all in black, his long inky hair tied back with a red ribbon, dancing in a clearing within a moonlit forest. In the background was Ronni's wolf lying against a lightly mossed log where Bodie's raven was perched, and he was leaning down to give her a peck on the cheek.

"Oh, Nel." Tears spilled from Ronni's eyes. "It's beautiful, but I can't accept this. Bodie and I aren't together anymore."

"Tristan said I shouldn't give it to you. I told him I had to."

"Why?"

"Because I believe." Nel squeezed Ronni's shoulder.

"When I saw you and Bodie dancing at Taylor's on the night we all had dinner, I *knew* you belonged together.

"Cassie told me once that I needed to have faith," she continued. "Now I'm telling you to believe in Bodie and yourself. Faith feeds the mate-bond. Feel it. Nurture it, but sure as hell don't ignore it. Bodie will come back to you. You'll see."

Chapter 33

Bodie flew into the open window of the camper and alighted on the kitchen counter. Sitting at the table, his mother peered at him over the rim of her coffee cup with the same disapproving look that she'd given him for the last three weeks.

Not up for argumentative conversation, he darted into the bathroom, shifted and quietly closed the door for a few minutes alone as if he hadn't spent most of the night by himself. He turned on the hot water, took a washcloth from beneath the sink, dampened it and slapped it to his face without looking at his reflection in the mirror.

Tonight he had expected Ronni to go to the wolf sanctuary. After all, he'd learned that Wahyas needed sex when the moon was full because it was a natural way to suppress the dormant wolfan hormones responsible for the emergence of the werewolf creature that Jeb had become.

Misery loved company, so Bodie had waited to see who Ronni would choose as her next lover, in hopes of tearing him to pieces.

No!

He pulled the tepid cloth from his face, dunked it in the hot water and buried his face in it again. The sting wasn't deep enough to cleanse the feral thoughts from his mind.

"Bodie?" His mother knocked at the door.

"I'll be out in a minute." He shut off the water and squeezed out the cloth.

All evening he'd watched and waited but Ronni never left her house to go to the sanctuary and no suitor came to her door. Neither had she stepped onto the porch for her nightly swing.

Worried something was wrong, he'd gone to her bedroom window. She'd sat curled in the reading chair, softly crying. He'd nearly come undone, wanting to punch whoever had reduced her to tears.

And then he heard her voice whisper through his mind, *"I love you."* Not knowing what to do, he'd flown straight to the camper.

Lifting his gaze, he stared into his own reflection, searching for signs of the monster who wanted to pummel the man who'd hurt Ronni. Wasn't it twisted that the man was him?

Bodie lifted his pajama pants from the hook on the back of the door and pulled them on. He was barely out of the bathroom when his mother spoke. "Does she know you still watch over her every night?"

No, he stayed far enough away so she wouldn't see him.

"Do you understand why you can't keep yourself from going to her?"

"I'm a glutton for punishment."

His mother frowned. "The Quickening, Bodaway. It is why you were drawn to her in the first place and why you hurt so much being separated."

"She's better off without me."

"Is that what your nightly visits tell you?"

Someone knocked.

Bodie went to the front door. "Who is it?"

No one answered so Bodie peeked outside.

"We need to talk." Arms crossed high on his chest, Rafe sat in one of the lawn chairs next to the camper.

"Are Ronni and Alex all right?" Even though he'd seen them tucked safe inside the house when he'd left, Bodie's heart drummed a hard, panicked beat.

"No, they're not all right!" The irritation in Rafe's voice was as harsh as a slap on the face. "Put on a jacket, then get your feathered ass outside."

Bodie turned around.

Standing behind him, his mother held out his sweatshirt. "Rafe asked me to call when I thought you might listen to what he has to say."

"When I get done with him, you and I are going to have a conversation about going behind my back."

Bodie pulled on the sweatshirt and stomped outside in his bare feet. The air was nippy but not cold enough for frostbite.

"Five minutes." He plopped down in the chair across from Rafe.

At least three of those minutes passed without Rafe making a sound or looking at Bodie.

"If you aren't going to say anything, I'm going inside."

"I'm listening," Rafe said.

"To what?"

"Your descent into madness."

"I'm not insane. There's a real monster inside me."

"The monster *is* you." Rafe finally met Bodie's gaze. "The key is to accept that part of yourself and live peaceably with it."

"Live peaceably?" Bodie's voice trembled with incredulity. "I killed a man."

"But you tried to save him first. Didn't you." It was more a statement than a question.

"How do you know that?" Bodie had tried to take the confrontation far enough away so that Ronni and Alex wouldn't witness any violence.

"We all do what is in our nature. You're a good man, Bodie. It's not your fault if Jeb didn't want you to save him." Rafe shrugged. "But fighting to pigeonhole that primal part of yourself is what will drive you to the edge and try to push you off. I know, because I've been where you are. The difference is you have someone with experience to help you cope."

Bodie stared at Rafe. "You became like Jeb?"

"I'm not like Jeb, so my beast isn't like him either. Mine knows my values because he knows me." Rafe leaned forward. "Keep fighting yourself and your beast will lose its connection to your humanity. That's when you'll truly become a monster."

"So I'm supposed to give in and let this thing control me?"

"Control you, no. It wants to live in harmony but the turmoil inside you is disturbing its residence." Rafe stood. "The key to sending the beast back to its cave is to make peace with what happened—you can't change the outcome. And stop punishing Ronni for your own insecurities and guilt. She deserves better."

Rafe walked to his vehicle. "You know where to find me."

Sometime after Rafe left, Bodie went inside the camper. His outer body was numb from the chilly air, but his insides were numb from the truth of Rafe's words.

"I want to show you something." His mother removed a pink present tied with a frilly purple bow from the upper cabinet and laid it on the table.

"When did you get Willow a birthday present?"

"This is from Ronni."

Bodie gingerly touched the wrapping paper and ribbon; his finger warmed at the thought that Ronni had touched it, too. "Clothes?"

"A transformation robe like the one Layla wore." His mother touched his shoulder. "Ronni said Willow had showed her a picture one night when she couldn't sleep."

"Willow asked Ronni to make this?"

"She didn't have to. A mother can sense what her child needs." Mary kissed Bodie's temple, then hobbled to the bedroom and closed the door.

Bodie didn't think his heart could hurt any more than it had been. But to know that his daughter had confided a desire so personal and that Ronni had turned that desire into a reality despite how Bodie had treated her—a jagged breath tore from his chest.

Somehow, someway, he needed to put his family back together. He just hoped it wasn't too late.

Jingle bells replaced the regular chimes over the door. Ronni glanced at the clock in the sewing room, ten fifty-five on the button. "I'll be right out, Elliott." She expected the faithful postal carrier had a handful of holiday cards to deliver.

Quickly, she finished marking the pattern on the fabric and put aside the tracing wheel. "I bet you'll be glad when the holidays are over so that mailbag won't feel like a mill-stone around your neck."

She walked into the front of the store and saw Bodie lock the door and flip the Open sign to Closed. Her fake smile fell.

Yesterday, she'd dropped off Willow's birthday present. She doubted Bodie's sudden appearance was a coincidence.

"I got your mail." Bodie held up a handful of cards but made no move toward her.

"Thanks." Heart thundering in her throat, Ronni walked stiffly to the register, putting the counter between them. She couldn't tell if the sigh echoing in the room was hers or his.

He strolled over and placed the mail on the counter. She didn't reach for it. Instead, she folded her hands in front of her. "What brings you here?"

"There's something I need to discuss with you."

"Is Willow okay?" If anything happened to the girl, Ronni would be devastated.

"She's fine, and excited by the present you brought by but my mother said she couldn't open it until her birthday."

"How is Mary?"

"She's walking without the knee scooter. Still a little slow, but should be back to normal in a few weeks."

"I'm glad to hear she's better." Ronni stopped herself

from asking Bodie how he was doing. He looked tired, with half-moon shadows beneath his eyes; his uniform hung looser on his frame. "I'm really busy today so—" she took a deep breath "—what do you want to discuss?"

She wouldn't be surprised if he told her to stay away from his family. And she would completely abide by his wishes. She'd done right by Willow; now there was no reason to cross paths with the Gryffon family again.

Except that her heart hurt so badly at the very thought of it. Nel had said to have faith but that was easier said than done when your faith kept getting shattered.

"Ronni."

"I'm listening." She looked at his chest rather than meet his gaze in case it still held the loathsome disgust she'd seen at their parting.

"Ronni, look at me."

"Just say it," she snapped. "Tell me to go to hell, to leave your family alone. Whatever it is, say it and leave."

"I love you."

Ronni's ears rang. "Wh-what?"

"I love you, Veronika Lyles."

"You love me?" Ronni's voice was barely a whisper over the pounding of her heart.

"I do." Bodie leaned across the counter, hooked his finger beneath her chin and tilted her head until Ronni looked at him. "I'm sorry for waiting so long to tell you."

The leaden weight that had been sitting on her heart shattered. "Oh! Oh!" She stepped back, waving a hand in front of her face. Still, tiny tears spilled from her eyes.

"Aww, baby." He came behind the counter and folded his arms around her.

If Bodie thought that would stop her from crying, he was wrong. A trickle of tears became a stream. Cradling her head against his shoulder, he gently stroked her back. Heat spread beneath his palm, but it was the gentle caress of his essence entwining with hers that calmed her turbulent emotions and warmed her soul.

"Why don't we sit down?" he said softly. "We have a lot to talk about."

Ronni eased back. "Yes, we do."

Taking his hand, she led him to a nook with a table and chairs. Bodie waited for her to sit, then he dragged over the other chair and sat in front of her, so close his knees grazed her legs. He leaned forward when he spoke.

"What I said after Jeb died was completely out of line and I'm sorry. It is not your fault he's dead. I blamed you because my beast emerged when I thought I could lose you. I struggled to keep myself in check, and I didn't intend to kill Jeb when I picked him up and flew away. I was only trying to protect you and Alex.

"But Jeb was unreasonable, lashing out at me midflight. I tried not to drop him. All he was focused on was destroying me because I stood between him and what he wanted." Bodie's gaze dropped. "I don't want to become like him."

"You're a good man, Bodaway Gryffon." Ronni reached for his hand. "You'll never be like Jeb."

"Alex isn't so sure."

"He's hurting and angry."

"What about you?"

Ronni walked to the storefront window. Wrapping her arms around her waist, she watched children playing in the town's park. "I never used you to *get rid* of Jeb. I wished him dead, hit by a bus or something. But I never entertained the thought of you killing him. And I'm sorry it happened that way."

"So am I." Bodie stepped behind her, encircling her in his arms. "But it's over and done. And I really don't want to lose you and Alex over him. Do you think it's possible to put our family back together?"

"We were happy, you know. Happier than we had been in a long time."

"Us, too." Bodie pressed his face against her hair; his breath tickled the shell of her ear. "I need you to know that even if you weren't Co-op, I would've chosen you."

A rush of his warm, masculine energy swept her being and joy filled her heart to near bursting. She closed her eyes, allowing her love to flow back to him.

"And I'm sorry for making you feel like the only reason I wanted you was for access to the wolf sanctuary."

"Well," she said, turning to face him and palming the hard muscles of his chest. "It is a really nice one. I can see why you were tempted by it."

Bodie kissed her sweetly. "The only thing I was ever tempted by was you."

Chapter 34

Butterflies fluttered in Bodie's stomach. It was hard to believe that sixteen years ago, on Christmas Eve, he'd held a tiny bundle of joy in his hands for the very first time. Now she was a beautiful young lady about to stretch her arms and receive her raven wings.

Ronni finished tying Willow's cloak.

"Turn around so I can see," his mother called from her seat on a nearby log.

Willow spun and the cape twirled with her. "It's perfect. Thank you, Ronni."

"You're welcome, hon." Ronni hugged her, tightly. "Happy birthday."

"It's the best one." Willow flitted about and Alex snapped pictures on his phone. He seemed okay with them moving in again, but when Bodie was alone with him, he sensed a subtle tension. A lot of work was needed to rebuild the bridge between them and Bodie intended to do whatever it took.

He checked his watch. The seconds were counting down to the exact time of her birth, the earliest moment she could safely transform.

"All right, Willow. Pick your spot."

She looked around the small clearing and chose a place where a single sunbeam streamed through the towering trees. "Come stand by me, *Enisi*."

"Don't lose your feathers, I'm coming." Although Mary was now allowed to bear weight on her foot, Bodie helped her along the uneven terrain. Once she was in the "perfect" spot, according to Willow, he joined Ronni and Alex off to the side.

Standing behind Ronni, he wrapped his arms around her, soaking in her warmth and the fresh, feminine scent of her skin. She leaned comfortably against him and he closed his eyes, hoping she sensed the absolute sincerity of his very grateful heart.

Forgiveness had come easily. Proving she could trust him again with her heart would take time. But he was a determined man, invested for the long haul.

"Dad, is it time?" Willow looked over at him.

Bodie checked his watch. "Almost."

He didn't realize his hands were shaking until Ronni covered them with hers. "Were you nervous during Alex's first shift?"

"Yes, and I am now. It's the good kind of nerves, though." Ronni glanced over her shoulder at him. "She's going to be fine." A sweet, gentle spirit filled him and he relaxed in the ebb and flow of Ronni's essence mingling with his.

When Bodie had confessed his love, Ronni did not say it back to him. Nor had she in the time since. Although it would be nice to hear the words on her lips, he saw her love in every look she gave him. Felt the depth of it in every touch. And recognized the power of it in every kindness she showered on his daughter and mother. So even if she couldn't say the words out loud, every little thing she did shouted how much she loved him.

His watch beeped.

Ronni held her breath. Alex had his phone's camera ready. Bodie's mother, wearing an old housecoat, opened her arms and began chanting.

"I should've made her a cloak, too," Ronni whispered.

Heart pumping happily along, he kissed Ronni's temple without taking his eyes off Willow. Following her grandmother's instructions, Willow lifted her arms. The black cloak stretched across her shoulders like beautiful wings.

His mother fell silent, then *poof.* The housecoat turned to dust and she hopped around on the ground, flapping her wings, but Willow simply stood there with her outstretched arms shaking.

"Why didn't she shift?" Ronni asked him.

Bodie shrugged. He walked over to Willow. "Sweetheart, are you okay?"

Tears trickled down his daughter's face.

Bodie hugged her. "It's okay to take your time. There's no rush."

His mother squawked and clucked.

"Mom, you're not helping," Bodie said.

Ronni joined them. "Hon, would it help if your dad shifted with you?"

"It's supposed to be my mom." Willow sniffed. "Dads shift with the boys."

"Alex, turn around," Ronni instructed.

"Why?"

"Because I'm going to help her shift."

"Really?" The tears stopped leaking from Willow's eyes.

"Yes, I am."

Alex's eyes widened and he quickly turned his back to them.

Returning his gaze to Ronni, Bodie understood why. No son wanted to watch his mother shimmying out of her clothes. Bodie closed his eyes. Seeing Ronni naked made him hot and hard and Neanderthalic. And all of that would have to wait until later.

"You can look now."

He opened one eyelid just a crack to be sure. She had squatted on the ground next to Willow, one leg tucked beneath her, the other knee bent in front and her arms shielding her chest.

Bodie quickly focused on Willow because the woman he considered his mate was sitting naked in front of him and the creamy, smooth expanse of her back and the curve of her hips were much too tempting.

"Willow, just close your eyes and breathe." Ronni took her hand. "In and out. In and out."

Bodie found himself following along.

"Feel the sunshine on your skin." Ronni's voice softened. "The air sifting through your hair. Now feel the energy inside you. It's in every cell. You don't have to force it to come—it's already there."

Bodie noticed a subtle change in Willow's demeanor. A confidence that had been missing during her earlier attempt.

"When you're ready, lift your arms and we'll count down from three."

Ronni didn't let go of Willow's hand until she began to raise her arms. Bodie's breath stilled and he willed his heart to thump quietly.

"Three," Ronni said. "Two." She placed both hands on the ground in front of her. "One."

His daughter disappeared and her cloak floated down to the ground next to Ronni's wolf.

"Willow!" Bodie's heart dropped into his stomach. The robe should've disintegrated, not his daughter.

Before he took more than one giant step toward them, Ronni's wolf grabbed the cloak in her teeth and pulled it back, uncovering a beautiful little raven dancing around on wobbly legs.

"So cool!" Alex shouted, hurrying over with his phone's camera set to record. "Bodie, you should've seen your face when Willow disappeared. Classic!"

Ronni touched her nose to Willow and gently licked her face. Willow's first caw was one of the most beautiful sounds Bodie had ever heard. Pride in his daughter nearly split him in two.

His mother hopped next to Willow, instructing her how to use her wings. It would be a few weeks before she could actually fly.

Alex, after shifting into his wolf form, loped over to her. After a few gentle nudges and playful barks, he lay down and put his chin on the ground.

Willow jumped onto his nose and strutted up his snout. In her attempt to get to the top of his head, her spindly toes slipped, scrunching his eyebrows.

Laughing, Bodie snapped a picture using his phone. "Classic!" he called out to Alex.

So much pride and joy swelled in Bodie's heart, watching his blended family celebrate Willow's special day. He was especially touched by Ronni's thoughtfulness and encouragement when Willow needed her.

He looked at Ronni, her reddish-gold fur slightly fluffed to keep her warm in the cool temperature. Daily he promised to love and cherish her every day for the rest of his life.

"Thank you, for everything," he said aloud, as the sentiment permeated his thoughts and filled his heart.

"You're welcome."

He sensed her spirit touch his, and no moment had ever been more perfect.

Long after everyone had gone to bed, Ronni sat leisurely on the back porch swing, conspicuously devoid of squeaks. Her mind seemed to have no "off" button tonight, replaying the ups and downs of last fall, and her utter contentment in the weeks following Willow's Transformation Ceremony.

Her raven form was absolutely darling. Bodie had even sent a few pictures to Willow's estranged grandfather, a peace offering of sorts. Despite their complicated history, he hoped, when the time came, Kane would convince the Tribunal to treat with the Woelfesenat and embrace some of the wolfan practices in order to revitalize their species.

Mary's foot had completely healed and she had happily gone to work at the Co-op's daycare. All the kids were now calling her *Enisi* and she doted on every one of them.

Alex was taking his role as big brother very seriously,

which caused a few tiffs with Lucas, but nothing lasting because Willow had learned how to handle them quite well.

And Bodie… She'd known all along that he was a man who loved his family. He loved her, too. Saying it often, leaving no doubt.

The door opened and she stopped the swing. He stepped outside, wearing only his pajama pants.

"Hey, beautiful." His hair was mussed and he peered at her with sleepy eyes and a cocky grin. "If you can't sleep, I can give you a workout that will tire you out." After all he'd been through, Bodie hadn't lost his sense of humor. She loved that about him.

She also loved that he never pressured her to say the actual words *I love you.* Even though she wanted to verbalize the sentiment, she choked every time. Because right when she was ready to tell him the first time, he'd flown away, shattering her heart.

What if it happens again?

"Baby, I'm not going anywhere." Barefoot, he padded toward the swing.

She opened the blanket for him to join her.

Instead, he took her hand, urging her to stand.

"You are the light in my soul. Without you, there is only darkness and chaos." Folding his arms around her and wrapping her in his warmth, he peppered kisses down the side of her neck to the sweet spot where her shoulder joined.

Chills, the good ones, swept her skin.

"And I will love you until the end of my days." Bodie touched his mouth sweetly to hers, nibbling lightly on her bottom lip before slipping his tongue into her mouth in a toe-clenching, bone-melting kiss. His essence merged with hers without expectation or demand, merely an unwavering declaration of love.

There was nothing left to fear.

Her family was safe, she was safe, and they had left behind the chaos to settle into a calm, steadfast routine.

When the kiss ended, and Ronni opened her eyes, Bodie's soft smile of acceptance and assurance filled her heart, which stretched and grew and beat in absolute contentment.

"I love you, Bodaway Gryffon." Her voice was barely a whisper but it carried on the wind and echoed through the woods.

"I know," he murmured, in utter faith.

Lifting Ronni into his arms, Bodie carried her into the house and continued to the bedroom, humming the tune she loved to hear.

Any hesitation that she had about forging a true mateship with Bodie had faded and she felt confident in their future.

He eased her down on the bed; the mattress dipping with their weight. She touched her tongue to her prickling canines as he settled his body over hers.

He kissed her deeply, lovingly and possessively. When he pulled back to gaze into her eyes, she cupped his face. "Bodaway Gryffon, will you be my mate, for now and always?"

"Baby, I'm already yours."

* * * * *